My breath caught in my chest and my heart began to pound uncontrollably at the shock of finding Lainey here. She wasn't supposed to come again until tomorrow. How could she be here now, and without me knowing it?

"Lainey, what are you doing here?"

"What do you mean?"

"The storm. The roads must be impassable. Wait, that's not even the point. I didn't know you were here. When did you come, and why didn't you tell me you were here?"

"Mom, I came last night before the storm started. I didn't want you to be alone. Don't you remember? I arrived just as you were finishing your supper—soup, I think it was."

No, it can't be.

"We spoke for a while about the weather, and if you were stocked-up for food and other supplies. And you told me about your meeting with Harvey."

No, no, no.

"Mom, you look like you've been crying. It's another bad day, isn't it? Come sit beside me."

I made my way to the end of the bed and sat. I couldn't face Lainey. Instead, I stared at the light switch on the opposite wall. It was a strange thing to focus my gaze on, but it was the first thing I saw while I struggled to process how she could be here, and my having no memory of spending time with her last night.

Praise for Colleen Coyne and Bewept

"…Tense, heart-wrenching and heart-warming as well, Bewept kept me up late, turning pages. I expect Colleen Coyne's next book to be equally enthralling."
~Roxanne Dunn, author of Murder Unrehearsed and Murder Undetected

~*~

"…Colleen Coyne offers a psychological thriller every bit as suspenseful and twisty as The Woman in the Window and The Girl on the Train."
~Steven J. Kolbe, author, the Ezra James Mysteries

Bewept

by

Colleen Coyne

Bewept

Cover Art by *Jennifer Greeff*

The Wild Rose Press, Inc.
PO Box 708
Adams Basin, NY 14410-0708
Visit us at www.thewildrosepress.com

Publishing History
First Edition, 2023
Trade Paperback ISBN 978-1-5092-4906-0
Digital ISBN 978-1-5092-4907-7

Published in the United States of America

Dedication

For my mother, Blanche Ann Coyne

Acknowledgments

I am incredibly grateful for the help and support I received while writing *Bewept*. I began writing this, my second novel, in 2017. My husband, Claus Frimodt, is my biggest cheerleader. His encouragement gave me the determination to persevere.

My daughters, Briana Boragine and Rachael Boragine, offered helpful comments on early drafts. Longtime friend Peggy Kilmartin also cheered me along and provided meaningful comments. I want to thank Author Karen Guzman, whom I met during her book promotion of *Arborview* (a fantastic read!) at Stonington Library in Stonington, CT. Her recommendation that I approach Wild Rose Press, Inc. led to the start of this book's publication.

Finally, but not least, by any measure, I thank Wild Rose Press Editor Kaycee John for her expert editing, her thoughtful guidance, and her unwavering encouragement.

BEWEPT

When in disgrace with fortune and men's eyes
I all alone beweep my outcast state,
And trouble deaf heaven with my bootless cries,
And look upon myself, and curse my fate,
Wishing me like to one more rich in hope,
Featured like him, like him with friends possessed,
Desiring this man's art, and that man's scope,
With what I most enjoy contented least;
Yet in these thoughts my self almost despising,
Haply I think on thee, and then my state,
Like to the lark at break of day arising
From sullen earth, sings hymns at heaven's gate;
For thy sweet love remembered such wealth brings
That then I scorn to change my state with kings.
(William Shakespeare, Sonnet 29)

Chapter One

Saturday, Anna

It snowed again last night. It was no longer possible to distinguish where the slope of the land met the lake's edge. The sparkle and purity of newly fallen snow once brought a freshness to the start of my day. The temporary stillness that allows a layer to form and delicately balance on the thinnest of branches once held the promise that anything is possible.

Now, the scene conjures a different feeling because I've learned that we cannot freeze time. Inevitably, a bitter winter wind will whip through the branches, shaking away the brief beauty and fleeting promise. Yesterday it was the promise that held my attention. Today it's the frozen branch laid bare.

I had just reached the bottom step when I heard my daughter Lainey speaking softly into her phone. "Mom is losing it! I'm sorry, but I didn't want to say anything before now. I wasn't sure, or maybe it's just that I didn't want to believe it."

What is Lainey saying about me? That's crazy. I'm not losing it!

"Like I said," she continued. "It's been lots of little things that, separately, didn't seem worrisome. I chalked it up to her grief over David's death, but walking to the mailbox barefooted, in the middle of winter when there's over a foot of snow on the ground, clearly isn't normal behavior."

Walk barefoot in the snow? I didn't do that. What the hell is going on here?

"No, don't come yet. You can't just suddenly leave your practice and the twins when we don't yet have a handle on what's happening. I'm here for the weekend. I don't have to be back in the city until Monday. Let's see how it goes. I'll keep you posted."

Clearly, Lainey was speaking to her brother, my son Trent. Silence now. The call must have ended.

Just as I was about to storm into the kitchen, scream my head off, and demand to know what she was talking about, a small voice inside asked if there might be some truth to what Lainey said.

"Don't say anything," that voice warned next.

I steadied myself and walked into the kitchen as if nothing was unusual.

"Hi, Mom," Lainey chirped.

"Good morning. Have you had breakfast yet?"

She turned to face me squarely and seriously. "We had breakfast nearly three hours ago."

I glanced at the wall where the clock clearly said 11:40 a.m. The morning was nearly gone.

"Mom, you seemed a little off this morning, so I told you to go back to bed for more rest—a little nap."

I didn't understand. I've just woken up from a full night's sleep, not a nap. And how would I not remember making, then eating, breakfast?

"You might be coming down with something," said Lainey. "You should take it slow and easy today. Go back up to your room for a while."

I felt confused and unbalanced. Lainey placed her

hands on my shoulders, laughed, and turned me toward the stairs. "Go back to bed for a while longer. Later, I'll make you some tomato soup and a grilled cheese sandwich just like you use to do for Trent and me when we were sick."

"I'm not sick."

"Let's not take any chances. Okay?"

She marched me toward the stairs, and like a good soldier, I trudged upward and slipped back into bed.

The nothingness of the newly painted white ceiling bothered me, so I turned on my side and looked out the window. Did I really walk to the mailbox in all that snow with no shoes on? What were the *lots of little other crazy things* I'd supposedly done, which Lainey reported to her brother?

Am I losing it? I admit I've been mad with grief over losing David. Could grief explain crazy behavior and lost chunks of time?

It happened during that space of time between Christmas and the New Year. To me, those days usually felt like a serene hiatus, a regrouping period, to recover between the two big celebratory holidays. It's difficult to believe it was less than two months ago that the pleasant interlude I anticipated would instead leave me crushed and broken.

That terrible scene played again. We were enjoying a glass of wine by the fire, and he was saying, "The house is finished. We should take a trip to somewhere warmer and sunnier after the New Year. I have a surprise for you…"

Then, before continuing, he grabbed at his chest and began to gasp. In seconds it was over. One minute, my new husband of barely eighteen months may have been about to tell me his plans for the honeymoon we had yet to take. The next minute I became a widow.

"Mom," Lainey said as she walked into my bedroom, "I've brought you some tea. The door was open, and I saw that you were no longer asleep. Dinner will soon be ready."

Dinner? Maybe I am losing it. I couldn't have been in bed for very long. I didn't nap. How could so much time have passed?

I glanced out the window hoping for a clue, but the winter sky darkens early, and it can be especially difficult to judge time of day when daylight becomes obscured by stormy skies. It would certainly be another starless night.

****

Lainey kept me cocooned inside a blanket on the couch for most of the weekend. I don't think anything else crazy happened, but then again, how was I to know? I wanted to talk with her about it, but that inner voice kept warning that I shouldn't. She might be embarrassed to learn that I'd overheard her talking to Trent and the things I heard her saying about me.

My gaze wandered from the television over to my daughter. I couldn't expose myself by asking questions. I already felt vulnerable.

"Okay, Mom," Lainey said when the movie's closing credits began to scroll, "I need to head back to the city. The groceries I brought here Friday should get you through the week, and I'll be checking in with you. Is there anything else you need? Are you okay?"

"I'll be fine, Lainey. Like you said, I was probably coming down with something. But after sleeping most of the weekend, I think I'm much better now."

"I'll be back next weekend," she said as she planted a kiss on my forehead and squeezed my shoulder. "Love you, Mom."

As I heard the front door close, I thought about how much my daughter had changed. She had grown into the woman that I always hoped she'd be, self-assured and loving. My daughter had come back to me after I lost David. I wish their paths had crossed. It would be a bitter irony to lose myself just after she and I had finally found one another again.

Keeping the faith all these years had been the right thing to do. Lainey was no longer a ghost.

Still, something about her continued to haunt me.

Chapter Two

Wednesday, Anna

My fingers slowly skimmed over each of David's shirts that still hung in the closet. Touching each one revived a cherished memory. I needed to spend time with him in any way that I could, and this was now the closest I could get to him.

With a mixed measure of irritation and embarrassment, I shrank away from the closet as I heard Cassie's voice behind me.

"Mrs. Simmons, my mom says to tell you that we are done cleaning on the main floor. She wants to know if it's okay for us to begin cleaning up here. She didn't know if you were busy or resting."

"I was just about to go downstairs. I'll tell your mom that it's fine to start up here."

Walking down the hallway toward the staircase, I glanced up at the towering cathedral ceiling and then peered over the railing to the living space below to take in what had been the dream house David and I had finished building and furnishing barely six months ago. This place didn't need cleaning every Wednesday. Somebody checking on me regularly to report that I was eating made my kids feel better and worry less. I also knew that my housekeeper Beth Taylor could put the money she was being paid her to good use, especially with the added cost of her daughter Cassie's university tuition.

I found Beth in the living room. Harsh ethereal wintery-white sunlight shining through the wall of windows this time of day made her features appear severe, and in stark contrast to the woman I knew. "I've brought you some of my famous chicken soup," she said, "and Cassie brought in the mail. It's in the office."

"Thank you, Beth. How much longer is Cassie here on winter break before she heads back to school?"

Beth's brow creased. "She isn't going back to school. She was asked to leave. She won't say what happened, but I'm betting that she preferred parties to books."

"I'm so sorry, Beth."

"Don't be. If she wants to continue to have a roof over her head and food in her stomach, she's now going to be my assistant. If she's happy with cleaning houses as her life's work, so be it, but I don't think it will take her too long to smarten-up."

"Cassie may just be going through a phase. It's a tough age. She'll figure it out."

"In the meantime, I hope you don't mind her being here regularly. Please, tell me if she gets in the way."

"Don't worry about it. Everything will be fine."

Just then, the doorbell rang. Through the sidelight window, next to the front door, I saw it was Harvey Duhamel, David's lawyer, and longtime friend. I'd forgotten that we had an appointment to go over estate issues. I wished now that I had put it off. Everything was still too raw.

The first time we met was over dinner at David's place in New York City. I had heard so much about him from David that I felt as though I already knew Harvey long before we met. That's why it was disturbing to feel his eyes on me too much throughout the dinner, and his behavior toward me when David disappeared to the bathroom was shameful. They had been best friends since college. Games of rivalry—over sports, girls, cars, practically anything—were at the core of their friendship. David would say that they still sometimes egged each other on, but these days it was more likely to be over a bottle of good wine or good-natured one-upmanship on the golf course. David trusted Harvey with his life. I wondered if it was wise for David to trust him with me. Harvey had three failed marriages behind him. David was fond of ribbing him that although he married at a late age, by marrying me, he had hit it out of the ballpark on his first attempt.

After Harvey stepped inside, we greeted one another with loose hugs. I hung his coat while he removed his snow boots. As I placed his gloves on the foyer table, I caught a quick glimpse of myself in the mirror hanging above it. It had been much too long since I last visited the hairdresser or applied any make-up. The coarse gray hair now framing my face added to my already bleached out and drawn appearance. With a shrug of smug satisfaction, I was glad to have not gone through any extra effort to improve my appearance before his arrival.

"How long did it take you, two - two-and-a-half hours, to drive here?" I asked while turning back toward him. "I'm so sorry. I should have thought to reschedule. More snow is coming."

"No bother. It's good for me to get out of the office sometimes. I'll have plenty of time to get back before the snow starts. Plus, I wanted to see for myself how you're getting on."

As I made coffee, I watched him withdraw a stack of files from his briefcase and arrange them into neat piles atop the dining room table. Could I handle this? He settled back in his chair and gazed out at the ice-covered lake. A conglomeration of ducks, geese, and swans always congregated in the one small pool of open water usually remaining. That particular spot never fully iced over. Sometimes, a thin layer of ice might form, but the waterfowls' body heat soon melted it. David sometimes spent hours watching the scene through his binoculars. There was a spring situated there that produced a robust upwelling current of swirling water. David and I loved swimming through the spring's powerful jet on hot summer days. The burst of icy cold water was refreshing. Tears welled up at the memories. I pinched my cheek to make them stop.

Harvey turned to me just as I was entering the room with the coffee tray. "I can see why you and David chose this spot to build your dream home."

Raw sadness flooded me as I flashbacked to David's unique smile on that beautiful day when we first discovered this property. My hands began to shake, and the tray started to tumble.

"Oh, Christ!" said Harvey as he jumped up to take the tray from me. "I'm so sorry, Anna," he continued. "How stupid and insensitive of me."

"I'm just more clumsy than usual today," I lied.

It took us quite some time to go through all of the files now scattered across the table. My head was spinning with details and wondering about how to make needed decisions. David's assets were held in a trust, which, as Harvey explained, provided several advantages over a traditional will. David directed the trust during his lifetime; now that he was gone, I was the successor trustee with Harvey named to manage the trust on my behalf for as long as I so directed.

"I knew that he owned a lot of properties," I said, "but I wasn't aware of the extent until now."

"He was also winding down and selling many of them," said Harvey. "He had money enough to live as he pleased. More than once, David told me that you were now his most important investment and that he wanted to concentrate full time on you."

Deciding to be stronger than I felt, I reached across the table and squeezed his hand. "That sounds exactly like something he would say."

With a smile, Harvey returned the squeeze, but something in his eyes was unsettling. He was watching me a little too closely.

I gently withdrew my hand but felt the need to say more to conceal the awkwardness. "After my divorce, I concentrated on my kids, and later I concentrated on my career. It wasn't until I met David that I began to think there could be more and that I was missing something in life. Being with him was a special kind of happiness. We didn't have very long together. Everything was still so shiny and new, just like this home."

Harvey gestured at the files spread out across the table. "David made me promise to manage his estate on your behalf if anything should happen to him. I intend to fulfill my best friend's wishes, which will also be one less concern for you. I wish I could do more."

"Thank you," I said, "I suppose you've probably been in this position before, advising widows and widowers. 'Widow'—what a terrible word. The sound of it is as unnerving as fingernails scratching across a chalkboard. The sound of the word feels more like an accusation than a descriptor, and the meaning doesn't come close to describing the overwhelming sadness, anger, and vicious injustice wrapped up within it. I'm shattered, exhausted, and sometimes so forgetful that I don't remember doing or saying some things. Is that normal?"

"Anna, dear, you've experienced a terrible shock. As you said, everything was so shiny and new. David's death happened so unexpectedly. Yes, I think what you're experiencing is completely normal."

He must have noticed from my face that I was struggling to believe him when he added, "I once had a client, then a recent widower, who drove into his driveway and forgot to put the car into park before getting out of it."

"No!"

"Yes. I've heard a lot of stories over the years. Grief can do strange things to a person, and forgetfulness is common. When a person is grieving, they aren't living in the present. They don't want to accept living in the present because that might mean having to let go of the past, and they aren't ready to do that. That great sadness is like a fog that settles over those that are grieving. They can't see through the fog. They are floundering in a limbo between the before and after. Some people even say that time passes differently initially—it's partially suspended—because of the limbo. It's normal, Anna. You might not believe it now, but you will get through this and out to the other side of the fog. Things will get better."

My body slumped in relief, and I settled more comfortably into the chair. "Thank you, Harvey. I needed to hear that."

"Anytime," he said as he checked his watch. "I need to get going if I'm going to beat the traffic and the storm. I promise to be available whenever you need me. I also expect you'll have some questions about some of what we reviewed and discussed today. I don't expect you to remember all the details. I'm leaving the files here with you. When you are ready, we can discuss what you want to do next. Do you need the proverbial bread and milk that people around these parts line up for before a storm? I can make a run to the store and bring it back to you before I get on the highway. I'd be happy to swing back."

"Thank you, but I'm fine. I don't need anything."

The last thing I needed was for Harvey to get stuck here with me during the storm. Or, maybe, I scolded myself, he was just kind, caring and, as David's best friend, trying to do what he could for me.

He was halfway out the door when he turned back to me and took my hand. "I hope I'm not overstepping my bounds here, but this place is very isolated. I worry about you being here alone. It might not be wise for you to remain here. You could consider selling. I can help you with that."

"There isn't any other place that I'm able to be. Thank you for your concern, but I don't have a choice right now."

Harvey gave me a long curious look. He didn't ask me to explain myself further, and for that, I was grateful. After seeing him off, I gathered up the files and carried them to the office at the far end of the house. Out of sight, out of mind—I hoped.

That evening I enjoyed Beth's soup. As I pulled crusty bread apart to sop up the last of the broth, I suddenly wondered how she knew I had been huddled under a blanket all weekend. I hadn't said anything to her about feeling under the weather. Then again, maybe I was psychoanalyzing myself just a little too much lately—after all chicken soup is also good for the soul, and...

My phone rang. I answered immediately, hoping it might be Trent.

"Hi, Mom!"

I smiled. "Trent, honey, how are you and the girls?"

"We're all good here. Karen is picking up the twins from a playdate. The weather is beautiful—not like in your part of the woods. I hear another Nor'easter is about to wallop you again."

"It has been quite a snowy winter."

"If it keeps up like this, next time you go to the mailbox, you'll need snowshoes," he said and laughed.

He's laughing at me because Lainey told him about my going barefooted out to the mailbox. Funny. Not.

"Mom, are you still there?"

"Yes, I'm still here. I heard you."

"Hey Mom, how about if you come out here to sunny California? The kids would be thrilled. Karen and I talked it over. We both think it's a great idea. We have plenty of room. If you decide you like it here, we could even make the arrangement permanent."

He thinks I'm losing it, too.

"No, Trent. Thank you for the offer, but there is still so much to do here. I'm not ready to leave. Just today, David's lawyer came by. He left lots of documents for me to sift through. There are a lot of decisions that I need to make."

If Harvey believed I was of sound mind, then Trent should accept it, too.

"Mom, think about it. The offer stands. Let us know when you are ready. I worry about you being alone in that big empty house out there in the woods."

"Don't worry about me. I'm fine."

As I hung up, I hoped he didn't hear the irritation in my voice. I remembered Harvey's words about the widower's car being still in drive when he got out of it and him mentioning that under these circumstances, forgetfulness and some crazy behavior is not abnormal. My kids need to cut me some slack.

Mounting irritation was suddenly replaced by overwhelming fatigue. The mentally taxing and emotional day caught up with me. It wasn't like me to leave after dinner cleanup until the next morning, but suddenly it seemed like too much to tackle. I dumped the bowl, utensils, and soup pot into the sink.

Wasn't I dealing with enough? Now, I also had to defend myself and to convince my kids I'm not crazy! Coping with this additional aggravation was unfair. I needed to go up to my bed and forget about it all.

****

At least, that's what I must have done because that's where I awoke the next morning.

I was still a little unsteady and feeling fuzzy as I reached for my robe and wrapped it tightly around me. It was only then that I noticed I was still wearing yesterday's clothing. Strange. I couldn't remember climbing the stairs or getting into my bed. I didn't even have any wine yesterday to blame on my memory lapse.

As I reached to get my hearing aid from its charger, I looked out the window. The day was already darkening. The new Nor'easter, whatever this one's name is, must be starting here soon. When and why did they start naming these things? It must be because there are now TV channels covering nothing but the weather. They probably have their biggest audience in Florida. I remembered my grandparents happily calling to report the beautiful weather conditions during reports of cold wintery weather. I just hope the power remains on during this storm. The remoteness of this beautiful place could be both a blessing and a curse. We lost electricity in almost every major storm. Tree limbs snapped from the strain of heavy snow and strong winds, taking power lines down with them.

David had been planning to buy a generator. It was something he was going to do the next day. *The next day that never came.* Tears threatened to overtake me again. I wasn't surprised to find myself standing in front of his wardrobe, caressing the fabric of the shirt that I loved most.

"David, am I going crazy?"

Then I remembered one of his many silly sayings, "Oogle Boogle." It was his way of referring to the famous and masterful search engine that people use when wanting to research something.

Chapter Three

Anna

After showering, eating breakfast, and cleaning up the kitchen, I made my way to the office. Passing through the living room, I paused to look out through the tall windows. The pounding winds had intensified; the heavy swirling snow mesmerized me. I could barely see any hint of the trees that I knew were beyond. The storm was approaching whiteout conditions. I again wondered where the waterfowl went when the weather turned this brutal. Certainly, they would find shelter somewhere rather than remain huddled around the spring. The Nor'easter was now in full force.

I made a mental note to check how long it would last and how much snow was expected. I was grateful for the snow plowing and shoveling arrangement we had with Old Bill and his son, Young Bill. It sometimes took them a while to get to us, but we were retired, and I was okay with being a lower priority than families that had to get off to work and school.

Sitting at my desk, I pushed aside Harvey's files and pulled out my laptop. I saw the sticky note stuck on top just next to the manufacturer's logo. Trent had put the note there as a reminder when he last visited because he sometimes used this computer. Password: *Lainey@4-ever*

After logging in, I started my online search and typed: *Can grief cause dementia?*

A variety of sites immediately popped up with answers.

From an elder group site: *Grief and emotional trauma can cause memory loss. Usually, as the person recovers, memory returns. Grief from bereavement can be especially painful...*

Okay. Good.

From a health site: *Being widowed and never remarrying may raise the risk of dementia and Alzheimer's disease... The risk of Alzheimer's disease, the most common form of dementia, was more than double in people who had been widowed...*

No, not what I want to hear.

From another site: *Physical trauma such as infections, injury, drug-reactions or interactions; dehydration and malnutrition, infections, or even anesthesia can bring on acute and temporary dementia, known as "delirium." If a person is already disposed to dementia, a single traumatic experience can trigger a sharp mental decline and onset of Alzheimer's or a related dementia. Emotional trauma, such as the death of a spouse, sibling, or child, has also been known to cause acute onset of Alzheimer's and other dementia...*

Next.

From a chat forum: *My father was diagnosed with traumatic psychological dementia after the death of my mother and his mother within a week of each other and for the next 4 years...*

Maybe I should search one of those medical sites for what this diagnosis—traumatic psychological dementia—means...no, not yet, let's keep going...

From a bereavement site: *Memory loss is quite a common symptom after bereavement, along with confusion, inability to concentrate, feeling that you are going crazy. But you're not losing your mind.*

There it is. Harvey was right. I'm fine.

I had read a lot and read enough. I had now been at this for hours. I logged out and closed the lid of the laptop. I glanced at the files left by Harvey and the stack of mail left by Cassie, but I no longer had energy enough to look into either.

I looked around the room. Everywhere there were photos of my kids when they were young and more recent photos of David. When the kids were little, I still took pictures with 35mm film that I developed and printed myself.

I carefully framed images, each photo a deliberate action. Yet, the best photos always had that something extra, a surprise. Maybe when framing the shot, I had not noticed a smirk, the elegance of a profile, or the extraordinary way sunlight dappled background scenery.

It was a beloved hobby that I started when still in my teens. If I closed my eyes, I could still recall the distinctive smell of darkroom chemicals. Those chemicals and the slow step-by-step process to develop negatives or slides and the wonderfully intimate process of seeing a print take form under the enlarger was meditative, soulful, and grounding. Then, like seemingly everything, film became passé. The thoughtful step-by-step process of creating was replaced by rapid clicks on a phone generating digital images that required little thought or knowhow. Images were no longer a distinctive celebrated memory.

Scrolling through images on a phone is as quick and unmindful as creating most images. Perhaps my criticism was simply a lashing out to avoid an inescapable truth.

Images capturing a moment and memory once added another dimension to my life, but now I could only see these images through the lens of loss. Lifeless replicas of something that was no more now brought only pain.

My heart grew heavier with each photograph that I studied. Only a few months ago, David hung these photos to be what he called my "Memory Walls." He said it would make me happy to be surrounded by photographs that reminded me about the people I loved and those who loved me. He even had small brass plaques made to commemorate each one. Each plaque noted the year, location, and names of the people appearing in the photo above it. He encouraged me to think about resurrecting my love of photography—done the old way—and, for a time, I was beginning to think I might find joy in it once again.

Before David, it would have been difficult to convince me that men like him existed. He never had children of his own and, from the beginning, his arms were spread wide open for mine. Looking over the photos now, I realized that I never thought to ask him how he came by the information for the plaques beneath pictures of when my children were young. I couldn't recall telling him about the trip to Yellowstone or the supper picnics at the beach house I rented one summer. I had almost forgotten some of these times.

Then, there was the last photograph taken of David. We were christening our new home just after moving in. Designing, building, and decorating this home had been our focus for more than a year. I snapped the photo just as the cork popped and champagne gushed out all over the deck. I couldn't have captured the scene or him better. His smile was a beacon that was my safe harbor, my refuge.

David had been only partly correct. These photos did bring back memories, but he was wrong about them giving me happiness. I started to cry, hard and uncontrollably, for all that I once had, and that was now lost. The photos disintegrated into blurry images through my tears, threatening to haunt me even more than they already did.

I left the office in search of tissues. Outside, the howling wind and swirling snow continued unabated. I never realized how alone and how isolated I was until this moment. With nothing else to do, but needing to do something, I began aimlessly wandering through each room of the house. We had so many dreams when we built this beautiful home, but now each room held only emptiness and sadness. Our just finished dream house was no longer complete. None of it felt finished without David here to fill it.

We'd been married only a few months when we decided to spend a long Columbus Day weekend in the area, hoping to escape for a few days to the quiet coziness the area promised. We hadn't yet taken a honeymoon or even had a wedding celebration. We had simply exchanged vows at the city hall. This trip was to be what David called our "mini-moon."

We enjoyed taking excursions, what we called "mystery rides," to explore unfamiliar areas. It was on one such ride that we stumbled on this postcard picturesque setting. At once, its extraordinary beauty claimed us. Noticing a "For Sale" sign half-hidden by tree branches, we jumped out of the car, and like children set free, we ran hand-in-hand down the gently sloping hill to the water. The beauty and its possibilities were mesmerizing. There could be no question. This place was meant for us.

Before learning the price or discussing our move to a state where neither of us had ever thought of living, we had decided where the house would be situated. It would have a vast wall of glass to take in the sweeping view outside, and a soaring cathedral ceiling over an open kitchen, dining, and living room for a commanding view inside. A massive stone fireplace would anchor the far end of the living room. Because we would build the house into the hillside, a must-have sprawling wrap-around deck would provide easy entry into the home from the street, and fantastic outdoor living space on the lake side. Every room would have access to the deck.

The realtor remarked that the land we were purchasing was "good solid ground."

David chuckled. "More important to me are the interstitial spaces."

The realtor's confused expression gave away his lack of understanding though his stumbling response was quick. "Yes, those spaces are important."

I didn't understand either, but I was too busy trying not to laugh at the poor young guy to ask David what he meant. Later that night, over dinner, I remembered and recounted the exchange. David laughed.

"So just what are the interstitial spaces?" I asked him.

"Everything!" David exclaimed.

"David," I demanded.

He smiled and said, "We think there is solid ground beneath our feet and our thinking about it stops there. But, although soil particles seem to touch and fit together, in reality, they don't. There are spaces in between called pores. When the soil is dry, the pores are filled with air. When the ground is wet, the pores are filled with liquid. It's those spaces in between that you need to think about for drainage at a building site, for growing crops, for all sorts of things. They are everything.

"You can't see the spaces between particles with the naked eye, but once you know they exist, it also becomes hard to unsee them."

"Are you about to get all philosophical on me? Are you trying to tell me that life is dirty?"

He smiled, raised his glass toward mine as if to make a toast, "Unseeing is believing!"

I raised my glass to his and chimed, "Sight unseen?"

"No. Hiding in plain sight."

We both became a little tipsy that night as our toasts continued and became steadily sillier.

"To 'interstitial', the unseen in between."

It became our standard toast, but only much later would I realize and appreciate how true its meaning.

Chapter Four

Anna

After buying the land, we hired an architect to transform our dream to paper. Construction started during the summer. We spent many afternoons swimming and splashing around in the lake while watching our dream house materialize. It was on one of those days that David found the lake's icy cold spot. He said the swirling current it produced felt like a cold-water jacuzzi. It became the spot we gravitated to for relief during the stifling dog days of August.

Now the house was here, but David was gone, and the dream was no more. Maybe I should sell. The thought of being closer to my granddaughters in California tugged at me, but there was something that I still needed here. I still needed David, and if I couldn't have him in the flesh, then maybe here, I could at least keep his memory alive for a little while more. And, of course, Lainey was back now, too.

But it was brutally lonely at times. There wasn't time for David and me to create a social life and ties to the area before he died. I only knew a handful of people here, and I certainly didn't know any of them well. Maybe that's an important reason to consider leaving. I remembered reading that isolation might also be a contributing factor to Alzheim...

Nope, not going there.

My aimless wandering had somehow brought me up to the second floor. I suddenly had the sensation that I was floating through each room, which made me start to wonder if I was the one that might be the real ghost here until I opened the door to the guest room, and an apparition appeared before me in the bed.

"Hi, Mom, everything okay?"

The breath caught in my chest and my heart began to pound uncontrollably at the shock of finding Lainey here. She wasn't supposed to come until tomorrow. How could she be here without me knowing it?

"Lainey, what are you doing here?"

"What do you mean?"

"The storm. The roads must be impassable. Wait, that's not even the point. I didn't know you were here. When did you come, and why didn't you tell me you were here?"

"Mom, I came last night before the storm started. I didn't want you to be alone. Don't you remember? I arrived just as you were finishing your supper—soup, I think it was."

No, it can't be.

"We spoke for a while about the weather, and if you were stocked-up for food and other supplies. And you told me about your meeting with Harvey."

No, no, no.

"Mom, you look like you've been crying. It's another bad day, isn't it? Come sit beside me."

I made my way to the end of the bed and sat. I couldn't face Lainey. Instead, I stared at the light switch on the opposite wall. It was a strange thing to focus my gaze on, but it was the first thing I saw while I struggled to process how she could be here, and my having no memory of spending time with her last night.

"It's okay, Mom. No worries. I was just about to get up anyway. I'll take a shower, and then I'll join you downstairs."

"Fine," I said as I rose.

I sat in my once favorite living room easy chair facing the windows and waited. I couldn't let myself accept that I didn't know Lainey was here. Because, if I accepted being surprised, then I would also have to admit that I couldn't remember engaging in conversations with her. It would be evidence that something much more than grief might be affecting me.

I waited, and I waited, finally becoming impatient even though I remembered that when Lainey was a teenager, her showers could often last almost an hour. Funny the things you remember, but not so funny when you don't remember what you should.

I looked over at the clock and then back out the window. I picked up the book I had been reading last, realizing that it had been some time ago that I last looked at it. I started reading, or at least I tried. It was frustrating that I couldn't remember anything about the characters or the story's premise. Focusing was impossible. I tossed the book aside and glanced back again at the clock. Much more time than I expected had passed. It was now nearly two hours since I left Lainey.

I started to wonder if everything was okay. Could she have had an accident in the shower? That single scary thought propelled me. I flew up the stairs and down the hall that anchored both bedrooms. The door to the guest bedroom was closed.

I knocked. No sound.

I knocked again and called for Lainey.
Nothing.
I pushed the door open. "Lainey?"
The bed was made, and the room appeared unused. I rushed into the guest bath, but nothing seemed out of place. Fresh towels hung neatly folded over the bar. I looked at the shower glass—no water spots. I returned to the bedroom to search again. No, there wasn't any sign of anyone having been in here until I noticed the dent in the bedspread at the foot of the bed where I had been sitting.

Swallowing the scream that threatened to send me over the edge, I backed out of the room, shut the door, and ran down the hall into the safety of my own bedroom. I grabbed one of David's old shirts from his closet and wrapped it around me. I paced the room hugging myself and the shirt, hoping both could ground me to another time, to the before or after, to a time that no longer mattered, because I just needed to escape the here and now. The present was becoming a far too dangerous place to be.

I willed my breath to find a slower and steadier rhythm. I sat on my bed and watched the swirling snow outside until my racing heart slowed. David's soft old flannel shirt boosted my courage. It also helped to combat the chill that tried to settle in my bones. It was now late afternoon, and I wondered how much longer it might snow. The simple act of wondering about such an ordinary, everyday concern helped. I decided that, for better or worse, I was stuck living in the present, and I needed to take control of my situation, whatever that may be.

I knew from experience how the mind could play

tricks. When Lainey first disappeared, I sometimes caught a brief glimpse of somebody that reminded me of my daughter. My mind became convinced it must be her. My therapist explained it was only my mind desperately wishing to find her that kept me chasing ghosts. My study of the memory walls earlier today must have triggered a momentary relapse into that in-between time—the time after Lainey disappeared to when she returned. The desperation that had overwhelmed me then was probably akin to the distress I feel now, wishing Lainey were here a day earlier. I must have been chasing ghosts so I wouldn't be alone in this howling storm and in another potential blackout.

I made my way downstairs and back to the office. I jotted a quick to-do list. I would start with getting back to the everyday, mundane tasks of life. The list was becoming pretty long, which made me realize just how much I had been avoiding life. I also couldn't hide from the fact that I might be trying to trick myself by making a long list to postpone listing the most crucial thing that I needed to do. With one hand caressing David's shirt for fortification, the other hand penned my last to-do bullet:

See a doctor.

My intellectual side, if I still had one, knew that I needed to put some effort into working through my grief, but my emotional side was quite comfortable to be in a sort of limbo because I didn't want to ask myself the bigger question tugging at me. *Is grief responsible for my behavior, or is it something else?* I didn't want to know the answer if it would be that *something else*.

That would be just too scary a something to face. On the other hand, I knew that I couldn't remain in this overwhelmingly sad and depressive state if it were just an excuse to avoid learning an answer that I didn't want to know. It would be selfish of me if that were what I was doing. I would be disrespecting the memory of David by labeling my sadness, depression, and that something else as grief. I suddenly felt ashamed and unsure of my true motives. Could I actually be losing myself?

I needed to find the answer, even if I wasn't keen on learning the answer or yet rejoining the land of the living without David beside me. I decided to start my reentry launch by forcing myself to complete routine tasks that I had been dodging. I took care to avoid looking at my memory walls. The first task was to sort through the pile of mail. There was a lot of junk mail. Sorting through it was a small, but satisfying, accomplishment—especially the act of tossing junk mail into the waste bin after barely a glance.

After sorting, I now had a pile of bills, and a separate stack of cards and letters that I knew would be condolences. The "sorry" pile could wait. It wasn't the right time to open those. I powered up the laptop and proceeded to pay utility and other regular monthly bills. The simple act of doing something so normal was gratifying. Maybe this was a sign that I really was losing it, I laughed to myself. After all, what sane person enjoys paying bills?

My credit card statement, as expected, had a zero balance. I started to push it aside when a thought stopped me. Picking up the phone, I dialed customer service and added Lainey to the account as an authorized user. I didn't know for how much longer she might be making the long drive from the city to check up on me, but it wasn't fair for her to absorb gas, grocery, and other costs.

After hanging up, I rummaged through the top desk drawer for David's card. I attached a sticky note, "For Lainey's use." She could use it until the new card came in the mail. I also made a mental note to tell Lainey I was getting better and that she shouldn't push her life aside just to be so much with me.

I returned to the task of paying bills and fell into a pleasing rhythm until the next one put a halt to my stride. I hated not paying bills on time, but I couldn't face this one just yet. I promised myself to deal with it tomorrow and then stashed it into the desk's top drawer. To keep myself—mostly—honest, I slapped a reminder sticky note on the desk.

Task one, done—bills paid.

Make hairdresser appointment.

This one was easy. I opened my online calendar to look for a date that might work. Everything that needed doing, every reminder, was on that calendar. I lived by it, or at least I used to do so. Seeing the empty calendar cells surprised me at first until I realized that it had been quite some time, and maybe even before…

Anna, you are wide-open so just call. I dialed the hairdresser.

"We are closed today due to the storm. Please…"

I hung up. I looked out the window, still snowing and now nearly dark.

Next, on the to-do list: *Check email.*

This was going to be a more difficult task. I skimmed my inbox. Ads and spam were quickly deleted, which felt gratifying. That left a list of emails from friends, former colleagues, and neighbors, people from where I lived and worked before moving here. All expressed their sadness at learning about David.

Forcing myself to read each one should feel like an accomplishment and one huge step forward. But as I started writing brief replies, I began to realize how disconnected I felt from many of these people. I could barely recall some faces or specific memories of them. Two steps back. I closed the lid on the laptop and pushed it aside.

A few emails—done.

Next, I turned to the files Harvey left. There was David's trust file, a file containing his real estate and other holdings, and a file listing numerous accounts and how David's cash flow was set up. David's trust was the first file that I placed in front of me and opened. It was a tome that must have numbered more than fifty pages. I was grateful for Harvey's carefully typed notes explaining each document or section, but I was slightly ashamed to feel even more grateful when the lights went out.

Pitch black. Another storm, another power failure. Not unexpected. We stored charged flashlights in every room. I reached into a desk drawer for a flashlight. Before leaving the office, I placed the stack of files neatly on the corner of my desk. I put my to-do list on top of the files and the credit card for Lainey on top of everything. Everything was neatly stacked and organized. It was okay to have a stack of to-do stuff on my desk. That didn't bother me as much as a messy desk. All throughout my career, and even after retiring, messy desks were my pet peeve. I could dig into neat stacks of papers, but I seethed inside if they weren't organized or if they were haphazardly strewn about.

I left the office and wove my way through each room to pull down the insulated window shades that would preserve the heat inside for as long as possible. Tonight, the act was an unnerving and frightening chore. Peering out windows while pulling down the shades, I sometimes thought I saw movement outside. I tried to convince myself that it was only the shadows of trees swaying in the blustery wind.

My stomach grumbled, echoing that it was also none too pleased by the lack of power. I felt my way to the kitchen guided by the flashlight's small beam. I informed my stomach that menu options were currently limited as I slapped together a tuna sandwich. Eating alone and in total darkness was a strange and uncomfortable feeling. The isolation of this otherwise completely normal act of eating somehow magnified my isolation, extinguishing any taste. I suddenly felt like I was chewing cardboard.

Outside noise was amplified. When the wind gusted, it sounded like a freight train rumbling toward me. I could remove my hearing aid, but then the feeling of not being able to hear anything would only remove another of my limited physical senses and not be at all reassuring. I gulped down the last of the tasteless sandwich, raced upstairs, and bored my way under the covers. The power would likely not be restored until sometime tomorrow, and the house was already starting to lose warmth. I wished I had thought to bring in more firewood before the snow began. Now it was too late.

In the safety of my bed, I could now remove my hearing aid and place it in its charger. I started to do so when I realized how silly that would be because without power there would be no charging. I lay there, my pulse racing too much to relax enough for sleep. I soothed myself by mentally listing the accomplishments I made today, and then I made a list of what I could do to achieve more progress tomorrow. I wasn't going crazy. I wasn't losing it. Grieving for David had simply overtaken me.

Lord, I miss him. Why did you have to take him from me so soon, I pleaded for the one-millionth time. We had so many plans and dreams. I still had trouble believing that David wouldn't suddenly walk through the door. He appeared so very fit for a man in his mid-sixties. He was more than fit. He was vibrant, vivacious, handsome, and charming beyond measure. He had been nearly addicted to staying fit, being sure to eat healthily and to exercise regularly.

We bought cross-country skis as presents to ourselves for Christmas. We planned to use them on the web of trails here. We only had to walk out the door, strap on our skies, and take off on one of the trails. Locals were known to pack down the ski trails with snowmobiles after every snow. We were looking forward to meeting people. Settling in here was a priority we shared. I was as excited as David about skiing this winter. Now, I might as well sell those skis. Without David, I no longer had any interest.

I still didn't know what the surprise was that David had in store for me and was about to tell me just before his heart attack. It was one of the things I couldn't let go of. It niggled at me. Early-on after David's death, I checked the mail, his emails, and credit card statements. Was it a trip he planned? Was it a purchase he made? I never found any clue. Whatever it might have been, it remained a mystery.

The incessant howling wind had me on edge. It was loud and frightening. I could remove my hearing aid, but tonight I felt more comfortable about leaving it in and having it last for as long as possible. There was nothing to do but sleep, but how could I ever fall asleep under these conditions?

The nursery rhyme about a little teapot that I sang and pantomimed for Lainey when she was little and couldn't sleep came to mind. It was her favorite song. Sometimes I could overhear her singing it softly to herself when she woke in the middle of the night. I found myself starting to hum the tune, and then singing the words. If it worked on Lainey, maybe it would work on me. I softly sang the song a second time but stopped halfway through when I thought I heard somebody singing along with me. I pulled the covers completely over my head and cried out for it to stop.

If I dared to look out from my covers, I knew I would see nothing. There was only darkness.

Chapter Five

Friday, Anna

I woke to bright sunshine and blue skies, glistening snow, and power restored. I decided if the universe could do all these things for me, the least I could do was to try producing a mood that matched. Temperatures had already risen enough that the snow was beginning to melt, though with so many inches now covering the ground, it would take quite a few days of weather like this to disappear. It was beautiful outside, maybe even more so after a harrowing night like last night.

I checked my cell phone and saw that it still had a lot of juice left in it and I wouldn't have to charge it again until later. I also noticed that it was Friday, which meant Lainey should be arriving later.

I placed my hearing aid in its charger. I could finally recharge the battery now that there was power and recharging it wouldn't take too long. I followed my morning routine and then put a load of clothing into the washing machine, I went from room to room to open the shades to the beautiful sunshine. I wondered how long it had been since I had ventured outside to breathe in fresh air.

Through one of the windows, I saw the Bills, Young & Old, busy plowing my driveway and shoveling the walkway to my front door. I was surprised that they had gotten to me so soon. Though when I glanced at the clock, I was stunned to see that it was already midmorning. I quickly dressed, inserted my half-charged hearing aid, and went outside to say hello to the Bills.

"Did you men get any sleep last night? To get to me so early, you must have been working throughout the night."

"We made a few passes in some places during the storm. Got some sleep, and then started again super early before the sun came up," Old Bill said. "We had planned to get to you earlier than now. Next time I'll make sure of it. We talked it over before this last storm and decided that we should make plowing you out a priority. We don't like the idea of you being stuck alone and out here, especially if the power goes out. If we can make a few passes during the storm, it might also be that much quicker the bucket trucks can get out here if they need to fix the lines."

"Thank you, Bill. Everyone I've met since we moved here has been so wonderful to us. There are such nice people here."

Old Bill lifted an index finger off the steering wheel and pointed behind me to my garage. "But, not to put my nose in," he said, "I can't plow out your driveway all the way with that cord of wood stacked in front in your garage, and if you don't mind me saying so, I don't understand why it's there. You can't get your car out of the garage now."

I turned and saw what he meant. He was right. It would be impossible to get my car out of the garage until all the firewood was removed. Why was it there? I had made arrangements to have more wood delivered, but that's not where the wood is supposed to be left. Plus, Wally usually comes to the door to let me know when wood has been delivered.

"I didn't realize the wood was left there. I don't know how or when that happened."

"I'd make a ruckus with whoever delivered that wood if I were you," said Old Bill. "And, if you haven't yet paid them, you shouldn't do so til they move it."

"You shouldn't be moving that pile yourself," Young Bill chimed in. "Let me know if they won't do it. I'll come back and move the wood for you. With more snow forecasted, it could be a while, but we'll be checking in on you when we plow."

"Thank you! You are both too kind."

I collected the mail from my mailbox and headed back inside. I was fuming. What idiot would dump a cord of wood in front of my garage door? We always bought wood from Wally, and he knew where to put it. David had built a firewood shelter midway between the front door and the driveway. I even paid Wally extra to stack the wood there. I grabbed my phone from my pocket, headed to the office to look up Wally's phone number, and dialed.

When the phone was answered, I said, "Hello, Wally, this is Anna Simmons."

"Hi Anna," said Wally, "I hope you made it through the storm okay. I'm glad I could get that last wood delivery out to you before. No doubt it was useful. I think out your way probably lost power again."

"I did lose power, but it's back on now," I said. "I'm calling because I don't understand why the wood wasn't stacked in my shelter like always? I pay you extra to do so."

"Is there a problem?"

I could feel my voice rise in anger. "It was dumped in front of my garage door. I can't get my car out of the garage now. I think that's a big problem."

"That numbskull!" Wally said, "I'm so sorry. I didn't know there was any problem. I'm laid up with a bum leg from a skiing accident, and I've had my nephew covering for me. The closest I can get to wood deliveries right now is hobbling over to my desk. Wait a minute. Let me check the receipts."

"Wally, I didn't sign a delivery receipt this time."

"He's done everything wrong. Wait until I get my hands on this kid," Wally said, "Wait, here it is."

How could there be a receipt when I didn't know the wood had been delivered, I wondered. *No, please don't tell me there's another thing I can't remember.*

"It was signed for," said Wally.

That can't be.

"Looks like the name is…'Lainey' no last name, but a note saying, 'daughter approved delivery.' Do you have a daughter named Lainey?" he asked.

"Yes, I do," I sighed.

"I still don't understand why the numbskull left the load of wood in front of your garage door. I'd come right out there now to move it myself, but with my leg, I can't," he said. "I'll try to get in touch with my nephew and get him out there, but with the weekend and him being a teenager…"

"That's okay, Wally," I said. "See what you can do and let me know."

"Again, I'm sorry. Your next delivery will be free."

"That's not necessary. Just feel better," I said as I

hung up the phone.

Still fuming, the phone still in hand, it started to ring. "Hello," I said into the phone, and shaking my head in frustration when I realized that my voice sounded a bit too testy.

"Anna, it's Harvey. Just checking in to see if you made it through the storm okay. I tried phoning a few minutes ago, but there was no answer, and I was starting to worry."

"I'm fine. I was probably just outside talking to the guys who shovel and plow for me."

"Good, good," he said, "I'd hate to think of you being so isolated that you can't even get into town if you need something."

"Well, that could still be a little bit of a problem. I've got a cord of wood blocking my garage. The kid who delivered it must have been half-asleep."

"That's crazy," Harvey said. "It's more than crazy, it's outright dangerous in this weather and with you living out in the boonies. I'll drive out tomorrow and move the wood for you."

"No that's not necessary," I said, not wanting him to be here. "I've made arrangements to have the wood moved before then." Under my breath, adding, 'hopefully.'

"Okay. Have you had a chance to review any of the documents I left with you?"

"I've started, but I haven't gotten too far yet. I plan to do so today."

"Perfect, Anna. It gives me another reason to see you soon and something to look forward to."

I cringed but said, "I'll let you know when I'm ready. Thank you, Harvey."

I hung up. Harvey was right. I shouldn't put off getting to those files any longer. After all, I had considerable motivation to finish. It would mean that I no longer needed to deal with Harvey as frequently. I made myself some food, again placed my hearing aid into the charger, transferred clothes from the washing machine to the dryer, and then went back into the office.

I glanced at the photos and focused on the one with little Lainey wearing the nurse's cap that I had made from paper. She was supposed to be doctoring to Trent who was sick in bed with one of the usual childhood illnesses. I had given her a tray containing tomato soup and a grilled cheese sandwich to deliver to him.

I could still remember the look on her face. She felt so proud, so grown up, to be given such a weighty responsibility. I watched her as she carefully made her way down the hallway focused on not spilling the bowl of soup and, at the same time, struggling to keep her head held high so that her nurse cap wouldn't fall off. I grabbed my camera, which was always nearby to capture special moments, and I tiptoed down the hall.

There, just outside Trent's door, I overheard Lainey telling Trent that he was too sick to eat and that I made the food for her. I peeked into the room and saw her stuffing half of the sandwich into her mouth. I had to put my hand over my face to muffle my laughter. I quickly snapped several photos to memorialize the scene, now titled on the plaque below it, "Nurse Feasts on Grilled-Cheese & Tomato Soup While Patient Starves." The scene made me smile yet again.

Okay, now down to business. I turned toward the desk and was surprised to see that it was not how I remembered leaving it. I had stacked everything neatly on the upper right corner of my desk. The credit card that I had left on top for Lainey was missing. My to-do list was now on the other side of the desk and the files were not in the same order. It wasn't that the desk was messy; it was just not how I remembered leaving it. I was annoyed.

And where was that blasted credit card? I started to look around on the floor for it, thinking that maybe the pile had toppled. That's when I noticed a few water spots shaped like a partial boot print on the floor around my desk. How did that happen? Maybe, I didn't remember to remove my boots right away when I came in from outside.

I was fuming so much about Wally that maybe I had forgotten, and because I was so agitated and looking for his phone number, maybe I also hurriedly moved things around on the desk. It was a reasonable explanation, but try as I might, I couldn't recall any of those actions. I also couldn't remember exactly when I did take off my boots or the act of searching the desk for Wally's number. I scolded myself to just let it go. It wasn't important. I moved my feet around in circles to make my heavy woolen socks soak up the spots of snowmelt, and everything was then fine again.

I looked over my to-do list. I should make that hairdresser appointment. I found the number and called.

"Fantastic Locks! How many I help you?"

"This is Anna Simmons. I need to make an appointment."

"Hi Anna, it's Carly. I think you already have an appointment scheduled. Let me check."

"I don't think I have an appointment. It's been a

while since I've been in."

"Hi again," Carly said. "Yup, it's here. I have you scheduled for a week from Tuesday at two. Do you need to change it?"

I started to shake. "Carly, when did I make the appointment?" I heard the quiver in my voice.

"Anna, it's the regular standing appointment you have every six weeks," she said. "Maybe, you just forgot about this one because you canceled the last time. You said you weren't up for it. It was so soon after your husband…"

"Thanks, Carly. Now I remember," I lied.

"So, the date and time still work?"

"Yes, thanks. I'll see you then."

I couldn't understand why the appointment wasn't on my calendar. Carly was correct about me having regular standing appointments to have my hair done, and they were also scheduled as repeat appointments on my on-line calendar. The appointment would automatically populate the same day and time every six weeks. I added the regularly occurring appointment back on to my calendar. Why would I have deleted the repeated event from my calendar, I wondered. I guessed it was more likely that when I deleted the appointment that I canceled, I also inadvertently deleted all future appointments. I also didn't remember canceling the last appointment, but I was still in a state of profound shock then. I shrugged off any more thoughts that tried to pull me along that terrible path. I was going to drive myself crazy if I started second-guessing everything.

Looking back over my list, my next task was to review the three files that Harvey left for me. I skimmed through the file of David's property holdings.

It contained a summary of his liquid assets and properties along with properties he had recently sold, and properties that were pending sale at the time of his death. Harvey had done an excellent job of condensing everything into a few easy-to-read pages.

Two things were clear. First, I was struck by the fact that David had accumulated more wealth than I had imagined. Second, I had no experience—or interest—in managing all these properties or their sale. As David's attorney and friend, Harvey recognized the opportunities and pitfalls associated with each property and investment as well as David. He knew David's approach to understanding when to invest and when to sell. It made sense that he should continue to manage everything. Admittedly, he should probably also continue to manage David's entire estate on my behalf. I was confident in Harvey's abilities given his experience, expertise, and history with David, but there was that uncomfortable feeling again about relying on him too much. Something told me that it could be a mistake in the long run.

To his credit, Harvey did suggest that Trent could handle everything if I preferred. However, we both knew that it would be a lot to ask Trent to take on. When David's estate matters were more settled it might make sense to turn things over to Trent or Lainey to manage, but it didn't make any sense to do so now.

I began skimming the summary that Harvey drafted for my own estate. One of the questions Harvey had jotted was to ask me to decide who my successor trustees would be if I became incapable of managing my own affairs. He again suggested that I could name Trent, but he also suggested that I could retain him as first successor trustee and Trent as secondary successor trustee. His logic was that he was already familiar with David's holdings that were now mine and because he was much closer geographically to me than Trent should I need medical care or other assistance.

I suddenly wondered why Harvey said nothing about Lainey. She was much closer geographically to me than Trent, and she was family. Could it be that Harvey was sexist? Or was it because Trent was also a lawyer like himself, which he might believe to be a more appropriate choice? I made a note to ask Harvey. I could feel myself becoming angry that Lainey hadn't been considered, or named, anywhere.

It was also frustrating to have all of this dumped into my lap. David's death was hard enough. Having to deal with all this crap was just too much. My frustration and anger were building. I turned to one of the photos of him on my memory walls.

"You think you had everything figured out!" I shouted at a photo of David. "Your lawyer, and so-called friend, here to synthesize and sanitize everything and to take care of me because you no longer can. I don't need you, or anybody, to take care of me and to control my life."

My voice became louder as I became angrier. It felt good. "Do you think you can control me from the grave? You are dead. Do you hear me, David? You are dead. I had a life before I met you. Life is messy. It's meant to be messy. Living is messy. How could you think you could keep me from suffering—you couldn't," I shouted.

"I had built a life of my own. I once had a career that I loved, friends that I enjoyed, and I didn't feel alone. Now, I'm alone, it's all I am now, and it's all because of you. You took away everything that I built for myself, and I'm somehow supposed to be content losing all of that and now living on what you built? You may have been rich, but you couldn't take it with you. I didn't have the money you had, but I owned my own life. I wish I never met you. I may have everything of yours, but I have nothing of myself anymore!"

I didn't realize I was pounding away on one of the photographs of David until the frame's glass shattered and large pointed shards fell to the floor, one narrowly missing my foot that was only covered by a woolen sock. I looked down at the broken glass. The pieces seemed to be waiting for me as an answer, as invitation, and I wondered how it might feel to slash one across my wrists.

Those pieces of glass were spellbinding.

Would I feel anything?

I couldn't look away.

Could I feel anything anymore? Even if there were pain, at least it would all be over quickly, and it would be the last pain I would ever feel.

I picked up the largest piece. I gently placed the slender, jagged spike across my palm. It was long and sharp enough. Ending it all was a familiar thought that I'd had many times before, but this was the first time that I had ever come so close. I was now holding the tool that could do the job. Before now I had never moved to that next thought, from wanting to end it all to envisioning doing it. I immediately thought of a bathtub.

But, of course, it's a must to slash your wrists while relaxing in a warm bath. Isn't that how it's supposed to be done? It's how everyone slashes his or her wrists in movies. I wondered why, and then I wondered if people slashed their wrists while in bathwater because they saw it in movies, or if movies portrayed it that way because of some unwritten how-to guidelines. I wondered if it might be a classic chicken and egg conundrum, which suddenly, made the idea seem funny. Laughing at myself broke my anger.

I walked over to the desk, picked up the trash basket from underneath it, and carefully deposited all the shards into it. I put the trash basket back under the desk, glancing at my computer as I lifted my head.

With my curiosity about why people slashed their wrists while in bathtubs still on my mind, I knew I wouldn't be satisfied until I had an answer. It was time again to consult the search engine. As I scrolled, I realized that a lot of people had asked the same question. I wondered how many of them went ahead with it. This window into the troubled lives of strangers struck me as deeply disturbing, and a kind of creepy voyeurism. I closed the laptop and left the office to head upstairs. The clothes were probably dry by now and my hearing aid should be fully charged. Passing through the living room I noticed the skies darkening again. The Bills had said more snow was forecasted.

With my clothing put away, I turned to the last item—David's shirt. I hated to wash it. Washing it was to renew it, which seemed wrong when he was no longer here to wear it again. On the other hand, my wearing his shirt gave me another kind of comfort that had helped me through the day. Lately, it seemed I was more in need of help wherever I turned. I opened his closet, reached in to grab a hanger—

And screamed.

Every one of David's shirts was shredded. They each remained on their hangers—but ripped to ribbons. I closed the closet door, stepped back, and screamed again. No, no, this can't be happening. It just can't be happening. This can't be real.

I ran out of the bedroom, down the stairs, and then didn't know where to turn. Where had I left my phone? I needed to find it.

The office. That must be where it is. I ran to the office and slammed the door shut. Grabbing the phone and gasping for air, I wondered what to do next. I tried to decide my next step as I desperately also tried to calm my breathing. There would be no way I could phone anyone until I was able to breathe and to think.

Holding the cell phone against my chest, I made a mental list of possibilities. I could dial 911, but that's such a serious call to make. Last time I phoned 911, was when David collapsed. Dare I phone Lainey or Trent? I didn't want to worry either of them. Trent is clear across the country. I despised people that were so needy that they tormented those who were dear to them with endless drama and worry.

I knew I was procrastinating, and I knew the reason. It was because I didn't want anyone to know if I were losing it. What would happen to me? Would I be placed in an assisted living facility, or would I be deemed too much of a risk for living in one? Would I be locked away in a memory care unit at some nursing home? No, I couldn't bear it. I would rather be dead than to end that way. I glanced down at the trash basket under the desk. I did have a choice.

How did those shirts get destroyed? There is

nobody else here. Could I have done this? Did I use one of the glass shards to do this? That would be some crazy behavior. It would be more than crazy; it would be unchecked anger. But why would I have destroyed things that mean so much to me? I couldn't bear to part with David's things yet, so why would I destroy them? But then I looked at the photograph that I had pounded away at. That too had been special to me. Am I really so angry inside? They say anger is one of the stages of grief people experience. But I couldn't quite remember what stage the anger phase was.

I sat at my desk, opened the laptop, and logged in to research the subject. There it was. The seven stages of grief are shock, denial, anger, bargaining, depression, testing, and acceptance. *Anger,* I read, *is a common reaction to loss, and it's one of the Kubler-Ross' stages of grief. You may be angry with the person who left you, or you may feel angry with yourself.* Well, that fits.

But I couldn't leave well enough alone. I then searched whether anger could also be a stage of dementia and found, *Anger, confusion, fear, paranoia, and sadness that people with the disease are experiencing can result in aggressive and sometimes violent actions.* Damn, that fit too. I read more and learned that these feelings are symptoms of *Moderate Cognitive Decline, which is a mild or early-stage of Alzheimer's disease. People reaching this stage should be under the care of a medical professional. Obvious symptoms can be:*

Having no recollection of recent events. Checkmark that.

The failure to perform specific math problems such as multiplication or long division. Not applicable—

haven't had to do that recently.

Not being able to take part in critical financial tasks like paying bills. I think I paid the bills correctly, but maybe I had better check.

Acting out or reacting negatively when faced with situations that test social and mental skills. Okay, I may have been short-tempered with people lately—Lainey, Trent, Wally, Cassie, and Harvey. Geez, that's just about everybody I've recently encountered.

Losing memories of personal history.

I quickly skipped over some information to scan the rest of the stages of Alzheimer's disease, and it struck me as a strange coincidence that Alzheimer's and some grief models both have seven defined stages. I glanced over at my to-do list. The last task on my list stuck out loud and clear.

See a doctor.

Chapter Six

Anna

I desperately wanted to believe that my grieving for David was the cause of my memory lapses, hallucinations, and crazy behavior. But I also couldn't dismiss the possibility that something more was happening to me. How long could I put off finding out the truth? I kept hoping that something would change to prove me normal. Prolonging learning the truth could be a disservice to me and a disservice to my family.

As a child I loved everything scary, especially the haunted house ride at the amusement park. I knew it was make-believe. I knew that I would be scared, but once it was over and I was back outside the building, in a world I knew, being scared would be over.

But real life was becoming more terrifying than any amusement park ride. I want to be normal again, but I also don't know what normal is anymore. If it's grief, there will be a new normal for me once I reach the other side. If it's dementia, normal will continue to slip away from me little-by-little and day-by-day. If I have dementia, then today I am closer to normal than I will be tomorrow, or any other day still ahead of me.

Trying to make sense of what I've been experiencing reminded me of the time, when I was still a child, that I had to undergo surgery to remove my infected appendix. My parents tried to keep me from being afraid by saying that I wouldn't feel any pain. I would be put to sleep, wake up after the surgery, and never remember a thing. I didn't believe that I would never remember anything so I challenged myself to remember everything I could, but try as I did, I was astonished at how one minute I was awake in one room and then the next minute I was somewhere else. I could never make sense of how that chunk of time was lost. It was a mystery, and a kind of magic then. Doctors had cut me open, took out something bad, and sewn me shut. It was incredulous that none of that time was something I would ever feel or could ever remember. That's what this feels like now. The difference is that I knew what to expect then. I now no longer know what to expect. Back then, I knew I would wake up and be on the path to healing.

Now, when I have memory lapses, I fear that I'm self-destructing.

Just as my hand reached out to shut the lid of the laptop, an email from a credit card company scrolled across my screen asking me to verify a recent purchase. The purchase was with an airline for nearly close to three thousand dollars. Something was clearly wrong. I went to the credit card website, clicked my cloud's stored password, and saw several pending charges that I didn't remember making.

Dare I dig deeper? How do I respond to the email? Did I, or didn't I? Damn it! What should I do? I'm starting to second-guess myself, and my every action. I'm paralyzed. I don't know what to do because I don't know what I may have done. I swear I'm going to drive myself crazy.

Is this what crazy feels like? I laughed, only to quickly realize that it was no laughing matter. Is losing a little more of yourself each day what dementia, or Alzheimer's disease, feels like? I had a newfound respect and compassion for anyone suffering from this interminable disease. I'd never put myself in the shoes of somebody suffering from the early stages of Alzheimer's disease. To be locked inside an endless nightmare where everything is so confusing is torture that defies understanding. Do people come to terms with losing themselves, or does the disease simply progress to a point that the torture stops on its own because it can no longer be understood or recognized by the person suffering? Maybe, it becomes easier once the disease progresses to the point where enough memory has slipped away and other people feed, bathe, and dress you.

Does a certain peace settle in when you no longer need to be responsible for anything? Do people give in and give up, or do they get to the point where they lack any self-awareness, and it's that stage putting an end to their suffering? How much worse does it get, before it gets better for the person with the disease. And does it ever really get better for the person? What am I thinking? There is no cure. Death is the only certain release from the grips of the disease.

I imagine that people, who are around other people, might learn through them that there is something wrong. How do you learn, and what do you do about it when you are on your own, alone? Do I exhibit more crazy behaviors than I realize? Harvey said David was selling off a lot of his properties and winding down his business so that the two of us could spend more time together.

What were the words he used? "I was David's investment now." Was that a plan carved out of necessity or desire? We were spending every day together, and he was undoubtedly the more active of us two—he loved to do the food shopping, cooking, etc. I glanced at my "memory walls" and suddenly wondered if the meaning behind the making of it was something different.

But if David recognized that something was wrong with me, wouldn't he have shared that information with my children? Would Trent or Lainey still allow me to live on my own? It's true that Lainey has been here on weekends. Beth and her daughter Cassie are here midweek. There are not many days when I'm entirely alone. Is that by coincidence or by design?

My cell phone started to ring.

"Hi, Mom," Trent said in his usual sunny voice that made me feel gloomy. "How does it feel to be buried in snow? Are you getting sick of winter yet?"

"Hi, Trent. Maybe I am sick...*should I go there?* of winter."

Then a thought occurred to me that could provide me with cover. "You know, how some people suffer from depression because of the lack of light in winter. Maybe, that's also happening to me, too."

"Mom, maybe you do have the winter blues on top of everything else. You are isolated out there, and you are still grieving. David's only been gone a short time. Those three ingredients make for a bad cocktail."

"Trent, I think you might be right."

"The offer still stands for you to come out here, live in the bright sunshine, surrounded by people who love you."

"That does sound wonderful! I promise I'll give it some thought."

How would Lainey feel about me moving across the country?

"Mom, another reason I phoned is to say that since you didn't seem to be planning to come out to us anytime soon, we've decided to come back east next month for a little vacation. We can spend some days with you and teach the girls cross-country skiing while we are there. What do you think?"

I couldn't imagine feeling cheerier than I was at this moment. Having my whole family near and having fun together is something that I'd missed for far too long. "I think that sounds marvelous! That news already makes me feel so much happier. Have you told Lainey yet? She'll be thrilled, too."

"What did you say?"

"Didn't you hear me? Lainey will be thrilled, too."

"I heard you, Mom. You've spoken to Lainey recently?"

"Of course. You know that she's been spending the past few weekends with me. In fact, she should be here again soon."

The silence that ensued began to fill me with an indescribable dread.

"Trent?"

"I'm here, Mom. Sorry, we must have had a bad connection for a minute. Did you say Lainey will be there again soon for the weekend?"

"Yes." I was about to remind him that I heard her speaking to him last weekend when she was here, but then thought better of it. I didn't want him to know that

I overheard their conversation about me losing my mind and cavorting around in the snow barefoot.

"Do you expect to see anyone else during the weekend?"

"No, I don't think so. Why?"

This was turning into a strange conversation. I thought for a moment about what Trent might be asking and wondered...

"Is Lainey seeing someone?" I asked him. "Does she have a boyfriend that I don't yet know about?"

"No, Mom. That's not what I meant. Never mind."

"Well, soon give me the dates of when you are coming. Lainey and I will make it special. It will be so nice for all of us to be together again."

"Mom, yes, it will be a nice time. We are looking forward to it. I think I saw that it's going to snow again soon where you are. So, I hope you don't mind if I phone a little more frequently. I'd feel better if I know that you are okay."

Why the extraordinary concern? I feel like I'm under observation, and it's annoying.

"Of course, Trent. But it's not necessary. You don't need to worry. Like I said before, Lainey will be here soon."

"I know, Mom. Maybe, I can tell her about our upcoming visit. I'd like to tell her myself if that's okay?"

"Okay. I'll save the exciting news for you to tell."

"Thanks, Mom. Take care. I love you."

"I love you too, Trent. Hugs to everybody," I said and hung up.

It had been a stressful day. I needed a nap. I wanted to be in a better mood and refreshed for when Lainey arrived. I made my way up the stairs and to the bedroom while thinking about how lovely it would be to see my grandkids. It had been under such sad conditions, that I last saw them for David's funeral. I wanted to hug them out of the joy I would feel by seeing them, instead of the despair of needing to be consoled. I smiled at the thought of watching them learn how to ski.

Distracted by these pleasant thoughts, too late, I realized that I was swinging open David's closet door. I didn't want to see those ripped shirts again, and I immediately began to close the door, but, too late, I had already caught a glimpse of the inside of the closet. Strangely, everything appeared normal. I open the door wide. All the shirts were okay again. Nothing was in tatters. There could be no more doubt. Here was my proof. I must be losing it. I quickly shut the door, crawled into my bed, and cried myself to sleep.

****

Waking sometime later, it was now mostly dark, and snow was again falling. I knew that I should go throughout the house and close the window shades, but I didn't have the energy. It didn't matter. The house was a cold, lonely, and a scary place to be. I can't do crazy things if I just stay in my bed. I need to tell my family that I may be losing it. If that's the case, they will need to take over everything much sooner than they probably guessed they would need to do. It's the right and responsible thing to do.

There is a noise downstairs. The television. I didn't remember turning it on, but, as I was now starting to learn about myself, that didn't mean I didn't do it. Or maybe Lainey had arrived. I got out of bed and walked to the hallway balcony. I saw lights on below and I heard more of the sounds from the television. I went down the stairs.

Reaching the bottom, I noticed a large tote bag by the front door filled with bags from the same two clothing stores that, along with the airline ticket, were the mysterious pending charges on my credit card. I wondered if those purchases had been made with my card, and if they had—when and how did Lainey get the card? I didn't remember giving it to her. Although I did remember that it was missing, which means that I do remember something.

So, maybe I just didn't remember handing it to her. Downward spiraling whirlpools of circular thought were overtaking me again. I was in danger of being swallowed by an ever-expanding vortex of never-ending second-guessing questions.

I heard Lainey call from the kitchen, "Hey, Mom."

"When did you arrive?"

"Oh, I don't know exactly—maybe an hour, or so, ago. You were sleeping, and I didn't want to wake you. I was just looking through the cupboards to see what there might be for dinner. I ate earlier. So, we just need to make something for you. What do you feel like having?"

"I don't know. I'm not hungry. I'll make myself something later."

"Can I get you something to drink?" Lainey raised a wine glass to her lips. "Would you like some?"

There was something different about her appearance tonight that I couldn't quite put my finger on at first—until I realized that she was wearing makeup, which she normally didn't use. It was overdone and didn't complement the blue of her eyes and her blonde hair. If she had been shopping, maybe she had let the people at the makeup counter try different eye, blush, and lip colors on her—but makeup professionals should know those shades didn't flatter her otherwise fair complexion.

"Wine would be nice. Thanks."

While Lainey got a glass and poured wine for me, I turned toward the direction of the foyer. I was still thinking about the clothing charges on my credit card and the bags inside her tote displaying the distinctive logos from the same major apparel chain and the same high-end lingerie store.

Turning back to her, I asked, "Looks like you've been shopping for some new clothes."

Lainey eyed the bag and then me for a second before answering, "Yes, I did a little shopping."

I couldn't think of a way to casually ask if she had used my credit card. It was nagging at me because I didn't remember giving it to her. It also bothered me that she might use my credit card for purchases unrelated to why I had made her an authorized user. The third reason I didn't want to say anything was that it felt wrong to say something that might sound as if I was launching an unfounded, and unfair, accusation. She could have made those purchases entirely on her own. I took a sip of the wine and decided to plow ahead anyway.

"I didn't know you liked to shop at those two stores. Do you have accounts with them?"

Lainey eyed me again, took a sip, and said, "No."

Her response, so quick, so direct, and somewhat off-putting left me little room to inquire more. "Show me what you bought. It's been forever since I've been shopping and maybe I'll get some ideas," I said, thinking I'd be able to tell by the price tags if the amount totaled the same as what was on my credit card. I felt guilty about the subterfuge and distrusting my daughter, but I also didn't deserve her flippant response.

"I'm quite sure you wouldn't be inspired by my selection of clothing. Let's go sit in the living room and see what movies are on pay per view."

"Okay, but first I really want to see what you've bought. I'm so curious. Humor me," I said as I walked to the tote and lifted the one of the bags. In one quick glance I saw the receipt on the top of the clothing. The total matched the amount I saw as a pending charge from that same store on the credit card statement.

Lainey swooped in and snatched the bag away from me. She shoved it back down into her tote. "Let's go," she ordered.

I walked into the living room and sat on the couch. Lainey's demeanor was disturbing, and now I had more questions than answers. Lainey had somehow gotten the credit card, used it, and, by failing to simply say so, is denying it. It's lying by omission. And what about the airline ticket purchase?

She handed me my glass of wine. "Drink up, Mom."

I obeyed.

Lainey settled into the easy chair and began browsing movie titles. I knew I should probably leave well enough alone, but I couldn't. Just as I was about to ask her directly if she used my credit card, my cell phone rang. The sound was coming from the kitchen.

Lainey jumped up, "I'll get it."

She came back into the room, with my phone in her hand, saying she didn't get to it in time.

"Is there a caller ID or voicemail?" I asked while reaching toward Lainey for my phone.

She backed away, my phone still in her hand and sat back in the easy chair. "No."

Then she casually placed the phone on the side table next to the chair she was sitting in and returned to browsing movie titles.

I took another drink of wine. Strange that she ignored me reaching for my phone and didn't hand it to me. I was starting to feel off balance—physically and mentally. Lainey was making me feel as if I were walking on eggshells. I was becoming increasingly annoyed.

"Lainey, did you use my credit card?"

"How many times are you going to ask me the same question?"

"What do you mean?"

"You keep asking the same question over and over. I'm not going to answer it again. I've tried to be super patient with you, but I've reached my limit. I hate to say it, but I think you might have Alzheimer's. I've read that it's a symptom when people start asking the same thing over and over."

I buried my head in my hands. "So, you think I may have the start of Alzheimer's?"

Lainey laughed. "I think you are going bat-shit crazy."

My head snapped up. "How dare you speak to me that way!" I bellowed, rising from the sofa.

She stared at me.

I was starting to feel woozy. Had I stood too quickly? What was happening?

"Geeze, Mom! What's gotten into you?"

"No, what's gotten into you that you think you have the right to speak to me that way." I shouted as I grabbed the arm of the sofa to keep myself from tipping over.

"I don't know what you are talking about," she said. "One minute we were discussing what we might want to watch on television and the next minute you are screaming at me. Are you okay, Mom? I'm starting to worry about you."

"You just told me that you thought I was bat-shit crazy and that I probably have Alzheimer's!"

Lainey again looked at me strangely and said, "Mom, I never said any such thing. That would be a terrible thing to say to anyone. Are you having trouble standing? I think that maybe the wine on an empty stomach has gone straight to your head."

I plopped onto the sofa. "I need to see a doctor. Something's wrong with me."

My cell phone rang again, and Lainey grabbed it. She stood, gave a quick glance in my direction, and headed to the office.

I knew that it was probably Trent calling like he said he would. If so, I'm sure Lainey's right now in the middle of telling him that she's sure I have Alzheimer's disease. Why else would she walk off to talk? The jig is up, and the cat is of the bag, Anna.

So, this is how it ends, I thought. I guess everyone, at some point, wonders how their life will end. Most people hope it will be quick and painless. I had done a fair amount of research on Alzheimer's disease, and I knew it wouldn't be quick. Nobody can answer if it's painless, because, by the time the disease reaches the end stage, the person has usually lost the ability to communicate. I'm clearly disconnecting more and more from reality, and my symptoms will worsen over time. I might live four to eight years longer after an official diagnosis, although the rate at which the disease progresses varies. I could live for as long as twenty years. I don't want to put my family through this terrible ordeal, but I don't know how to prevent it either. I am becoming the burden I never wanted to be.

I've always been organized and efficient. These strengths got me through everything until now, but they won't get me through this. Those strengths are seeping away from me. At some point those skills will be totally lost to me, and I will then be totally lost to myself. I shaped a career that had me crisscrossing the globe to advise some of the most powerful corporations about marketing strategies for their products and services.

By the time I sold my company, I had five offices worldwide. The frenetic pace of managing the business and those offices kept me on my toes. What would be considered stressful to some was what fueled me. The next big products to hit the market, or how to draw attention to the newest service, were games that I was good at playing. When somebody referred to me as a CEO, I corrected them and said that I was not a CEO but a "CPS" because I often thought of my job as Chief Puzzle Solver. Solving puzzles was play, not work. Not a lot of people understood what drove me. David understood because he had that same self-drive and skill set. I was an expert at solving puzzles. Now, I fear that if psychological tests and investigations include puzzles, I'll certainly fail.

Lainey came back into the room. I noticed she didn't have my phone with her. It struck me as odd that she would leave it in the office.

"Was that Trent?" I asked.

"Yes."

"Well, what did he have to say?"

"Not much. Everything's fine there," Lainey said as she slid back into the easy chair and again began browsing movie titles.

"What did he have to say?" I asked again. I knew that he wanted to tell his sister the news about coming for a visit.

"There you go again sounding like a broken record, barking the same question over and over."

"What has gotten into you? I've never known you to be so mean."

"No, Mom, it's what has gotten into you that is the problem. You do need to see a doctor."

"Tomorrow we will have a serious talk about what may or may not be going on with me, but starting immediately, you will treat me with respect. Is that understood?"

"Goodnight, Mother," she said dismissively, turning her attention to the television.

"I don't recognize you tonight. There is something wrong here, and it isn't completely about me. Be prepared to talk tomorrow," I said before walking away.

I wasn't feeling well, and I was scared and angry. My feet felt like they were caked in cement as I struggled to climb the stairs to my bedroom. Harvey had described grief as being lost in a fog, but I had also read that many people with Alzheimer's also say they often feel that way, too. Those same people also described heaviness in their feet the same as what I was experiencing now.

Crawling in between the covers was comforting. The coolness of the sheets soothed my skin. I stretched out and tried my best to relax, but my mind wouldn't cooperate. Thoughts were swirling, but I couldn't grab onto one that could explain anything. Something was wrong—that much was obvious. That something was wrong with me, I accepted as being quite likely. But what I couldn't understand was Lainey's demeanor. I had never known her to act that way before toward me. Tonight, patience was missing. She displayed only a cold nastiness.

Maybe, I am repeating things over and over. But that doesn't excuse her rudeness. I've never known Lainey to be hostile or belligerent. The look in her eyes tonight left me feeling as if I were looking at a stranger. Her behavior tonight was not characteristic of the Lainey I knew. She wasn't interested in sharing with me the conversation she had with her brother. Certainly, she would have remarked about them coming to visit. I expected her to be happy about the news. Her reaction made no sense.

Something suddenly occurred to me. Maybe, the conversation with her brother had not gone well. But why wouldn't it have? Something might be going on that I was not privy to knowing. Is it because of my suspected disease or is something else happening that I'm not able to see or make sense of? More and more, I sensed that there was something wrong about everything and that it was not entirely everything that was wrong with me. There was something more, but I couldn't put my finger on what.

Tonight, I didn't like Lainey. Something was unsettling and strange about her, and I began feeling guilty about not liking my own daughter. Am I redirecting my anxiety over my own mental health to a false anxiety over my daughter? Maybe, I'm trying to protect and distract myself from now knowing the eventuality of what will happen to me when I am no longer to make my own decisions and when my care is left in the hands of others. She came back to me after David's death. The comforting I've received from my children, and Lainey's spending time with me has been the one good thing to happen since David's death. Tomorrow, I need to have a serious talk with her. Tonight, my brain is fogging over. It's as heavy as my feet were earlier when it was difficult to lift them one-by-one up the stairs.

Chapter Seven

The Lawyer

It was shaping up to be a memorable evening—a fantastic dinner with a beautiful woman. As I poured us another brandy, I could tell from her body language that she was also looking forward to what might happen next, which certainly wasn't supposed to be the ringing of my cell phone.

I checked caller ID before saying, "Why, hell-o, Trent. To what do I owe this call?"

"Hi, Harvey, have you spoken with my mother recently?"

"I phoned earlier today to check in on her. Why? What's up?"

"Did she sound okay?"

"Yes, but she was angry. Said somebody dumped a pile of wood in front of her garage so there was no way she could get her car out of the garage. Crazy, stupid people! I offered to drive up and move the wood, but she said somebody else had already offered to do so."

"Did she say who?"

"No. What is all this about? Why the twenty questions routine?"

"Did she say anything about Lainey being there with her?"

"Lainey? God, no!"

"That's what she told me," Trent said. "My mother said Lainey's been spending a lot of time with her. She's been staying there with her on weekends. I told my mother that I would call again later so that I could speak with Lainey myself, but now my mother's phone is going to voicemail when I call. It's unusual for her not to take a call from me, especially when she knew that I would be calling again soon. I don't like it, Harvey. I'm worried."

"What about the police. Have you thought about having them check on her?"

"If they show up and everything at that moment appears normal—what then? The arrival of the police would just tip her off that we think something is up. The odds that police would walk in and find themselves in the middle of a dangerous scene are slim. They don't know what to look for in a situation like this, and they don't know my mother. How could they judge?"

"What about the housekeeper—Beth something or other? I met her and her daughter when I was at the house a few days ago. Maybe Beth can check in on Anna without raising too much suspicion?"

"Good thinking. I'll give her a call."

"Okay. Keep me posted, Buddy." I quickly hung up, happily turning my attention back to the pretty little lady waiting for me. But—damn it! Something about the call gnawed at me.

Trent phoned me back only a few minutes later. Beth wasn't answering her phone. In less than ten minutes, I had deposited my lady into a taxi, and was now in my own car, weaving my way toward the interstate. Something wasn't right. It was just an instinct, but I had to follow my gut.

Anna was my best friend's wife. He was the best friend that I still woke up missing every day. It's not even two full months since David passed, but his loss still feels as acute as when I first heard the news. I had doubled-over in pain that felt as real as if I'd been sucker-punched.

Once David found Anna, nothing else mattered. It was ironic that he, a confirmed bachelor who'd always said marriage was not in the cards for him, finally found the love of his life. Me, multiple marriages behind me, and I'm still looking. David always said that I looked too hard, that I was impulsive, and I had a weakness for beautiful women. He called that a lethal combination that was guaranteed to generate nothing but alimony bills. David, as usual, had been right. I had a string of support payments to make each month, and I still haven't learned my lesson.

As I drove on, I thought about how easy it would be to fall for the lovely lady that I had to disappoint tonight. I wondered if she would give me a second chance. A small voice that I recognized from memory as sounding just like David's laughed inside my head, and as he had often said in life, again said, "I probably just saved you from more alimony payments!"

It had started to snow, and it was coming down in a good clip. I winced as the radio reported the beginning of another big storm. Travel advisories had been issued. Here I was—heading into the woods during a massive snowstorm. There was plenty wrong with this picture. Was I playing hero, or did I need to be one?

I owed David lots. I loved him like a brother, and his business dealings made me quite comfortable, financially speaking. I wasn't as wealthy as David, but he paid me generously for the legal work. David was that golden client that few people ever have. I'll never have another friend or another client like David. Those are the two reasons why it's so important that I look after Anna's interests. Anna and Trent must continue to want my services. Keeping both satisfied is priority number one. Trent is completely capable of administering David's estate on Anna's behalf. Every time I've spoken with him, I've sweated bullets that he wouldn't pull everything out from under me.

Anna never trusted me after that stunt I pulled the night I first met her. I'd heard plenty about her from David. I knew how much he was in love with her. He even starting to talk about marriage. This was entirely different from the guy I knew. There was no excuse for how I acted.

I had been invited over to his place in the city to meet her. Anna's cooking was superb. Everything about her was fantastic. She was beautiful, smart, funny, and capable. I still regret the combination of too much wine mixed with envy. When he made his way to the toilet, I made my way into the kitchen under the pretext of helping to clear the table. Anna was at the sink spraying off the dishes before loading them into the dishwasher. I came up behind her and slowly placed the serving dishes that I held in each hand onto the countertop, trapping her in the middle between my arms. I purposely moved in much too close. When I was up against her backside, I whispered a teasing remark about how if she tired of David…

I still hate myself for how I acted. I was a fool. She was right to turn the sprayer on me. I haven't forgotten how lousy I acted, and I doubt if she has. I've tried to make up for my stupidity a hundred times since, but I get the feeling that she'll never trust me. I've been wrestling with bringing that past event out into the open and apologizing for my behavior, but the right moment hasn't yet presented itself.

David and I constantly tried to outdo the other, but I had gone too far, and I've been sorry about it ever since. To her credit, I knew she never said anything to him about the scene. She's a class act, that woman. It's unfathomable what she's been through. How David managed to pull her through it all is a testament to the kind of guy he was. I acted like a complete jerk.

I'll need her trust if I'm going to be able to continue managing his estate. If I can't earn her trust, I'll have to resort to plan B. It might be a dicey situation tonight, with me showing up suddenly, and if it starts to spin out of control, it could get ugly fast.

I should make sure my cell phone is fully charged. I reached into my coat's breast pocket, but it wasn't there. I felt around inside all my other pockets. When I came up empty, I realized that in my haste to get on the road, I had forgotten to grab it. In my mind's eye, I could see it still on the table in my entry foyer. I had put it there when I grabbed my coat. Suddenly, it became a good idea to drive even more carefully and to be much more careful once I got to Anna's.

Chapter Eight

The Daughter

Sometimes "Mommy" sits, staring out through the wall-to-ceiling windows at the snowy landscape and ice-covered lake beyond, but I know that isn't what she's seeing. She's lost inside herself, struggling with grief and loss. Whether the struggle is for the loss of a loved one or her sanity is still in question. Whatever the cause, loss is taking her over. Loss is consuming her, and she is losing her mind over it.

I love turbulence—of every kind. I first discovered the excitement of it when I was still a young girl taking my first flight. That day changed my life. It would lead to me making a study of how to play with and change the lives of others.

I was excited about going up into the sky and looking down on the world from a birds-eye vantage. But there were thunderstorms, and I grew more and more impatient waiting in the gate area for our plane to get the okay for departure. Each delay announcement further blackened my mood. I was tired of waiting in the confines of the gate area. There was nothing to do there, but to look at the other people around me all feeling the same. When would the action ever start or, worse, would the flight be canceled?

After what seemed like an eternity we boarded, our

plane raced down the runway and began to climb. It was exhilarating and everything I hoped it would be—for a while, at least. Then I grew bored. Being restricted to the confines of my seat made me restless. Suddenly, turbulence jolted the plane. It took everyone, including me, by surprise. The flight attendant's voice warbled through one bump after another as she ordered everyone to stay in his or her seat and to keep seatbelts tightly fastened. It was intriguing to see how scared the adults around me had become.

Suddenly the plane dropped about twenty feet. In rollercoaster fashion, our bums rose off the seats as our stomachs fell. I was the only one exhilarated by the ride. Up and down the aisle, for as far as I could see, people were gripping their armrests and mumbling prayers or pleading with God to keep them safe. The more panicked the person, the more audible the prayer.

I started laughing when the heavily muscled-bodybuilder guy across the aisle began rapidly pleading, "Please God, Please God, Please!" His neck-to-toe Star Wars battle scene tattoos didn't match his horror-stricken face.

Even though I was only a kid, it was at that moment that I realized how predictable humans behave when facing fearful situations, and I wondered how easy it might be to produce and manipulate those predictable behaviors. People will reach for anything when they are afraid, sad, or in pain. They can be made to do anything. They can be made to believe in anything. They can be made to believe in me.

Gripping an armrest won't help anyone survive a plane crash, and neither will prayers. When prayers to your Almighty for relief, respite, reassurance, rebirth, resurrection, or restoration is all you have left, that's when you become mine to shape and control into whatever pleases me. When you have lost control or when you believe that all is lost, that's when I take hold over you and when my fun begins. I become the Almighty, but I'm not going to grant the help you beg for in prayer.

My phone lights up with a text message. Trent is concerned. Can I check on her and call him back?

Trent is a hoot. He believes he can take care of dear Mom from three thousand miles away by making other people responsible for doing so. You'd think with everything there is at stake, he'd want to do the job himself. By all accounts, David had a lot of money. The distance between Trent and all that money is short. How grateful will Trent be for the help I'm providing to lessen the waiting time?

He has no idea who he's dealing with. I conducted my first experiment in manipulating people to do what I want shortly after that experience on the plane. The Wassermans were an old couple who lived next-door. They sometimes invited me over for tea and pie when Mrs. Wasserman baked. When she was outside gardening, I sometimes invited her into my playhouse for play tea and cookies. I sang for her as I poured. She would laugh, clap, and tell my mother that I was the daughter she always wanted.

They didn't have a daughter. They had one son, and he was a soldier away in Iraq. She died of cancer while he was away. Not long after her death, an exploding mine killed their son. I never saw Mr. Wasserman smile again. It became a near-daily ritual for me to deliver meals my mother had prepared or things she had picked up for him at the market. The old man thought I was a nice little girl by visiting him and listening to the stories about his son. But this all happened soon after that experience on the plane, and I decided that old Mr. Wasserman would be the perfect specimen for my first experiment.

Kids are expected to say the unexpected. So, when I would say something hurtful, he couldn't be offended, because I was just a child that didn't know any better. "Your son must have been so brave, Mr. Wasserman. You must miss him so much. It's so sad that you will never see him again. You must feel so lonely. Tell me another story about him."

I made sure the old man's already fractured heart shattered into even more pieces with the telling of each story. I had the power to make him hurt worse. He had the need to talk about his son, and I was a willing audience. So, he excused and endured my lack of appropriateness. Talking about his son was all he had left. He suffered each dagger because I gave him what he needed. An addict might hate needles, but the jab only lasts a second. The addict turns a blind eye to what the needle delivers and the more lasting devastation it causes.

Each night, I carefully recounted and studied that day's events. I noted what I had said, and I made a study of the impacts. I knew that my next step would be to shred the happy memories Old Mr. Wasserman recounted. Taking away those memories, which was all he had left, made him increasingly desolate.

"That's amazing how he led the football team to their big win. It's so sad that somebody so special isn't here anymore. Had he lived, he probably could have been anything he wanted to be. Now he's gone, and you have nothing left but those special memories."

He wasn't out much before his wife died. He transformed into a crippled up old man who mostly kept to himself after his wife's death. After his son's death, he never left the house. Despite my mother's best efforts, Mr. Wasserman's appetite never recovered. He couldn't sleep, and he began forgetting to take his pills. He slowly gave in and gave up.

One day when I came to visit, I noticed how strangely still he seemed. The television was turned on, but he was now turned off. That's how I thought of it. He was dead. I carefully reached out and poked his cheek. His flesh was cold to the touch. His face appeared strangely calm. The creases in his face were less noticeable. He looked like he was at peace. I accomplished what I had set out to do. I was surprised to realize that I had probably done something good for the old man in the process.

His death was my first success, and I felt good about it. As I helped myself to Mrs. Wasserman's gold jewelry and his coin collection, I imagined them as ghosts happily reuniting. The jewelry and coins were my rewards for a good deed done. My mother's concern over my unimaginable trauma from finding the old man dead made her treat me super special for a long time after.

Chapter Nine

Anna

I woke with a start. I didn't remember climbing into bed. I barely remembered climbing the stairs. I glanced over at the bedside clock and saw that I must have been sleeping for several hours. It was still the middle of the night. The insulated curtains had not been drawn, and yet darkness covered everything. The fog slowly lifted from my brain. I lay there, wondering why I didn't close the drapes before getting into bed. Something was troubling me. Most everything was troubling now. And that, unfortunately, seemed to be the only constant.

I tried to remember back to a time that wasn't troubling. My mind rolled back over the decades. Like waves rolling to the shore, when the water reached a blockage, the water spread around it and kept moving forward. Was that how my life was—a meandering stream that simply turned the next bend when an outcropping of riverbank blocked its way?

My first job after university was with an advertising agency. It was the first time I had struck out on my own. Initially, my status was more gofer than my actual title of marketing assistant. Not many women were yet in the workforce, and of those that were, most never advanced beyond low-level secretarial pools.

Corporate-think at the time was that it would be bad business to invest in women that would invariably leave within a few years to raise a family. Business was a man's world. Few women were ever even given a chance.

That's why it was so unusual when I did quickly advance. I was lucky to have a mentor that respected somebody with a good head, even if that head was feminine and boasted shoulder length hair. Mr. Cummings, the agency partner, was an advertising legend. People vied for a job at our firm and for the opportunity to work under him. For some reason, it was me that he chose to take under his wing. There was tremendous jealousy among the all-male team, but I was focused on learning as much as I could and on doing my best. I loved the high-energy creativity that came with marketing the next hot toy, best cereal, or clothing brand. Five years in, and there was already corridor buzz about me making partner.

I once overheard a junior partner remark that I was probably being hoisted up the corporate ladder so that the higher-ups could get a better view up my skirt. Mr. Cummings, who happened to be walking by, shot back that unlike most of the men in the firm, I had a natural instinct for the business. He said that I had already captured more accounts than most men with double my experience. Mr. Cummings had my back. So, the occasional lewd comment or snide remark directed at me easily rolled off.

I had a cozy apartment just off the park and an active social life. There were parties, dates, and summer getaways with friends to the Vineyard, Fire Island, or the Hamptons. I didn't think I wanted for anything more until I met James Blackwood. One of the partners had hijacked him from a rival firm. Gossip was that he was hungry and would step over his own mother if it meant landing a big account. We locked eyes as he was being introduced to everyone around the table at our weekly strategy meeting. I flushed and quickly looked away. In that briefly intense moment, I had noted that he was handsome and self-assured, but there was something different about him too. As luck would have it, his first assignment was to work with me on the branding and marketing strategy for a new clothing line by a top, and well-known, designer.

That was the beginning of it all. We spent the next two months focused on developing a branding strategy and marketing campaign. Days spilled into evenings, which spilled over into weekends. Although our energies were focused on the project, we also got to know one another better. James Blackwood was originally from a small Kansas town, and he never looked back after heading to the big city. He was drawn to everything big, bright, and expansive—throngs of people, skyscraping buildings, and the city's fast pace. I preferred life on a somewhat smaller scale. The frenetic city could sometimes be overwhelming.

When working on the project hit a roadblock, and our creative juices began to run dry, we would plan restorative breaks. James took me to Central Park and taught me how to ride horseback. I took him to Rockefeller Plaza and taught him how to skate. The breaks were fun, relaxing, and just what we needed to return to the project with fresh eyes.

James put excitement and sizzle into everything he touched, which was why I was careful not to let him touch me. I didn't want to become the cliché stereotype of that woman looking for a man to marry her so that she could leave the working world behind. I didn't want the men at the agency to boast that they had been right all along about me. I couldn't let myself down. I loved my career and my life. Most of all, I didn't want to let Mr. Cummings down. I took a step backward if I sensed that James was taking a step toward me. He always sensed my concerns, and he gave way.

It wasn't that I didn't feel attracted to James. It was impossible not to be. He was handsome, charming, vivacious, and appeared to be everything a woman could want. That was the problem. He had a love for sonnets, particularly Shakespeare's, which he would charmingly recite, in barely a whisper, while working out some media ploy or ad buy problem. Meeting him took me by surprise. Getting to know him was another surprise. Discovering that we were a perfectly matched business team didn't surprise me in the least.

Our pitch spellbound the clients. Mr. Cummings stood at the back of the room grinning during our presentation and later said that he knew from the get-go that it would be a winning campaign if it came from the two of us. He jokingly took the credit by saying that his pairing of us together for this project was brilliant. The client requested not a single change in the campaign, even though we had proposed one of the most expensive media campaigns of the time blanketing print, radio, and television. Ads using top models and actors were just the tip of the campaign expenses. The revenue and visibility that the campaign generated would soon catapult our agency to the top. Our multilayered media campaign was about to make the clothing brand a desired wardrobe must-have throughout the country. Of course, we didn't know any of that just yet.

James poked his head through my office door as I was getting ready to leave one evening and asked if I was free for a drink. I was tired. It had been a long day and an even longer week, but I gave in.

As we walked along, I asked where we were heading.

"It's a cute little place right in the center of Times Square," he said.

We soon arrived. Darkness was descending, and the lights of Times Square were beginning to pop and dazzle. I noticed James glance at his watch.

"Where's this cute little place you are taking me to?" I asked.

"You'll see. Close your eyes."

"What?"

"Close your eyes," he demanded.

I laughed and closed my eyes as instructed. He turned me around to face the opposite direction. I heard a clattering sound nearby.

"What is going on?"

"You may open your eyes now."

I opened my eyes and saw James standing directly in front of me. His eyes were twinkling, and he wore a mischievous grin. "James, what is going on?"

"Look up," he said as he moved aside.

I looked up, and seconds later, there it was—our campaign debut—a ten-story high brilliantly lit billboard ad appeared out of nowhere. Everyone stopped, looked up, and began remarking about the smartly done ad. The buzz we intended to create had begun, and we were witness to its very start. There was an audible buzz growing all around us because of what we created. It was the most exhilarating feeling I'd ever experienced. James smiled, I jumped into his arms, and we twirled under the bright lights.

"We did this!"

"Yes, *we* did this!" he echoed as he sat me down into a chair. A bistro table and two chairs had somehow magically appeared on the sidewalk behind us. People stared at us as they walked by. A waiter appeared, he uncorked a bottle of champagne and presented us with two glasses.

"How?" I asked.

"Just enjoy."

I glanced again at our magnificent billboard. I glanced back at James; he was magnificent, too.

We were the advertising agency's best and brightest, and we instantly became the darlings of our industry. Stereotypes were pushed aside. Nobody questioned our professionalism as we demonstrated a successful partnership, both on and off the clock. We successfully partnered on several more high-profile projects while partnering as a couple.

I had both a career and a man that I loved dearly. Mr. Cummings, my beloved mentor, approved. He was proud to have introduced us and to have created our partnership. He was happy for me. He was happy for us. We received substantial bonuses for acquiring some of the biggest accounts of the day. Our reputations within the industry surged. We were on top of the world, and I couldn't believe my good fortune.

We married fifteen months after that initial blockbuster campaign. James wanted to make a big splash. He was always all about big splashes, and he was good at it. The wedding reception guestlist numbered well over two hundred, and it was held at the exclusive Plaza Towers Hotel. I felt like an imposter in that setting but James radiated happiness, and that was more than enough to make me happy as well.

He rose to make a speech. "First of all, I want to thank everyone—our family, friends, and colleagues—for sharing in our special day. The first time I laid eyes on Anna was in our agency's boardroom, and the first thing I noticed was her beauty. The next thing I learned was how talented and capable she is. She is one spectacular package, and I look forward to later unwrapping my present!"

James was a natural storyteller and speechmaker. He continued his speech by detailing how we became working partners and what a good match it turned out to be. Our guests laughed as he described instances of how I rebuffed his attempts to ask me out. He had everyone roaring when he detailed how he plotted and planned and finally wore me down.

He paused, turned to me, smiled, and turned back to the guests. "We also have another announcement to make today. Another big change is in the making."

What? What announcement? I noticed everyone looking at one another, and I heard whispers. *Oh, God, is everybody expecting James to announce that I'm already pregnant? I'm not!* Say something, James.

He slowly looked around the room, letting the anticipation build. He called me to his side, took my hand to his lips, and asked, "Ready, Dear?"

I didn't know what to think or what to say. I felt foolish for not understanding what was happening. I nervously smiled toward the crowd.

"We want to announce," James started, "that becoming married is not the only new partnership we've created." He smiled and while continuing to look into my eyes, said, "Anna and I are opening our own advertising agency, Blackwood & Associates."

I was dumbfounded. I scanned the room for Mr. Cummings and spotted him just in time to see his face fall. His hurt expression haunts me still. I cannot imagine the depth of betrayal that dear man must have felt at that moment. I wanted to run to him and to tell him it wasn't so.

But James still had a tight grip of my hand. Guests were clapping.

"James, what?"

He leaned in and kissed me. "My present to you, my darling."

"But, James?"

"Later," he said firmly, with a look that was something unrecognizable and strange. A chill ran through me.

As soon as I was able, I sought out Mr. Cummings. I didn't know what I would say, but I knew that I had to find him and try to explain. I finally spotted him smoking a cigarette at the far end of the ballroom. James also somehow turned up by my side just as I reached Mr. Cummings. "I'm sorry, Mr. Cummings, I didn't know…"

"What Anna means to say," James interrupted, "is that she didn't know that I would make the announcement here and now…"

"What, no, I didn't know…"

"Anna, that is what I'm trying to explain if you'll

just let me do so," James again interrupted. "Look, I'm sorry that we didn't talk privately with you beforehand. I admit that I got a little ahead of myself and carried away by the celebration, but I do hope that you will give us your blessing."

I was so upset. I couldn't speak. I wanted Mr. Cummings to know that I had nothing to do with this, but how could I say so without going against James and making him look foolish in front of all our guests.

Mr. Cummings looked at me, his eyes searching mine, beseeching me to say something. Then, finally, he said, "I wish you every happiness. Please excuse me now. I'm suddenly not feeling well." He turned and left.

I was furious. James expressed remorse for his actions. He said that he intended Blackwood & Associates to be his wedding gift to me. It was to be a surprise he intended to announce later when it was just us two. But he became so swept away in the moment, so happy about our being wedded to one another, and his good fortune, that he chose an entirely inappropriate moment to make the announcement.

"It's not just how you did it that was inappropriate, it's why you did it in the first place that is entirely inappropriate," I said. "What made you think that you could go behind my back and play around with my career?"

James grabbed my hand and said, "Just imagine how the trades will report the news. I created a sensation with that announcement."

He promised to make things right with Mr. Cummings, which softened me. His explanations made some sense. Ours was a competitive industry, and only the strongest survived. The actions James took would be understood and even respected. I wanted to believe James. I knew it would take some time for all of this to sink in and to become my new reality. I capitulated and acquiesced.

I would later learn, upon returning from our honeymoon cruise, that Mr. Cummings died from an apparent stroke two days after leaving our wedding reception.

****

The early days of our marriage and business were fast-paced and exciting. The glass offices situated on an upper floor in one of Manhattan's tallest skyscrapers became the headquarters of Blackwood & Associates. James had been right about the timing for launching the agency, though how it had come about remained a raw wound in my heart.

Our clients were A-list, our portfolio was strong and diversified. We continued to make a spectacular team. Working together flowed easily but as the agency expanded, and as our clients demanded more and better ways to advertise, it began to take a toll. Work was taking over our relationship. When I discovered I was pregnant, I knew it was imperative that we create a balance between work and a private life. Although James didn't seem to see things the same way.

We kept our downtown apartment while we settled into a charming colonial outside the city. We had a two-acre lawn delineated by beautiful old stonewalls that were surrounded by three acres of trees. A fenced-in pool was set off to one side and a play area for the children that came along, one after the other, was installed on the other side of the grounds. Country living was idyllic, and I thought our happiness was complete the day we introduced a cuddly puppy to our children. I loved our home, although I knew that James wasn't as fond of it as me. He clearly thrived more on the energy that came with busy city life.

We employed a live-in nanny so that I could put in three days a week at the office. James and I rarely shared time together despite working in the same space. To be effective, I had to maximize my time at the office. James took care of the must-do events and the showy launches our clientele expected, which meant he often also had to spend nights at our apartment in the city. Family time was scant. Looking back, it came as no surprise that our relationship began to suffer. That James's behavior took a turn for the worst probably shouldn't have come as much of a surprise either. There were plenty of signs that I chose to ignore or to forgive once too often.

It was an unspoken point of contention when we realized that our successful business partnership relied equally on both of us to be effective. Through experience, we learned that I was the one who had the instinct for creativity and ideas. James was the one who had the knack for launching them. The stress of trying to shoulder half of the business responsibility and the pull of family life created conflict between James and me. My creativity suffered, which left James unable to effectively conduct his side of the business. Clients began to take notice, and some began to turn away. James turned to alcohol. The three-martini lunches, business standard for the time, led to evenings that poured into more of the same.

James mournfully began repeating his favorite Shakespeare sonnet when he had his first of too many drinks. His face tightening and the anger building was when I knew to quickly put safe distance between him and the kids and me. The Bard's prose became as close as James could ever get to having heart for anything. In everything else, there was only the good or bad, the black or white. I was to blame for everything gone wrong. For him, there was nothing in-between. He shouldered none of the blame. He couldn't see that his drinking, and what it was doing to our relationship, was also a reason why the agency was in decline.

I began to dread those weekends when he did make a family appearance. Too often he would stagger in, drunk and sneering. Verbal barrages were hurled, and the children were exposed to his disgusting behavior. Gradually, the verbal attacks escalated into his shoving and pushing me around. One night, things reached the limit.

"Hello, happy family," James slurred while staggering into the house.

The children ran to him and hugged his legs. James, sloppily drunk, couldn't maintain his balance and viciously pushed the children aside. They cowered.

"James take control of yourself. Go upstairs and take some rest or a shower."

"Don't tell me what to do, you *bitch*!"

"Don't speak that way in front of the children. Go, James!"

He lunged at me, and I screamed for the kids to get up to their rooms. As I watched the children run up the stairs, James grabbed me by the throat and threw me down hard onto the floor. I could hear the children screaming, "Stop, Daddy, stop!"

He was a man possessed and didn't hear them. He

tried to pin me underneath him but, in his drunken state, he couldn't balance himself well enough. All his weight came crashing down on me. My pelvis was being crushed. I had no air to scream. He slapped my face and boxed my ears, one then the other, alternating from side to side.

His spittle fell into my eyes, as he muttered, "You lost our biggest account today. Are you happy?"

"Stop, James. Please!"

"You are worthless to me," he said. "You've always been worthless. You are nothing without me. You could never be anything without me."

I could hear the kids still screaming in the background as he continued his tirade. "You try to embarrass me and tear me down. You tear down everything I've built."

He unzipped his pants, pulled out his limp member, and tried to pry my mouth open with his other hand. "This is the only thing you've ever been good for."

I couldn't stop crying. I tried desperately to catch my breath through locked jaws.

"Take it."

I locked my jaws together as hard as I could using every ounce of strength left. His fist coming at me was the last thing I remembered.

****

I woke in an ambulance. Our nanny had heard the ruckus and phoned the police. James, contrite at first, would eventually, and with predictable regularity, build himself up to another tirade even after a domestic protection order was in place.

I gave my lawyer a letter to present to James and his attorney. In it, I acknowledged my share of responsibility for the downturn in our business and marriage, but I refused to take any responsibility for his shameful decline. I hoped he could turn himself and the company around, but it was not healthy, or possible, for me, or the children, to any longer be part of the picture. I offered that he could buy my share of the business, and in exchange, I would forgo any alimony or child support. He could keep the apartment, and I would keep the house. He would be entirely free to live his life, and to run the business, as he pleased. I wanted a divorce, and my terms were non-negotiable. If he fought me, I would take it all down.

I knew he would recognize that these terms would be the only way that he could keep and rebuild the business. I also knew that his ego wouldn't let him take any responsibility for everything that had gone wrong. His ego also wouldn't let the opportunity escape him to show everybody that he could rebuild the business on his own and better than ever before. He had a need to prove to himself, and to everyone around him, that I had held him back. He needed to show that he alone had always been the shining star, the best and brightest.

James agreed to my terms. I sold the big colonial, bought a modest cape, and found a wonderful new position with another family for the nanny. I needed a break from the corporate world and, more so, I needed to heal my children. They had been through too much, and they deserved a happy and carefree childhood.

Our lives became easier, far less dramatic, and healthier. James bowed out of the picture entirely, which as far as I was concerned was perfect, but I knew it wasn't good for the children. I had hoped that he would turn himself around and when he did so, would want to come back into the children's lives to be the kind of father they needed and that I hoped somewhere inside him, he needed too.

James, however, did a complete disappearing act. He never returned to them. I did everything I could to make up for his not being there on birthdays, Christmas, and every other holiday or school event. I left messages at his office, begging him to get into contact with the children, but he had left them as completely as I had left him. I wondered if this was punishment aimed at me or if he was indeed so cold-hearted to punish the children, who just by being born, became liabilities to achieving everything he wanted. I hated him for what he did to the children. It was hard on them both but hardest on Lainey.

I did the best I could to be both mother and father to my children. I had enough money set aside so that I didn't have to work, and I could focus my love and attention entirely on them. But I could never make up for, or take away, the hurt their father's absence inflicted. By him completely turning away from them, he said loud and clear that they no longer existed for him, and they didn't mean anything to him.

Trent tried to conceal his hurt through bullying other kids around. It was something I couldn't tolerate, and together with the guidance of a therapist, we helped him through it. I also had Lainey in therapy, but she never benefitted. Lainey was often home sick from school. There were times when she just couldn't cope. Then, there was that day, the awful defining moment.

I had made a quick run to the pharmacy and the grocery store after dropping Trent off at school. Lainey was home again, not feeling well. I wasn't gone for more than twenty minutes. I walked in to find her on the edge of the couch, glued to the television. She was crying and screaming.

I looked over at the television and saw the carnage happening at the World Trade Center twin towers. That's where the agency was situated. My first instinct was to shut off the tv, but I also knew that what was happening was bigger than just what was happening on our screen. There was no way to hide this from her, from us. I sat down beside Lainey and wrapped her in my arms. Both of us were crying and unable to believe what was taking place. People were actually jumping from windows. I couldn't help but wonder if I knew any of them. Had one of them been James? I had heard that he had sold the apartment to keep the business afloat and he had taken to sleeping in the office. I began shaking at the horror of it all and at what my poor daughter was experiencing. I was helpless to shield her from it.

Just after her father's tower came crashing down, Lainey wiped her eyes and snotty nose with her pajama sleeve. A freaky calmness overtook her. She looked at me and declared, "Well, that's that isn't it? It's over. My father's dead and nothing can ever change that."

I reached out for her, but she rose, slipping through my hands. I wanted to tell her that we didn't know for sure. There was a chance he wasn't in the building. But I instinctively knew, as surely as my daughter, that he was gone. She calmly walked into her bedroom, shut the door, and slept for two days straight. She was never quite the same again. Nothing in my power could change the course of events. She was right about that. It was prophetic.

I desperately tried to get into touch with some of the people that I had known at the agency. I had to be sure that he was gone. It was for my children's sake that we needed to know. It was unbelievably painful to make calls only to learn that some of the people I was trying to reach had also died that day. We never received any concrete evidence that James died. There was no body, no witnesses who may have seen him that morning, or after. James had died an unimaginable death along with many other people I knew well or as casual acquaintances with whom I had regularly shared elevator talk.

I was out of my depths for knowing how to help my children. How many of us were in the same position? I brushed aside and locked away my own feelings to concentrate on my children. I dared not open that wound to examine it until many years later. One day, with David by my side, we visited the newly opened 9/11 memorials. I fell apart and wept uncontrollably when I found his name etched on the fountain wall. David's strong, loving embrace was all that kept me standing. I wept for James. I wept for everyone. I cried for everything that could have been and now could never be. I wept for my children and the horror of how that day scorched them, leaving them as wounded and as scarred as if they had been inside the building. They too were victims.

****

About three years after that horrific day, as I was aimlessly pushing a shopping cart down the grocery aisle, I heard, "Anna, is that you?"

I turned. "Denise. Yes. Hello!"

"How are you, Anna? The kids? I've thought of

you often over the years. It was so tragic what happened to James and so many at the agency."

Denise Webb worked at Blackwood for a time. She was good. She was very good. Lucky for her, another agency noticed her talent and stole her away long before that dreadful day.

"It was tragic," I replied. "The kids are still coping, probably always will. It's the tragedy that never ends. Every year, there is the haunting reminder—on television, radio, everywhere. It's a scab that gets pulled off again, and again. How can anyone ever heal?"

"I heard that you left the business after you split from James. Did you ever go back? Are you with another agency?"

"No, I took a hiatus from the industry to focus on the kids."

"Have you ever thought about getting back in?"

The truth was I had lately been thinking I needed to do something more. The kids were in high school, and I had too much free time. On the other hand, I still wanted to be available to my children. I didn't want anything too demanding. I had been eyeing the part-time help wanted ad that was posted in the window of the florist down the street. "I'm not relevant anymore in the ad world."

"Who says? Your breakout clothing campaign that lit up Times Square, and then the rest of the world, elevated that designer to the top of his industry. It is still legendary in the ad world."

"Denise, I'm a single parent. I don't have the time, energy, or desire to get back into that rat race."

I wasn't entirely truthful. I still had the desire. I

still had ideas that flowed and wouldn't stop. Ideas that nobody knew about or therefore needed. As if Denise was reading my mind, she pointed into a refrigerated case and said,

"This brand of yogurt—do you have any ideas to better position it?"

As if from nowhere, I listed four things to consider.

She smiled, and we strolled on. "How about this cheese?" she asked.

My insides tingled with that old familiar excitement as ideas just flowed into my head and out of my mouth.

"My agency, *any* agency, would be thrilled to contract with you as a consultant on special projects," she said. "You could name your price and work when you want and only on the projects you want."

"I don't know."

Denise must have noticed my lying eyes when she said, "I'm serious. Give it some thought and give me a call—soon."

She slipped her business card into my hand, smiled, and continued down the aisle.

****

I thought about nothing else over the next few days. I drove around town, viewing storefronts and local businesses. I thumbed through magazines, watched television, and perused the Internet. I made a study of looking at advertisements and quizzing myself over if they worked—how they worked. If the ad didn't work, I considered how I would change things. I found online resources that provided me with demographics, consumer spending statistics, and consumption data. It was so easy and fast now to come by needed data. I could do this. Discovering that I hadn't lost the touch was invigorating.

I phoned Denise to tell her that I was game at trying my hand on a project. That old energy came back the instant I walked into her agency's boardroom two weeks later and confidently launched a promotion pitch. The feedback was better than I hoped. One project led to another. Soon my name was back in the trades as a sought-after freelance consultant. I cherry-picked projects based on my available time and interests. The kids were older and not home as much. It felt good to no longer be sitting around and waiting for them. I had new interests of my own, and I banked away funds to put the kids through college.

Sifting through my memories of meeting and marrying James, our divorce, his death, and the relaunching of my career skidded to a sudden stop.

I was propelled back into the here and now when I wondered how is it that I can remember these details about my past, yet I can't remember if I cooked a breakfast or walked around in the snow with bare feet? That I can remember these things should be a good sign. Then again, I've read that people at the onset of dementia can recall past events with more clarity than they can remember what happened five minutes before. I've also read that people deeply grieving have similar experiences.

All I know for sure is that I'm constantly second-guessing myself now because I don't understand what is happening with me.

And I'm scared.

All the second-guessing just makes me slip-up more. Lainey clearly thinks something worse than grief might be what's going on with me. I need to make arrangements as early as tomorrow to see a doctor. Starting tomorrow, I'm taking control of myself, and I'm not going to let anyone treat me as badly as I was treated tonight. Lainey's behavior was inexcusable.

Reliving the emotional trauma of the past was draining. I had no strength left. Sleep settled in.

Chapter Ten

The Lawyer

I finally saw the highway exit I needed to take and gratefully offered up another silent prayer of thanks that I'd made it as far as this point in this nasty storm. I looked down at my hands and wondered if they were now fused to the steering wheel. I'd been gripping the wheel so tightly that I could no longer feel my fingers. I wasn't sure I'd have control over loosening my grip when I finally did reach Anna's house. After looking first right, then left at the bottom of the exit ramp, I realized it might still be some time, and trouble, before I was finally there. It was unlikely this sleepy rural town had a fleet of snowplows. I'd be skeptical about believing they had one. More likely, some private people plowed on the side to earn some extra money.

I still had farther to go, and the closer I got to Anna's, the less populated it would be, which inevitably meant still worsening roads. Most people with houses out her way were only there in the summer. Smarter people.

"Hang on a little bit more," I said aloud as I pried one hand off the wheel to pat the car's dashboard.

I still didn't know what I should say or do when I saw her. According to what David told me, and what I later learned from Trent, this business about Lainey was nothing but bad.

Then there is Trent to consider. Should I spill the beans and tell Anna about his plans and what he's up to? There would be hell to pay with her son, but she also has a right to know. Still, I don't know her so well, and it's tough to judge what her reaction might be.

I don't know how I got in the middle of this mess. I don't have a clue about what is going on. I'm no mental health professional. I know only that something is very, very wrong and I'm damn sure there won't be a welcome mat laid out ready to receive me.

If only I hadn't forgotten my phone. I could have phoned Trent to ask his advice about how to deal with the situation when I got there, or even when I'm in the middle of it. I'd also be able to call the police if needed. Why didn't I try phoning Anna before I left? I'd at least have gotten some measure of what I might be walking into. I can't get in touch with anyone—Trent, Anna, or the police.

At first, the roads weren't any worse than the highway, which I found to be a little surprising, but the more distance I put between the town and me the worse it was looking. The town, "hamlet" might be more accurate, was shut up tight. I wasn't even sure there was a local police station here. The gas station was also deserted. Gas was soon going to be my next problem, especially if I got stuck along the roadside somewhere in the middle of the woods—and without a phone—and in the cold. The gauge showed I was already dangerously low. Damn, another thing I should have checked before coming out here and another thing I should have planned on better beforehand. It would be just my luck to get stuck out here and freeze to death.

Chapter Eleven

The Daughter

I poured myself another glass of wine and settled into the comfy leather chair. I began to think about the need to now move a little more quickly than I had initially planned. How to do so, without losing any of the fun I looked forward to, would require careful consideration.

The human psyche and how easy it is to manipulate fascinates me. A thought, an experience, and an emotion—all can be triggers to what makes a person believe in a specific something or act in a certain way. Getting to know somebody, gaining their trust, finding their weak spot—and everybody has one, or more—is phase one of every experiment. Seeding their self-doubt is the next phase. How it's done depends on the person. Leading that person to their tipping point is simply a natural progression of inconspicuously planting one seed, then another. Watching the person tip and fall, and the satisfaction of getting away with it thrills me.

I've always had a good instinct for seeing into people, finding what fear they hide, and using that fear to push them over the edge. Mandy would attest to that. If she could.

Mandy was my university dormmate. She was overweight and self-conscious about it. That self-consciousness led her to become introverted and socially awkward. Hapless bouts of depression seized her regularly and comfort food was her medicine of choice, which only intensified the next round of the vicious circle she was trapped in. I pretended not to notice her weight problem, which naturally drew her to me. She believed I saw something better when I looked at her. I gained her trust because I appeared to want to be her friend.

As psych majors, we had a few of the same classes together. Mandy also doubled with an English major. She faithfully kept daily journals from the time she could first write. Writing was her outlet. Writing was her contribution to self. She also believed she could make it her contribution to others. Her greatest wish was to write something that could have a lasting impact on her readers' lives. I decided to help her do that.

I imagined myself having a career as a psychologist who would listen to people's problems and profit from it. Not too much unlike what all psychologists do. My practice would, however, have a decidedly different twist.

I introduced Mandy to some of my friends from the classes we shared and to some other people from around campus that I hung out with. People, reluctantly at first, gave her a chance because of me. There were even one or two people that genuinely liked her and she started to flower. She was becoming a happier person than she may have been for most of her life. She trusted me. We spent long evenings in our room sharing a pizza, chicken wings, and beer. Soon, she began to share the secrets of her past.

Mandy had been a victim of sexual abuse. The

neighbor's teenage son sexually assaulted her, starting from when she was seven and lasting until she was twelve. It only stopped after he went off to some distant college. Mandy's parents had been best friends with his parents since moving to the same street a couple of years before Mandy was born. The two sets of parents often went out to the movies or dinner together, and when they did this boy was responsible for babysitting Mandy. Mandy and the boy were each an only child.

I remembered her recounting of the first time. They were on the sofa together watching a show. He was sitting at one end, she was sprawled out over the length of the couch. His hands moved under the blanket they were sharing to first hold her toes. It happened so slowly that she barely noticed when his hand began to move farther up her leg. He began gently and lightly rubbing her leg. She was comfortably snuggled under a blanket, enjoying the show, and totally trusting of Tad, a boy she had known her whole life. She enjoyed the feeling, which she described as cozy. Tad asked her if he should stop, and she said no. She said that it was nice and to keep on doing it. He continued gently rubbing her leg. It seemed innocent. Mandy was only seven and an innocent. Gradually, Tad's fingers moved farther up her nightgown to her thigh. His fingers lingered there for a while, still gently massaging her.

A short while later, she felt his fingers slipping under the elastic band of her underpants. His fingers tentatively probed. She noticed the different feeling and now wondered what to do because somehow it didn't seem okay anymore. As she turned to look at Tad, she noticed his other hand moving rapidly under the blanket. Just as she was about to ask him about what was going on, he sighed, stilled, and withdrew his hand from her. He leaned back and closed his eyes. Whatever it was, it was over. Tad got up refilled their soda glasses and then sat in her dad's chair. They kept on watching television like nothing had happened. Mandy even quickly forgot about it, and if things had stopped with that instance, she probably wouldn't have remembered it at all now.

But things didn't stop there. He became bolder each time he babysat. Soon, he became overtly sexual and not just when he was babysitting. He made her see and do frightening things. He would find her and corner her inside her backyard playhouse. There was that time when he led her into the nearby woods. He sometimes offered to pick her up from school, or a friend's house, and he would make her do things while driving her home in his mother's car. The nice Tad she had known was now blaming and threatening her afterward. It grew more and more uncomfortable to be around him, his parents, or even her parents. She became reclusive—afraid to leave the house, especially her room, because he might be in the next room waiting for her. She was afraid to tell her parents because of Tad's threats of what he would do to her and to them. He said it would be all her fault.

That was when food became her comfort. Junk food was her only friend. When you live behind a closed door, and you don't have the opportunity to exercise off all those extra calories or to make friends, your weight balloons. Her parents worried. But she insisted she was okay and because they didn't see any downturn in her school grades, they chalked it all up to a phase.

"But it wasn't a phase," said Mandy, "It became me. Or, maybe, I became it."

"Or, maybe the more weight you gained, the more invisible you hoped you might become," I offered.

"What do you mean?"

"Subconsciously, you were packing on the pounds as a means of self-protection."

Mandy's eyes pleaded with me to continue seeing into her.

"You are not alone in your room anymore. You are living on a campus among fifteen thousand other people. Being overweight is still your protection. Chances are nobody is going to approach you and try to hurt you again, or to expose you."

"Expose me?"

"This secret you are keeping. Part of you remains fearful of Tad. Another part of you probably wonders if you are to blame for it happening. Did you buy into any of the guilt he threw at you when he said that if you told you would be responsible for splitting up their parents' friendship?"

"My parents and Tad's are in Hawaii on vacation together right now. It's like they are as much a part of the family as any of us. Or, maybe more than I am."

"And that's why you've never told anyone?"

"Pretty much, I suppose. I only told my journal. Every account and all of my feelings are documented there. It's how I dealt with everything." She pulled a stack of paperback journals out of a knapsack she had hidden under the bed. "It's all here," she said. "You are the only other person who knows about these."

Bingo! I thought to myself.

"Do you know that I carry this knapsack with me

wherever I go? I couldn't leave these journals at home and take the chance that my parents might find them. I carry them around with me every day, all day long, so that nobody here will find them. I also need to haul them around on holidays and school vacations. They are always with me, and I'm sick of it."

"That's a lot of weight to shoulder and more than anybody deserves to carry," I replied.

My dredging up of her old memories began to again put them in the forefront. For the first time, boosted by me to become so, she became angry about what happened. She began to understand that she had been victimized. I insisted she needed to deal with what happened so that it could no longer haunt or hurt her. I told her that she could become a healthy, happy person if she did so. I gave her self-confidence. I gave her the courage to tell.

She begged me to spend Thanksgiving with her and her family. If I were there, then she would have the courage needed, and she wouldn't feel so alone. I promised to back her up. Her parents were thrilled to have a friend of Mandy's join their Thanksgiving. It would be the first time, as far as they could remember, that Mandy invited a friend home. Thanksgiving was always a joint venture with Tad's family. Mandy's mother was especially happy because Tad was bringing home a girlfriend. It was rumored that he had become pretty serious about her. The new faces, Tad's girlfriend, and Mandy's friend were sure to add another layer of joy to a tradition that Mandy's mother especially loved.

I didn't want to spend time at home with my mother, and I certainly wouldn't miss this Thanksgiving at Mandy's. I'd worked too hard. I spent countless hours planning how, and when, I would push her over the edge. I had to be ready to improvise if necessary. Timing was crucial.

We took the train to Mandy's. Her home was a traditional ranch on an unremarkable street. Each house sat on the same size postage-stamp lot. The people who lived there, apart from their perfectly manicured lawns and gardens, were probably also unremarkable. It only took one sweeping glance to know that nothing truly bad ever happened here and probably nothing spectacularly good either. These were even keel folks, marked by a gentle caring camaraderie. The setting was perfect.

We arrived a few days early. Mandy borrowed her mom's car and showed me around town. She cheerfully pointed out, "This park is where kids hang out. That mall has the best stores. Over there, is where everybody likes to eat."

"I'm guessing you never hung out there, shopped much, or liked to eat at that restaurant?"

Her face fell. Her lower lip quivered.

"Tad stole these things from you. He robbed you of everything. Will you be strong enough to do it?"

She gave me a questioning glance. She was faltering. I knew it, but I also knew that she didn't want to let me down.

"It's now or never," I said.

"I know. But seeing my mom so happy…"

"Mandy, she's happy because you brought a friend home. She thinks that you are happier now, so she is happier now. But you'll never be able to be truly happy until you confront your past. Your mom wants you to be happy. She would want you to do this."

Mandy wavered back and forth over the next few days. She was too afraid to make a scene. She was coming to terms with being too much of a coward to stand up and speak for herself. So, I asked her to let me do it. I asked her to let me choose the time, the place, and how. I convinced her that as her friend, I could step in and do for her what she couldn't do for herself. Reluctantly, she agreed.

I stayed close to Mandy on Thanksgiving Day. I smiled and joked and put her at ease. Tad and family arrived at the appointed hour. Mandy immediately began to shrink and withdraw. I found her in the laundry room, shaking. Tears welling as she said that she was having second thoughts.

"He has a girlfriend now. Maybe he's changed. She seems nice…"

"Stop, Mandy! This must be done. She has a right to know. You have a responsibility to say something. Suppose he does this to other little kids still and nobody ever knows!"

At that, she looked up at me and said, "Okay. I trust you."

Everyone took their place at the beautifully arranged dining table that Mandy's mother had carefully set. Wine was poured and conversation flowed easily. With a nod from his wife, Mandy's father stood, welcomed each of us to their table and expressed his love and thankfulness for his family and for good family friends. Then the tradition of each person around the table stating what they were thankful for began. When the two sets of parents had finished, Tad stood and announced that he was thankful that Lela, his girlfriend, had agreed to become his wife. The table exploded with congratulatory remarks, kisses, and hugs from Tad's parents, and Mandy's parents, to Tad and Lela.

Mandy looked at me, and I knew that she was remembering our talk in the laundry room. Her anger was boiling. She shook her head at me as if to say, "Let's do it."

When the congratulatory dust settled, Mandy's father noticed the unfinished round of thanks still to be given, and he asked Mandy to continue. She drew a deep breath, looked down at her hands folded neatly in her lap, and didn't say a word.

"Mandy?" her father asked.

"I don't know where to start," she croaked.

"Let me help," I said.

Mandy gratefully shook her head.

"One second, please," I said.

Mandy looked confused as I rose and went into her bedroom. I returned with half a dozen of Mandy's journals. Her eyes opened wide as fright took her over. I patted her and said it would be okay.

I passed the journals out around the table, one journal each to all the parents, then Tad, and finally to Lela. "These are Mandy's private journals that she's kept since age seven," I said. "As I look at each of you. Please read aloud the year of the journal you are holding."

Mandy was again staring into her hands. I don't think anyone noticed that anything was unusual. This was probably her go-to behavior when surrounded by them.

Among the others, anticipation mounted. Everyone

smiled at this creative and fun game we were about to start. I began with Tad's parents, then Mandy's parents, then on to Tad's girlfriend and finally Tad. Each excitedly read the year Mandy had written on the cover of each journal.

"Good!" I said. "As you heard, each journal represents Mandy's life from the ages of seven to age twelve."

Everybody smiled warmly at her.

"When I give the word, everyone is to open his or her journal to the marked page and read aloud the passage that I've highlighted. We'll proceed again in the same order as before."

Mandy looked at up me in terror.

I walked behind her, placed my hands on her shoulders, and said, "Let's start."

Tad's mother read, "I don't understand what happened last night. Why did he do that to me? It really made me feel strange."

She looked up in confusion. Everybody was confused. The atmosphere at the table was changing from jubilant to weary. I slowly massaged Mandy's shoulders to steady and bolster her as I instructed Tad's father to continue next.

He read, "I'm getting more and more afraid of what will happen next. Last night, Tad…"

He choked back words none of us could make out. He stared at his son.

"What is going on here?" demanded Mandy's father.

"Everyone now open the journals and read the highlighted passage," I said.

All at once, the table erupted.

"Oh my God, that's sick!" exclaimed Tad's girlfriend as she jumped away from the seat next to him and backed against the dining room wall.

Mandy's father jumped out of his seat and tried to lunge across the table to attack Tad, but Tad's father intercepted with a blow that knocked Mandy's father to the floor.

In unison the two mothers screamed, "Stop!"

They looked at each other, instantly realizing that it was probably the last thing they would ever do together again.

"This is all lies!" screamed Tad, and as he tried to grab across the table for Mandy. Mandy's mom grabbed the carving knife to defend Mandy, but stumbled over her crumpled husband on the floor, causing her to fall into Tad and accidentally stab him in the jugular.

Time stilled. Everyone froze while I admired my handiwork. I remembered reading once that it takes a person about four minutes to die after being stabbed in the jugular. I checked my watch. Afterward, I phoned 911. While Tad's parents were crying over his body, Mandy had run to her room, and her parents had run after her. Tad's girlfriend had disappeared.

I looked out the window to see all the red and blue lights that began to arrive and light up the street outside—police cars, ambulances, even a fire truck. Christmas had indeed come early.

Mandy's parents moved into a hotel and listed their home for sale within forty-eight hours of the catastrophic events. They were told to remain within the city because there was still a lot that the police needed to unravel. Investigators agreed with Mandy's parents that she would be better off going back to university. They didn't need her because they had her journals and those spoke volumes. Everyone's lives were shattered. The two sets of parents would never speak to the other again.

Word spread quickly on campus. Mandy's parents tried to arrange counseling for their daughter, but she refused. She said that she had me to talk with, and that was good enough. They were skeptical but didn't want to cause Mandy more stress.

I stayed by her side and forced her through the motions of attending class. Her weight melted away, revealing quite an attractive woman, but everyone still gave her a wide berth. Nobody knew what to say or do.

I was still Mandy's sole confidante. She didn't feel any better for having told. She said she never wished Tad dead. She felt sorry for his parents and hers. She was responsible for it all. She didn't believe any of them could ever recover from this.

I agreed.

"Nobody planned for Tad to die. It was an accident," I said repeatedly.

"My parents don't know what to say around me," she wailed repeatedly. "They blame themselves, and each other, for not recognizing his behavior or what was happening to me."

"Listen, maybe they should take some of the blame. I can't believe they ever cared enough if they let you turn into an overweight recluse. They had to have some clue that something wasn't right. But they chose to look the other way."

"What an awful thing to say! My parents love me!"

"Then where are they?" I asked. "They've sent you

back to school again, so they don't have to deal with you! That's not how loving parents act. That's what everybody here is saying," I lied.

It didn't take long to twist Mandy into a tangled pretzel of emotions. I helped her slide into a depression that was so deep nobody, but me would ever be able to reach her. She stopped going to classes. She barely left her room. The meals I brought to her were left untouched. She said she couldn't deal with any of this anymore. She didn't want to see her parents at Christmas break. Nothing would ever be the same. Everything was torn apart and broken. She begged me to help her, and so we made a plan. I convinced her it was the only solution.

On the appointed day, I peevishly twirled my pen across my notebook impatiently waiting for class to be over so that I could run back to see if she was yet twirling in the air like some twisted ballerina? We planned that she should do it while I was at classes so that I would have an alibi. I hurried back to the dorm, held my breath, and opened the door. She was finally beautiful.

I looked up toward the second-floor balcony as my thoughts returned to dear sweet Mommy. Trent knows something's up. I've listened to the voicemails, and I've read the texts. I thought there would be a little more time. No matter.

Chapter Twelve

Anna

I had fitful dreams about running through fog desperately trying to catch up with Lainey. The dreams turned nightmarish when she suddenly stopped, turned toward me, and began singing the little teapot song. The worst of it was the realization that I was no longer asleep.

The soft singing was coming from somewhere in my bedroom. I sat up, turned on the bedside table lamp, and took my hearing aid from its charger. My brain, still fogged, couldn't determine where the sound was coming from, even with the help of the hearing aid. I looked around the room and saw nothing unusual.

Quietly, I rose from the bed and tiptoed across the room. The singing seemed to be coming from the direction of the closets. It was coming from David's closet. I was petrified, but I couldn't avoid opening the closet because I needed to know what was happening, but I really, really, also didn't want to know. I drew in a deep breath and reached toward both knobs. As I swung the doors open, my eyes couldn't believe what I then saw. David's shirts were no longer in tatters. They were whole again.

I screamed.

The singing continued, more softly now.

I fell to my knees and covered my ears. "Stop, please stop!"

None of this could be real. I screamed for Lainey to help me. When she jumped out of the closet at me, I realized that help was not something she would be offering. She stood over me, still singing.

I desperately tried to scuttle away from her. Crab-walking backwards was all I could do, but she was towering over my every move. It wasn't working.

She lifted a bat over her head. "Be quiet, bitch!"

As I jumped back and instinctively turned my head away, I slammed into the dresser, and all went black.

Chapter Thirteen

The Lawyer

The roads were narrowing, or did it just seem so because no plows had been this far out yet? There weren't any streetlights this far out of town. There was only darkness, wind, swirling snow, and bitter cold. I wasn't dressed for a hike through the snow, and I couldn't remember how much farther it was to Anna's. Could things be any worse? The car fishtailed again, stopping sideways, and blocking the road. I was damn lucky not to have gone off the road. I remembered the steep drop down to the lake. The car wouldn't budge now. I'd have to alert the authorities once I got to Anna's. It wouldn't be possible to plow unless I could get help to first move the car off the road.

I reached into the glove box, thankful as my hand found the flashlight I hoped was still there. It turned on, but the beam was weak. The beam became stronger after shaking it a couple of times, but I didn't trust the batteries to last long. The whipping wind caught my dress pants as soon as I opened the door. *Please, God, don't let Anna's house be too far, I prayed.* I tucked my chin into my chest and began walking. I concentrated on putting one foot in front of the other to keep from thinking about how cold I was and how my shoes, socks, and pants were now soaked through.

The flashlight gave out about ten minutes in. I hurled it into the woods along with every nasty epithet I could muster. Now, I was in total darkness and forced to concentrate on walking a straight line to make sure I was sticking to staying on the road. That might have normally been an easy thing to do, but mounds of drifted snow were making the way even more difficult.

It was slow going and then no going when I tripped over a tree branch under the snow, fell, and then began falling more, head over heels, down the hillside. A tree finally broke my fall and nearly broke my head. Everything hurt. I tore off my glove, reached for my cheek and felt something warm, runny, and thick. I knew well enough that it wasn't tree sap. My suspicion was confirmed after I brought my index finger to my lips and tasted the unmistakable metallic aftertaste of blood.

This was quickly becoming one of the worst nights of my life. I tried standing and felt a sharp pain in my ankle. I was surprised I could feel anything because my feet were now mostly numb. The incline was steep. I needed a few minutes to gather my strength before climbing up to the road.

I tried to recall the lay of the land here and how much farther it might be ahead before I came to Anna's. The last time I was here, just a couple of days ago, there was also a lot of snow on the ground. The snow-covered landscape hid things that may have stood out as landmarks. I tried to remember the few other times I had been here. The time before had been the day of David's funeral and the time before that had been the day he and Anna married.

They'd been married the year earlier by a justice of

the peace, just the two them, but they renewed their vows here on the edge of the shore. It was a small and casual affair, just a few of their friends, Trent, his wife Karen, and their twin daughters. The twins made the cutest little flower girls. They looked like something out of a magazine, with their matching gowns and a crown of fall flowers atop their little blonde heads. A couple of grill masters David found in town put on a barbeque spread that was some of the best food I've ever had. The sound of a trio of local acoustic musicians in the background, and the beautiful colors of fall foliage against a perfectly blue sky, everything came together to make it a picture-perfect day.

That was the first time I met Trent, Anna's son who lived on the west coast. I knew a little bit about him from David, but not much. There was something David said about Anna and Trent not being able to enjoy as close a relationship after everything that had gone on with Lainey. From what I gathered, both mother and son loved one another, but their relationship had become strained. One of David's goals was to change that. He was intent on restoring their relationship.

He was also intent on finally having a family. The way he danced and laughed with those two little girls made me smile. I remember thinking that day how he would have made a wonderful father, and although that never happened, at least he'd make a wonderful grandfather. Too bad David didn't live long enough.

Trent was a lawyer like me, which gave us some common ground for getting to know one another during the celebration. After the standard questions: what type of law do you practice, how big is your firm, etc.—we learned that we had a lot in common career-wise. Our practices were similar. That led to a discussion about differences in state laws over various common issues and complaints. It was sometime around that point that David joined us. With arms around both of us, he joked that he hoped we weren't comparing billable hours. That's when he told Trent that I handled most of his business dealings and that's when he said to me that Trent was working on a special project for him in California.

They seemed comfortable enough with one another. Knowing David, I'm sure the project was probably an excuse to get to know Trent. He was a likeable enough guy when I first met him at the wedding, but I also noticed an edge about him. He was guarded. When I mentioned it to David, he said that I was right-on. He thought Trent was naturally guarded given all the trauma he'd experienced. That's when I learned that Anna's first husband was one of the 9/11 tragedies. David said it was one of the reasons that Trent was on the opposite coast. He went to California for university and never came back east. It was too painful. David spoke highly of Trent and enjoyed getting to know him as they worked together on their project. David was an expert judge of character, which I reminded myself of every time I now needed to deal with Trent. He remained guarded with me, but then again, it has only been a short time since David's death.

Nervous about his mother's condition after David's death, Trent contacted me for help. I shared David's trust information and the fact that Trent could be named trustee to oversee the estate that was now his mother's. It was something I was obligated to do, and I knew it was also something David would have wanted him to know. It was a kindness David extended to Trent from the grave. I've wondered what Trent thinks about it all, but I dare not ask, afraid, as I am to learn if Trent might decide it better to pull everything away and to administer the estate himself.

I swear I'd give it all up now for a chance to be warm and dry again. I've never been what somebody would call impulsive, but tonight I acted too quickly and without thinking things completely through. My lack of planning was inexcusable. I hoped that Anna's house was not too far away. I started climbing my way back up to the road. I couldn't see a damn thing. I hoped I hadn't fallen too far down. I had to pull myself up hand over hand to keep weight off my ankle. I vowed to spend more time in the gym if I survived this. I hadn't realized until now just how out of shape I had become.

Finally, the steep incline gave way to something a little more level. I guessed I must have finally reached the road. I used a free tree branch that had been in my way as a cane to help me along. I might be able to make it a little farther, but if I didn't find Anna's soon, it would be unlikely that I would survive for long.

The snow stung the side of my face as I hobbled along. Then, and just when I thought I couldn't make it much farther, wouldn't make it all, I saw a faint light up ahead.

Chapter Fourteen

The Daughter

Dear sweet Mommy lay crumpled on the floor. I made myself comfortable on her bed and waited for her to wake up. I was having a bit of fun imagining all the different ways she might meet her unfortunate end. I could easily throw her over the balcony, but no, I still need to get what I wanted from her first. Plus, too easy is simply not my style.

It was too bad that it would have to now happen sooner than I planned. I was having such a good time. She's way too easy. I'd even started to like her. There are a couple of believable and wonderfully satisfying ways I could kill her. It would just be a matter of tidying up a few loose ends before settling on one.

Ah, movement. She's waking.

"Mom, are you okay?"

"What happened? What's going on, Lainey?"

"I was crossing over to my room when I saw you here on the floor. What happened?"

"There was singing from the closet. Lainey, it was you!"

"Mom, you sound super crazy right now. That doesn't make any sense."

"But that's what happened. Isn't it? And there were the shirts too? David's shirts aren't all cut up anymore!"

"Mom, you are not making any sense. Listen to yourself. I was singing in the closet where David's shirts are okay now? I'm not sure what happened here. Somehow you fell. Maybe, you bumped your head while falling. I was just about to call 911. Thank God, you regained consciousness and seem to be okay. But you aren't making any sense. Maybe that bump on your head did something to you. I better keep my eye on you for a while. Can you make it downstairs?"

I helped her up, and we carefully made our way downstairs. I sat her at the dining room table and made her a cup of tea. Anna slowly raised the cup to her mouth. Her shaking hands threatened to spill most of it before it reached her lips.

Perfect.

Chapter Fifteen

The Lawyer

I was close enough to the house that I could see
Anna sitting at the dining room table. I almost tumbled
again down the slope to her door. My legs were giving
way from the numbing cold. At least, I barely felt the
pain in my ankle anymore. I startled her when my
banging on the door was a little harder and my voice a
little louder than I intended. I saw Anna start to rise
from the table, but somebody else opened the door.

"Harvey?" Anna called out.

I staggered inside. I must have looked a sight—all
covered in snow, and ice sticking to my drenched pants.
A girl caught me in mid-slump. "Here, let me help you
out of these wet things," she said.

She pulled off my coat, hat, and gloves. I could
have sworn I saw a slight smile on her face as I
screamed out in pain when she removed my left shoe.
She ran down the hall and was back in a flash with
large bath towels. Then she led me over to the table
where Anna sat in strange stillness, watching.

"I'll make you some tea," the girl said, and backed
away into the kitchen.

"Harvey, what are you doing here?" Anna asked.

"I just want to make sure you are okay," I said,
half-watching the girl in the nearby kitchen. She was

hovering by the door, obviously listening.

"You could have phoned. You didn't need to come all the way out here."

"Trent tried phoning you several times, and when there was no answer, he called me."

The girl stepped back into the room, placed a steaming cup of tea before me. "But I spoke with Trent. He knows everything is fine here. Didn't he call you back to tell you?"

"He might have tried," I lamented, "but by then I was probably on the road and stupid that I am, I forgot my cell phone."

Anna must have noticed me staring at the girl. "Harvey," she said, "this is my daughter, Lainey. Lainey, Harvey is my estate lawyer and was David's best friend."

Our eyes locked. I felt as if the girl were daring me to say what I wanted to say next. "Pleased to meet you, Lainey," I said, even though it was about as far from the truth as possible. She knew it too. I didn't know what kind of game this was, but I had the feeling the stakes were steep and that I would need to tread carefully.

"Anna, I'm sorry to be a bother," I said, "but my pants are soaking wet. Might you still have a pair of David's old sweats that I can change into while my pants dry?"

She seemed as tense as me, but then again, she's always been anxious around me. "Of course," she said. "Lainey, could you go get them? Third drawer down in the tall chest of drawers."

"I'll be right back," she said with a tone that sounded eerily like a warning.

As soon as the girl disappeared, I said, "Anna, is that really Lainey?"

"Of course," she replied, with a voice implying that I was an imbecile.

"But how can it be?"

She didn't turn her head to look at me as she replied. She continued staring ahead, and her voice was completely flat. "She is here, and that's good enough. Plus, I guess you should know there are a lot of things I can't figure out anymore. Everything is sometimes all jumbled up. I think I'm losing it, and so does Lainey. I heard her singing in David's closet. His shirts weren't ripped up anymore."

Oh shit! That wasn't the explanation I had hoped to hear. What the hell is she talking about? "Does Trent know you are feeling this way?"

"Lainey told him."

"Trent spoke to Lainey? When?"

The girl reappeared and handed me a pair of sweats. "She'll be fine. She bumped her head, and she's a little foggy still. Besides, nobody's going anywhere tonight in this weather."

Anna stared straight ahead, zombie-like. Her increasingly monotone voice, her growing lack of emotion, and her lack of physicality were disturbing.

"Anna, are you okay?"

"I'm fine."

I wasn't going to get much more out her for the moment, but did I dare push any of Lainey's buttons? I finished the tea. "You said you spoke with Trent earlier. It must have been a long time since you both spoke. How long has it been?"

"I'm sorry, but I don't like to talk about family

matters with people outside of the family, especially with people I don't even know. I hope you can understand."

"Understood."

This girl's shrewd and Anna's acting strangely. "I'll just go change in the guest bath. It's down the hall, isn't it?"

The girl responded affirmatively with a shake of her head. Anna continued to stare off into space. I felt wonky and a little more off balance than I expected as soon as I rose from the chair. I guessed my body was still thawing. My ankle was throbbing. At least I didn't have frostbite. I limped down the hall to the guest bath. After closing the door, I nearly fell onto the toilet seat. I was feeling a little foggy too. Maybe, my brain was still thawing out as well.

I needed to speak with Trent. Lainey really was here. There was strangeness about that girl and Anna, too. I wondered if there was a landline phone anywhere in the house. The house was new, and I knew that a lot of newly built homes were forgoing old landlines now that cell phones dominated. Then again, being out here so far away from cell towers, maybe there still needed to be a landline. I couldn't remember how my cell phone's reception had been here or how strong the signal was. I wasn't sure that I even used it while here before.

I felt David's loss keenly again as I slipped into his sweatpants. I remembered him telling me what a number Lainey's disappearance had done on Anna. He was instrumental in pulling Anna back into accepting reality and beginning to enjoy life again. I wished he were here now. I don't seem to be able to reach her.

She's practically catatonic. You'd think she would be ecstatic to be with her daughter again.

Anna said that she thinks she's losing it and then some crazy crap about Lainey singing in a closet and David's shirts not being cut up. I wonder if she is losing it. Maybe David's death affected her more than anyone realized. She's so listless. Perhaps, it's depression. Maybe, it's as Lainey said that she bumped her head. But, if so, why isn't she resting in bed? There's something about that girl that's off. I wish I could get into contact with Trent.

I wasn't sure what to do with my wet pants, so I just held on to them. Slowly, and as quietly as possible, I turned the knob of the guest bath door and looked out into the hall. I didn't see anyone. Quietly and slowly, I made my way down the hallway, opposite from the way I came before, and looked everywhere for some sign of a phone—landline or cell. I scanned the living room. Nothing. I wasn't sure what was beyond the living room.

"Harvey, can I help you find something?" asked Lainey as she peered at me from the dining room area.

"I was hoping to find a landline so that I could make a call about my car. It's straddling the middle of the road. I'm going to need a tow truck."

"No landline here and cells aren't working either right now. The storm must have knocked out power to the cell tower."

Damn, this woman has a ready-made and convenient answer for everything.

"Why don't you come back into the dining room?" she offered.

Truth was, I was beginning to feel dizzy. I

complied and made my way toward Lainey and Anna. As I passed by Anna's line of sight, I noticed that she didn't flinch or blink. It was as if she were staring right through me. I stopped and turned back toward the living room. The girl was beside me in a flash.

"Just admiring the place," I said. "Your Mom and David built a beautiful home together. Did you ever meet him?"

No response.

"He was quite a guy. I miss him. You would have loved him."

Nothing.

"Something's wrong with Anna. She's not herself."

"How would you know?" she sneered. "How well do you know her?"

Damn, she's strange! I was becoming progressively dizzier. I returned to the table and again sat next to Anna. The girl refilled my mug with more tea. Feeling scrutinized by Lainey and not knowing what else to do, I drank the tea. The chill in the room was growing, becoming worse and more dangerous, than the cold outside. The girl disappeared into the kitchen with the kettle.

I leaned closer to whisper, "Anna, do you know who I am?"

"Harvey," she replied.

Relief spread through me. Just as I was about to continue, Anna leaned into the table, closed her eyes, and dropped her head into her arms. She was out.

"Lainey, can't you see that something is wrong with your mother?" I said in the direction of the kitchen.

"How are you feeling, Harvey?"

I wasn't feeling so good either. Wooziness. I had trouble focusing on the mug before me. I stared at it. There was something…

The girl came back from the kitchen and began singing. It was little's kid's song about a teapot. It wasn't cutesy; it was downright chilling. She leaned over the table and pulled the blonde wig off her head. She peeled off contact lenses to reveal brown eyes instead of blue.

My jaw dropped, then snapped shut as my face hit the table.

****

I'm not sure how much later it was when I woke, though I could see that it was still the dark of night outside. I could hear the television from the living room beyond. My face was still on the table, and I was facing Anna. I tried to lift my head from the table but was unable to raise it more than a couple of inches. Anna, still out of it, made a pained sound when I tried to lift my head. That's when I realized that a length of rope was coiled around each of our necks.

When I lifted my head, it caused the rope to tighten around Anna's neck. Each end of the line was likely wrapped around the table's legs. If I tried to lift my head too high, or too fast, the rope would choke Anna. I would be choked if she did the same. If we both raised our heads at the same time, at best we would only be able to rise about six inches. Another length of rope was coiled around my waist and then wrapped around my hands to bind them together behind me. Anna, of course, was likely bound in the same fashion. Neither of us could move.

Anna's eyes opened. Our heads sideways on the

table we were inches apart and eye-to-eye. "Harvey?" she said and began to raise her head.

"Don't lift your head," I warned in a whisper.

The fright in her eyes when she saw the rope and the realization that we were bound up made me wish I could reach out to comfort her. "What's happening?" she croaked.

"Anna, that girl is not your daughter."

"Who…then is…"

"She's the daughter of your cleaning woman. I remember her from my last visit here."

"Cassie?"

"She's been wearing a wig and contacts to change her eye color, Anna."

Tears pooled in Anna's eyes and began falling onto the table.

"I'm so sorry, Anna. Lainey's been gone for a long time now. She's gone and never coming back. She can't come back. Lainey died. David was helping you to accept it and to live again. You were doing so well up until he died. I guess we didn't realize…"

"Stop, please!" Anna began moaning softly, her tears pooling on the tabletop.

I'd never felt so much sadness for another person. My gut wrenched at the thought of what she must be going through.

Chapter Sixteen

Anna

Harvey had just ripped out what was left of my heart.

Lainey was gone. David was gone. James was gone.

But it was because of James and what he did to us, to her, that she was gone, and I wasn't able to prevent what happened to her. The trauma my children experienced from losing their father the way they did was beyond measure. The public spectacle of his horrifying death on 9/11 was unfathomable. They were already battling the hurt of his rejection when their father turned his back on them after the divorce. His rebuff of them was surely meant to punish me, but I also couldn't accept that he lacked any awareness for what he was doing to the children. He believed that their births were what came between our agency and our relationship. He thought he could only be all into our marriage if I remained all into the agency. A part of me always knew that he resented the children.

His rejection of us was a festering wound that ate away at the children and me. When James died, that wound didn't go away. Instead, it became a painful malignancy. There would never be a time, or a chance, for the children to reconcile with their father. Any opportunity for his embrace, a smile, words of love, or encouraging support was lost forever. That does something to a person, especially to a child.

Trent reacted by becoming loud and obnoxious. He threw things, he was disrespectful and always testing my patience. He hated me. I became the whipping post he needed to release his hurt and anger. I understood that. But, when he started bullying other kids at school and acting out in class, that was when I had to step in for his sake as well as the sake of everyone around us. I arranged for family therapy, which seemed to benefit him. His outbursts became fewer, and the complaints from school stopped. His grades recovered. He learned to feel his way through the hurt. He came to terms with it and was then able to move on from it. Even at that young age, he found a strength that I still lack.

It was more challenging to tell how Lainey was coping with the death of her father. It was more difficult to reach her. Maybe I never did. Her reactions were completely opposite to Trent's. She became sullen after the divorce. At home, she spent a lot of time in her room. She maintained her friendships and her involvement in sports, but her heart wasn't into anything. It was as if she were merely going through the motions. No highs, no lows, barely present.

The therapist was most worried about her. On the surface, there seemed to be less to worry about. But still waters run deep. A lot was going on beneath the surface. None of us knew the depths of her suffering. Her agony was beyond our reach.

It was more important than ever for me to generate an income. Maintaining a roof over our heads, having food in the fridge, and paying for health insurance to cover mounting therapy bills forced me to take on more projects. I was still able to work mostly from home. If I had to make a presentation or meet with clients, I usually had the luxury of doing so during school hours. When the children grew older and were out of the house more, I spent more time working.

Family life morphed into a different kind of normal. The kids were more guarded, less spontaneous. Though a couple of friends that I confided in told me that it was merely teenageritis and nothing more. I hovered, and then felt guilty about it. If I found myself starting to smother one of them, I backed off. Looking back now, I wondered if I sometimes needed to back off, and to create distance, because I was afraid that if I wrapped them tightly in my arms, I would never find the strength to let them go.

I prayed for them to believe that a full and happy life could still be theirs. I was consumed by gnawing doubts over whether I could grow them well enough. I was both mother and father now. I sucked at both, but I became an expert in "what ifs" and worrying. Second-guessing myself because I had to get it right for the kids' sake was my new norm. I was decisive and bold in my work life. I was an emotional wreck holding on by a thread in my family life. Helping my son and daughter to become happy, healthy adults was all that mattered.

Trent left the nest first. He flew as far away as he could, choosing a university in California. It didn't take a therapist to tell me that he needed to put the devastation he experienced as a child far behind him. He needed to create distance. I understood, and I supported his decision. Trent being far away also gave me the chance to focus more on Lainey. Of the two, she worried me more. There was a fragility about her now. She was too quiet. I longed for her to laugh wildly and uncontrollably about something. She never expressed enthusiasm for anything. She was a serious student, a devoted friend, and a well-behaved daughter. Her self-control was obsessive, and I was afraid for her.

Trent found excuses to avoid coming home on breaks and summers. He thrived in California. He said he found his groove. I was happy for him, though I missed him sorely. Lainey then also went off to university. She didn't have an overriding need to go as far away as Trent, because she had perfected an inner distance, and detachment, that was much greater than any geographical space. Lainey chose a school in Florida because of the school and what she wanted to pursue as a major. Dutiful daughter that she was, she kept in close touch, which eased me considerably.

That first semester was tough. Lainey spoke of feeling lonely and out of place. Maybe she should find a school closer to home she'd say. I told her to give it a chance and assured her that many a freshman felt that same way at first. Toward the end of that first semester, she made some friends, and her calls soon became filled with energy. She expressed enthusiasm for her classes and the things she discovered with her new friends. I had begun to think everything would turn out okay for both children. Those next years flew happily by.

I took on more projects, some of which took me to other countries. I found the challenge of international work fulfilling and I began doing more of it. My life was expanding and pleasurable. Eventually, the work grew to the point where I needed to establish distinct bases of operation. The first office was in New York, I opened the second operation in Paris, and the third office was in partnership with a well-known agency in Shanghai.

Trent, now in law school, became involved with a delightful young woman. Karen made him happy. I was surprised when they announced they spontaneously eloped while vacationing in Napa. Soon after, we were all surprised by the news they were expecting twins. Trent began working at a good firm, and they settled into a lovely home. I saw in Trent a determination to be the father he never had.

Lainey, having recently graduated with a major in communications, was still trying to find her footing. She was working at an internship in Miami and was planning to start graduate school in Chicago, a few months later. She began dating a young man whom she described as "intoxicating." She said he lavished her with attention, and he always had so many plans for things to do together that she sometimes had trouble keeping up with his zest for life. Lainey certainly needed some excitement in her life and, at first, I was happy for her. But sometimes the way she described how he monopolized her time made me uneasy. If I asked her about it, she would say that it was because he loved her so. My concern grew when he convinced her to postpone moving to Chicago and to instead move in with him there in Miami. A couple of times when I tried to talk with her about it, she would cut short the conversation because Matthew needed her for this or that—at that very moment. Interruptions became a deeply unsettling routine.

Lainey had dated throughout college, nothing

serious, but she became serious about this guy too fast. I wanted to meet him. He was too busy to get away when I invited them to come up north for a long holiday weekend, and since he also didn't want to be without her, that trip didn't pan out. A few months later I offered to visit them in Miami, but at the last minute, something came up, and Lainey told me they would have to cancel. Lainey was all apologies. I could sense her feeling torn.

That was about the same time I met David. We were seatmates on a flight over to Paris. Like most people who travel often, I barely spoke to anyone I might be seated next to during a flight. Flights were a time to either get caught up on a backlog of work or to indulge in a good book or movie. I also sometimes got my best sleep under business class comforters. The home was too quiet now with the kids gone, and hotels just sometimes seemed too sterile. Napping on long flights somehow could make me feel more recharged than sleeping a whole night in my own bed. But there was no napping during that flight when I was seated next to David. There was also no computer work, movies watched, or book read. We chatted the entire trip. He was easy going, and I enjoyed his company. It was one of the most relaxing and enjoyable flights I had ever experienced. Two days later, we literally bumped into one another, spilling champagne, during an American business reception at the U.S. Ambassador's Residence in Paris. Though I still barely knew David at that point, it was like bumping into an old friend. We again fell quickly into conversation. He invited me to dinner after that reception. We saw one another two more times over the next week, and we made plans to reconnect once back home. He would be returning to his place in Manhattan, me to my home just outside the city. Though we wouldn't connect right away because I was planning to make a side trip first.

Something gnawed at me about Matthew. I hoped I was wrong. I decided to fly from Paris to Miami and not give Lainey a heads-up beforehand. I would use the pretext of visiting a client for an unscheduled, and last minute, meeting. I arrived in Miami and waited outside the office building where Lainey worked. Finally, I saw her coming through the door, but before I could get her attention, a young man swooped in, grabbed her by the forearm, and began leading her away.

"Lainey!" I called out.

She turned. "Mom?"

I quickly caught up with them and saw by the grimace on his face that the man was none too pleased. "Hi, Honey," I said while trying to hug Lainey. It was an awkward physical maneuver because the man wouldn't let go of her. I managed, at least, to give her a kiss.

"Mom, what are you doing here?"

"I was on my way back from Paris when a client here said they needed a meeting to address something right away. I didn't have time to get in touch with you," I lied. "I've only just landed a few hours ago. I thought I'd surprise you."

Lainey looked nervously from me to the man, and back to me again.

"You must be Matthew. I'm very pleased to finally meet you," I said as I offered him my hand.

"Yeah, good to meet you, too," he said unconvincingly. His right hand never let go of Lainey's arm and shrugged off my attempt to shake his hand, adding, "We've got to go."

"I know that I've taken you both by surprise and I don't want to interrupt any plans you might have, but I thought that maybe we could just spend a few minutes catching up over a coffee? There's a cute little café just across the street. I've missed you, Lainey."

She gave Matthew a pleading look. His grip on her tightened in response. Surprisingly, and much to his obvious annoyance, Lainey then said that it would be possible to spend just a little time together.

After we settled in at a table, I noticed small drops of perspiration forming on Lainey's brow and upper lip. I didn't know if it was from nervousness or because she was wearing a sweater over her blouse. The weather was hot, certainly not sweater appropriate. She shook her head nervously and negatively when I asked if she wanted to remove her sweater to be more comfortable.

It was evident that we would only have precious few moments together. I was becoming increasingly nervous, too. The woman before me seemed to be just a shadow of my daughter. Conversation was awkward and stilted. Matthew was clearly itching to get going. I reached across the table for Lainey's hand, and as I did so, I noticed bruising on her wrist. A few minutes later, as she swept her hair behind her shoulder, I noticed what looked like a thumbprint size bruise on the side of her neck. She saw me noticing—and so did Matthew.

I needed to get her alone.

"Time to go," Matthew said tersely. "Sorry, Anna, but we've got lots to do."

"Lainey, do you have any time to get together tomorrow? It's a Saturday. Maybe I could take you shopping, and we could do lunch?"

Lainey looked pleadingly at Matthew.

"Sorry, Anna," he said curtly. "We're very busy this weekend. You caught us at a bad time. Maybe next time you are down this way, letting us know in advance would be helpful."

He practically pulled her out of the chair. It broke my heart to see her leave.

I paced back and forth in that hotel room throughout most of the night trying to figure out what to do. I repeatedly tried to call and to text her cell, but she wasn't picking up. It was evident that my daughter was suffering from physical abuse at the hands of Matthew. I went to the police the next morning to see what help they might be able to offer. The police said there was little they could do without me having proof or without my daughter reaching out to them.

There was little I could do, but I had to do something. I remembered that I had been standing in front of a bank just next to Lainey's office building while I was waiting for her. I went back to that bank still early that Saturday morning to open a joint account with Lainey. I deposited five-thousand dollars into the account. I then mailed to her office address the account details and a signature card for her to sign. I wrote that I knew something was wrong, that she was in danger, and that she needed help. I wanted her to use the money to purchase an airplane ticket back home and whatever else she might need. I wrote that I would be coming to her office to talk with her before I left for home.

I arrived at her office that Tuesday, just before lunch. My mail had already been received because she was clearly expecting me. She introduced me to her coworkers and then she motioned for me to follow her to a small conference room in the back. She shut the door behind us and immediately flew into my arms. Lainey cried uncontrollably. "I'm so sorry, Mom," she managed while choking through her tears.

"I don't want you to be sorry. I just want you to be safe. You must leave him."

"I don't know. I know he can be rude, and he sometimes gets angry, but he can also be very sweet sometimes, and I know that he loves me."

"Loving you does not mean isolating you, controlling you, and hurting you!" I said as I rolled up her sleeve and saw a line of bruises extending from her wrist to her forearm. "Lainey, you can't allow anyone to treat you this way."

"Matthew says that he loves me so much that he wouldn't be able to live without me. He needs me and wants to be with me always. Nobody has ever felt that way before about me."

There it was. I sat her down; I took a seat across from her and gathered her hands in mine. Looking deep into eyes and trying to reach deep into her heart and soul, I said, "Listen, baby, don't confuse Matthew's behavior, or your father's behavior for love or the lack of it. Your father had demons, just as I imagine Matthew does, but you can't extinguish his demons any more than we could your father's.

"James' behaviors had nothing to do with you. Matthew's behavior also has nothing to do with you. You are not broken. Matthew is the one who is broken and no matter what you do to try to make him happy, you can't. You can't fix him."

We talked throughout her lunch hour, and I thought

I had finally reached her when she conceded that she was in a bad situation. She agreed that she needed to do something about it. She reached up and lightly traced the slender hearing aid tube that traveled from the inside of my ear to the apparatus behind my ear.

"I know why you need this," she said. "You didn't wear a hearing aid when we were very little. You didn't need one until that night when Daddy was drunk and on top of you, slapping your face, and slamming your ears. That night he killed your hearing in this ear. You never told us, but we knew it all the same. You handled ending things with Daddy your way, and it made you stronger. Please let me handle things with Matthew my way. I won't let it get as bad for me as it got for you."

I pleaded with her to leave with me that very day, but she said that she needed a little time. She said she didn't want to run away. She wanted to do everything in a way that she wouldn't feel like a coward running home to her mother. She would give notice at her job. She would tell Matthew that she was leaving, and why.

I begged her not to give advance warning to Matthew. I told her that it might not be safe to do so, but my dutiful daughter would not be swayed. I said that he might promise to change, he might charm her into staying, and that he might do a thousand different things to make her change her mind. But it wouldn't last. When a person's first instinct is to resort to physical violence to control another person, they don't suddenly change. That type of behavior is instinctive, and it doesn't change overnight, or maybe at all.

She was wavering. I could feel it. "I'll stay here," I said. "I'll get a short-term apartment rental. That way I can be close by if you need me."

"No, I must do it my way, and when the timing is right. No, Mom. Go home. I'll be fine. I know how to handle him."

"Lainey, please reconsider."

"Mom, maybe you are overreacting because of what you've been through in your life. It might not be the same kind of situation. He deserves a chance to change. I won't be able to live with myself if I don't give him that chance. I might even suggest counseling. It could be that he loves me so much that he is willing to change, for me. I can try to make him understand that he doesn't need to be afraid of losing me."

"I need to know that you are safe."

"I'll phone you from the office every morning during the week. I'll call you on weekends. I promise I'll use the funds you've set aside in the bank here to leave in a hurry, if necessary."

I wasn't comfortable with her plan. But at least she was thinking ahead now, and at least I would have more frequent contact with her. I relented. I had no choice. She was an adult, and I couldn't force her. She walked me out to the front of the office. We hugged and said our goodbyes. I had to force myself to leave her. As I turned the front office doorknob, I turned back around to get one last look at her. Lainey blew me a kiss before disappearing to her office carousel.

I was supposed to see David again shortly after my return home. I was emotionally exhausted, and tense as could be. I considered canceling. I was too preoccupied to be good company to anyone. But, when he called to ask if we were still on and to discuss plans, I was drawn to his calming voice, and I thought the distraction of seeing him again might be good for me.

Nevertheless, Lainey was always on my mind. Every moment was filled with obsessing about whether she was okay. I tried to block the "what ifs" from my mind and I held my breath until her call each day.

She said that after our talk, she began viewing Matthew through a different lens. Instead of letting every angry outburst overwhelm, overpower, and paralyze her with fear, she was sometimes now able to think through ways to diffuse his anger. She believed she was getting stronger. She thought therapy might be helpful for their relationship, and she was soon going to bring up the subject with Matthew. I was skeptical, but she wouldn't be swayed. She wouldn't listen when I asked if she was making excuses for him.

Seeing David again was delightful. We had a wonderful dinner at that cozy small Italian restaurant I can never remember the name of. He was easy to be with. We were still at the stage where we hadn't yet shared deep dives into our pasts, and that was particularly okay with me. We made plans to see one another again that Sunday for brunch, followed by a walk in the park. I found myself looking forward to it more than I initially thought I might.

Lainey didn't call on Saturday. I kept my phone even closer to me on Sunday. I explained to David that I was expecting an important call from my daughter. We were walking through Central Park and chatting about our favorite places there when my cell rang. Assuming it was Lainey, I answered without looking at the number.

"Hi, Lainey!"

"Am I speaking to Anna Blackwood?" an unfamiliar male voice asked.

"Yes, this is Anna Blackwood," I answered, looking up at David with a casual shrug.

"Mrs. Blackwood, is there somebody with you right now?"

I was confused. I looked up at David, "Yes, there is somebody with me. Who is this?"

David looked back at me, also seemingly just as confused.

"Ma'am, if you trust that person near you, I think it would be helpful if you were to put me on speaker."

I did so. At hearing the next words, I froze. Blood ceased to course through my veins.

"I'm sorry, Mrs. Blackwood. This is Detective Stanton with the Miami Police, and I have some terrible news. It's about your daughter Lainey."

I'll never forget that detective's calm and measured voice as he delivered news that would forever change my life. How could he be so calm?

"Boaters discovered Mr. Matthew Barre's boat seemingly drifting unmanned yesterday. As they pulled closer, they found Mr. Barre lying dead in the boat. He apparently shot himself with a flare gun."

"Oh, my God! But what has this to do with my daughter?"

I must have been swaying because David then gripped my arm to steady me.

"Perhaps, I should continue by speaking to the person nearby you, Mrs. Blackwood?"

"No, just tell me!" I cried. At that, David wrapped me protectively in his arms.

"There was a lot of blood on the floor of the boat, and in a streak up along the side of the boat. It didn't seem to match how Mr. Barre died. There was also a bloody knife. We strongly suspect that it may be your daughter's blood on that knife…"

I don't remember anything more. David later told me that I screamed, dropped the phone, and fainted in his arms. He continued speaking to the Detective. Extensive searches of the area had so far not turned up any sign of my daughter.

David said that when he asked the detective how they could be so sure the blood was Lainey's or that she had even been on the boat, the detective explained that eyewitnesses saw them leave the marina earlier that same day and the marina personnel said the boat didn't return. The blood type they found on the bottom and sides of the boat didn't match Matthew's. They needed to do a DNA analysis, but all indicators presently pointed to Lainey having been on the boat and Matthew shooting himself with the flare gun.

David immediately booked flights to Miami. He insisted on being with me. I was unable to speak coherently so it was David who also broke the news to Trent. It wasn't until much later that I realized it was the first time they spoke to one another. I'm not sure I had even told Trent or Lainey about David yet. Our relationship was that new.

Trent had just walked in the door from a business trip when David called. With suitcase still in hand, he left again for Miami. I was glad to have them both at my side. The DNA analysis confirmed that the blood on the floor and up the side of the boat, and on the knife, was indeed Lainey's. Murder-suicide was their theory. Relentless ocean searches came up empty. No trace of Lainey was found.

Unable to accept that she was gone, I was wracked

with guilt. I should have stayed in Miami. I should have forced her somehow to leave him. I should have found a solution that would have gotten her away from him. She could be alive now if I had not failed her. First, James, now Lainey—I couldn't bear it.

And I couldn't believe it.

I couldn't give up on her like the police had done. Despite Trent and David's compassionate attempts to convince me otherwise, I was relentless in my search for Lainey. I spoke with their neighbors, her coworkers, and everyone I could at the marina where Matthew docked his boat. Everyone confirmed what the police had already uncovered, and the detective in charge of the case said there was no doubt in his mind, after hearing from me that Lainey was in an abusive relationship. If an abuser who has little impulse control over inflicting physical hurt is confronted with threats of his partner leaving, demanding counseling, or any attempt to change the partnership's dynamic, that person might resort to murder of their partner and suicide for themselves as the last, only, and best solution.

Intellectually, I knew all of this. I've watched enough of the news to know that this kind of thing happened all too often. Knowing of it, its prevalence, and the telltale signs were also the reason why I initially became concerned about Lainey. The red flags were there. I couldn't forgive myself for not having done more, or better, to save her from him.

When I couldn't bear the suffocating weight of the pain, I hoped against hope that maybe she had found a way to escape. Maybe she jumped out of the boat when Matthew came at her with the knife. Perhaps, she had hit her head before falling from the boat, and Matthew only thought her to be dead. Maybe, Matthew thinking her dead then killed himself? Perhaps somebody else came upon them, saw that Matthew was dead and found Lainey had been hurt but was still alive and they dragged her aboard their vessel. That could explain her blood smeared up the side of the boat.

If she survived, then where was she? Maybe a passing ship had rescued her. Cuban fishermen, a passing cargo ship, or small craft people sailing from Miami northward or to the Caribbean—none of them would have likely heard about this tragedy. Maybe she didn't know that Matthew was dead and that's why she was afraid to let anyone know that she was alive. Her rescuers could be helping her to cover things up for the time being. Maybe, she was waiting until she felt safe enough. I had to cling to any hope until I could again cling to my daughter.

David and Trent became an irritation. They slowed me down. I told them to both go back to their homes. I was staying in Miami until I had answers. Neither wanted to leave me, but I didn't want them near me. They had accepted what I wouldn't. I didn't need that negativity circling around me and trying to dissuade me from doing everything I could, and what I felt the police had given up doing. The police considered this a clear-cut, open-and-shut, textbook case of an abusive relationship that ended in a murder-suicide.

The cops lost patience with me. Lainey's neighbors, coworkers, Coast Guard officials, marina staff, and boaters with slips nearby Matthew's began to give that "Not again!" look when they saw me coming. Pity was tattooed across everyone's face. But I didn't want pity. I wanted answers.

I wanted to find my daughter.

Trent talked me into letting him hire a private detective to help me before he and David left. They made me promise that if no leads turned up within thirty days that I would accept the fact that Lainey was never coming back to me. My promising was the only way to rid myself of them and their mistaken views. Reluctantly, I complied.

Initially, I had high hopes that the independent investigator could turn up information that nobody else had yet discovered. He insisted on letting me give him the freedom to conduct his own interviews without me present. I had already worn out my welcome with everyone he needed to speak with, and he said my presence would only hamper his investigation. While he investigated without me, I needed something to fill my time and calm my unending overdriving brain. So, I spent time researching people who had been lost at sea and presumed dead. There were other cases, there were instances of people surviving for long periods undetected, and there was hope still.

Though now far from me, David and Trent remained annoying, still continually begging me to get some rest, to eat some healthy food, and to come to my senses. Both were kind enough not to voice that last part directly to me, but I knew what they thought. It was inferred by their attitudes. It was the pity for me they tried to hide but couldn't. I told David to stop contacting me and to get on with his own life. I said that I wasn't interested in him, or in anything, except finding my daughter.

I tried to balance the irritation and annoyance I felt

for everyone and everything with frequent visits to church. I had never been much of a churchgoer but sitting alone in a pew and talking to God seemed to somehow fortify me. He wasn't yet answering my prayers, but I had faith.

While the investigator busied himself by going over the same ground that I had, I posted missing person notices at supermarkets, banks, marinas, churches, and libraries all along the coast. I contacted news outlets and radio stations. I began a social media campaign and broadcasted photographs of my daughter wherever I could. I used my company's influence to gain media attention. I wore everyone out.

At thirty days, and after the investigator reported to us that he too believed Matthew had murdered Lainey, Trent begged me to stop what they viewed as a foolhardy quest. But I couldn't give up. Giving up, and giving in, was not an option.

Needing fortification, I decided to light another candle, to pray, and to again use sitting in the stillness of a church to contemplate my next move. I entered the vestibule and glanced, as I always did, at the missing person photo and description of Lainey that I had posted there. I noticed an old woman, bent from aged bones, reach up to touch the picture of Lainey. I was moved. I then followed some distance behind as she entered the church. After lighting a candle, I seated myself in the pew behind her, and I watched her pray. I thought about how she was the only person I'd ever seen pay attention to Lainey's missing person poster. This woman, this stranger, suddenly became an all-important person in my life.

As I struggled over how to approach her, she

suddenly turned to me. "You are praying for the wrong thing."

"What? Excuse me?"

"Your prayers will go unanswered if you do not change knowing what to pray for."

In a flash, I became angry with her and at myself for thinking this woman held any importance for me. I said, "You have no idea what I'm praying for, and it's none of your business."

Then she shocked me by saying, "I pray for your daughter's soul, and I pray for you to accept what you refuse to accept. I see the photos of your daughter everywhere, and I've seen you on television, and I've heard you on the radio. The reporters say that all leads have been exhausted and they say what the police believe happened, but you refuse it. I pray for you to find peace. I pray you accept that your daughter cannot come back."

I had to get away from her. I started to rise, but she covered my hand with her own. "I also had a daughter who died tragically. She was young and beautiful like your daughter, and I could not bear to believe it. The images of how they say my daughter died and the pain she must have suffered is unthinkable. Those images haunted me. I could not accept it, and I couldn't rid myself of the guilt of failing to protect her."

I fell back down into the hard pew, my misery unleashed, and it couldn't be pushed back inside. I couldn't suppress it anymore. The old woman suddenly beside me, her arthritic hands offering a handkerchief as I wept uncontrollably. She wrapped her bony arms around me. She told me to cry for Lainey, for myself, and for everyone who mattered.

As I cried, she patted my hair and my face while whispering soothing words in Spanish, which I didn't understand. But those words helped me claim the depths of my pain and sorrow, giving me a strength that I didn't know I had.

I thanked that old woman. I went back to my hotel, booked a ticket for the next flight home, and packed. I texted Trent to let him know that I was headed home. I was emotionally and physically drained. I fell asleep at the gate and woke just in time to board the plane. I slept the entire flight. I was still groggy at baggage claim, and so I didn't at first believe my eyes when the first face I saw at Arrivals was David's. The man I had callously thrown away walked toward me, hugged me, and kissed my forehead. He grabbed the trolley cart containing my luggage and proceeded to leave the terminal. I followed. Neither of us said a word.

We drove in silence, arrived at an apartment building that I guessed was where he lived. I followed him into a bedroom and collapsed. David was then beside me. He wrapped his arms around me while I cried tears that couldn't be stopped. This was how we spent our first night together and the ones that followed. I sobbed into his chest until fatigue overtook me, only to awake again to my real-life nightmare and begin to cry all over again. Grief's floodgates opened. David held on to me to keep me from being swept away while my tears baptized me into acceptance.

There was before, and then there was a new reality. I never knew why David stayed with me, what he saw in me. In the beginning, I didn't have the energy or the desire for a relationship. I treated him shabbily. It didn't matter to me if he were there or not. So, I don't know why I mattered to him. But slowly I did retake notice of him, his kindness, and his attentiveness. He was incredibly patient. If I took one halting step forward, I usually also then took two awkward steps back. David was always there, behind me, ready to catch me from falling.

I was just beginning to feel joyful and hopeful again, without guilt. David helped me to cope with losing Lainey. Did I think that Lainey came back to me to help me deal with losing David or did I want to believe so badly that Lainey was really with me to keep at bay the guilt still buried within?

Chapter Seventeen

Anna

"Wake up!"

My cheeks were being pulled. Rough punches pummeled my arm. I knew the situation would likely only worsen after I opened my eyes, but Cassie wasn't going to leave me alone until I obeyed. As I slowly opened my eyes, her face filled my line of vision. How could I ever mistake her for my own daughter? Without the blonde wig and blue contact lenses, this evil creature before me bore little resemblance to Lainey.

"Had you fooled, didn't I?" Cassie laughed. "Your dear daughter is really dead! So sad!"

An icy chill ran through me. "Why are you doing this?"

"It's fun."

"What kind of monster are you?" Harvey demanded.

"Oh, be nice now!" Cassie said and gave him a hard poke in the forehead. "At first, it was just a fun experiment, but when I couldn't believe how easily convinced you could be that I was Lainey, I thought my hypothesis might be correct."

"What hypothesis?" Harvey sneered.

"Be nice, old man. I'm not going to warn you again," Cassie said, and then continued. "Trent hunted around to get home help for you after David's death, because you insisted on staying here in this house, but he had to get back to his life, his wife and kids and couldn't stay. That's how he found my mom and me. You can probably say that we were meant to be found. You were upstairs resting. Trent showed us around the first floor, and we finished in the office where he said we could talk privately.

"The good part came when he said he did a double take when he first saw me because I looked so much like his sister. He pointed to a photograph of her on the wall behind us. Even my mother commented about how much we looked alike. Trent said I could practically be her twin if my hair were blonde and my eyes blue. When I asked where his sister was now and why she didn't come back for the funeral, Trent explained that she couldn't. He told us that she had died and how. Wow, that was some crazy way to die! Do you think that fish and crabs and other things ate her and that's why they never found any body parts?"

I groaned as the horrific image of my daughter again appeared in my mind's eye. It was an image I had often fought to push away. It was as if she knew it. This girl was pure evil.

"How dare you," Harvey bellowed at Cassie.

Cassie simply laughed. "Trent told us how bad you took her death and how instrumental David was in helping you. Trent thought you may have been suicidal after Lainey died. David helped you through it all. He said if it weren't for David... Anyway, then he continued by saying that it was all very complicated, and he didn't know if you could survive another loss, so soon and again so traumatic. He described how David died right in front of you."

Cassie smacked the top of my head, then said, "You are one unlucky lady, aren't you? He said you refused to leave here and to go back home with him. House cleaning was only one thing he needed. He also needed somebody to look in on his mother and to let him know if she seemed to be getting worse.

"My mom, she acts like such a pushover, and says that of course, we would do it. She also asked why there were so many photos and why there were plaques under each picture. When Trent referred to the walls of photos as your 'memory walls', I expected him to then say you had Alzheimer's. He didn't say that, but he told us about some of the photos. He said that David had asked him for the captions, and he made the plaques to help you revisit happier memories. He wanted you to remember the happy times instead of only reliving the worst times. It was then that you started to intrigue me, Anna. Trent's use of the words 'complicated' and 'surviving another loss' spoke to me—and in that instant, the plan took shape."

Cassie crossed to the side of the table that was behind Harvey and still mostly in my line of vision. She squatted and rested her chin on the table's edge so that I could plainly see her face. She gave me a glaring once-over stare before continuing.

"After our talk and after my mom agreed that she would work for you, Trent put on some tea and went upstairs to wake you. He wanted to introduce us. Granted, you had just awakened, but you were a complete mess. You weren't with us. It was clear that your mind was in some other realm. Pain was etched across your face. You went through the motions of meeting us, but it soon became quite awkward when there wasn't much more you were interested in saying or learning about us."

"It explains how you know my son Trent," I lamented. "And asking about the memory wall explains how you knew about the grilled cheese sandwich and tomato soup." I shook my head slightly, aware that any larger movement would result in pain from the rope around our necks. "What a fool I've been."

"Now, Anna don't be so hard on yourself. You still don't yet know the half of it. I'm quite good about getting into people's minds and psychology—that's my thing. Trent said you had suffered from Complicated Grief Disorder. Or 'CG' for short. Isn't it, Harvey?"

Harvey, his cheek still pressed to the table, like mine, didn't respond. His stare was going through and past me. His mind was elsewhere.

Chapter Eighteen

The Lawyer

This girl was beyond frightening, and she was also eerily accurate. Was she really that smart to figure everything out herself or did she have help? Cassie just explained how she knew Trent. Maybe Trent told Cassie and her mom a whole lot more than Cassie was letting on to us. I wondered what her end game was.

David was close to Trent from the onset, drawn together by their shared concern for Anna. It was Trent who alerted David that Anna was coming home from Florida—even though she didn't want anything to do with him. He met her there at the airport, and when she followed, he knew he had made the right decision.

I remember David telling me that he convinced Anna to go for counseling when months later she wasn't much better. She wouldn't accept that Lainey was gone. Anna thought she kept seeing her. Poor David was subjected to near-daily reports of how Anna thought she saw Lainey walking the other way on a crowded street or while getting off the subway she might see Lainey getting on the subway a few cars away. She sometimes swore she spotted Lainey in a restaurant window. She'd run into the restaurant and check everywhere for her. Lots of times she never made it to her office or wherever she was supposed to be headed because she had started on another wild goose chase to find the Lainey she supposedly saw. I never did understand how David could put up with it. The accounts and the sheer number of them were maddening and tiring, but David never complained. The therapist said Anna was suffering from Complicated Grief Disorder. I had never heard of it before. It's some kind of super intense grief characterized by a preoccupation with thoughts of the deceased, searching and yearning for the deceased, disbelief about their death, and unable to accept the death. That was how David described it.

Anna lost interest in her business and couldn't see herself returning to it. David talked her into selling her stake in some of the overseas offices and just closing others to prevent the business from hemorrhaging losses. He convinced her to do it before Anna's industry learned she wasn't any longer a worthwhile investment so that some of the offices could be sold and her employees hopefully retained under new management. The sooner they were sold, the more profitable they would still be. I helped David with closings, sales, and transfers. We were able to amass a fortune sizeable enough to provide Anna with continued financial security. She was in such a fog that I'm not sure she ever realized the full extent of what David did for her or my role in all of it.

This Complicated Grief thing, or CG as David referred to it, meant Anna couldn't make sense of her loss and couldn't work through her pain. She wouldn't, she couldn't, accept losing Lainey. CG could be triggered by witnessing the death of a loved one, especially the violent death of a loved one, and particularly a child, or husband, or more than one death close in time. Damn! Anna's had a trauma trifecta, her ex-husband dying on 9/11, the murder of her daughter, and David dropping dead right in front of her. Cassie's correct about one thing. Anna has been one unlucky person. David's death may have triggered a big setback. After what Anna's been through, I wasn't surprised she'd be vulnerable to somebody like Cassie pretending to be Lainey.

People with unresolved guilt, or CG, were either obsessed with the memory of the loved one they lost, or they were intent on finding them. They could feel extreme guilt over the loss of their loved one. They may even believe they can sometimes see, hear, and talk to the deceased person. They tend to lose interest in anything else, just like Anna did with her business and the total lack of interest she had in David for a time. They prefer isolation, which is pretty much how Anna's been after David's death by stubbornly wanting to stay here in this house. After Anna's daughter died, David feared that Anna might harbor thoughts of suicide, which happened to be another sign of CG.

Chapter Nineteen

The Daughter

"Do you know what was quite interesting to me during this whole experiment?" I asked.

Neither Harvey nor Anna made a sound. But that didn't matter. "I knew about Anna experiencing CG after the death of her daughter. I became suspicious that she was again sinking into CG because of David's death. Remember when I found you in front of David's closet rubbing the sleeve of one of his shirts across your cheek?"

No response.

"Hey, Anna, remember how you screamed when you later saw all his shirts in tatters? Then, how you screamed again when the next time you went to his closet all the shirts were whole again!"

Anna groaned.

"Neat trick, wasn't it? Do you know how I pulled it off? I shredded one arm of every shirt and then when I wanted to shock you again, I just turned the hangers in the other direction!"

Anna's groaning continued.

"Getting sidetracked here. What I had started to say was that it was quite exciting to make the correlation between grief and Alzheimer's. It was so easy to convince you that you might be losing it because a lot of what a person feels while grieving is the same as what they might experience in the early stages of Alzheimer's.

"You wondered too, didn't you, Anna? I looked up the browsing history on your laptop. You looked up a series of websites on grieving and Alzheimer's disease. I bet you realized the same as I did! Harvey, did you know that both grief and Alzheimer's have seven distinct stages?"

"Grief has five stages," Harvey replied.

"That's a commonly held notion. The seven stages of grief are described as Shock or Disbelief, Denial, Anger, Bargaining, Guilt, Depression, Acceptance, and Hope.

"Sometimes, people think of Shock, or Disbelief, as being the same as Denial. Bargaining and Guilt are also sometimes combined. Under that scenario, there would be five stages. See Harvey, you can learn something new every day.

"I wondered how easy it might be to convince somebody in the throes of grief that they were actually losing it. I was genuinely amazed when I began this experiment how easily I could persuade you, Anna, that I was Lainey. Having you believe that I was your long-lost daughter was phase one of the experiment and key to conducting the rest of the operation. You needed to think that I was Lainey for me to gain your trust. I needed that trust to lead you down the path I was laying out for you. My experiment was an unequivocal success. Don't you think, Anna? I had you believing you were losing it."

"What now, you sick, twisted bitch?" Harvey bellowed. "Your so-called experiment is finished. What were you planning afterward?"

"My original plan now needs to be modified. I didn't count on Trent sending you my way, Harv. Although, it was probably a stroke of genius on his part. Anna, are you listening? You're awfully quiet."

Anna groaned a response. Her eyes remained tightly shut.

"Maybe I put a little too much gabapentin in her tea this last time."

"Gabapentin?" asked Harvey.

"It's a medication sometimes used for nerve pain. I found it in my grandparents' medicine cabinet. It was prescribed for my grandfather. He uses it when he has an outbreak of shingles, and I know how it affects him. He hates the stuff and tries not to use it. So, sometimes my grandmother slips it into drinks and meals. It was perfect to use on Anna because it can cause brain fog. It works by slowing down neurons, and since your whole brain is neurons, it will slow it down a bit too. Side effects are drowsiness, dizziness, and fatigue. The drug can also affect short-term memory, focus, and concentration—all of which I needed Anna to experience so that she would fear that she might be losing it. The drug can cause hallucinations and swelling of the feet, making people feel like they are walking in cement shoes.

"Originally, I was just going to ask Mommy-Anna here for a little financial help. Then I overheard you and her discussing David's estate when my mom and I were here cleaning. I learned that she is loaded. Real loaded."

"How did you think you would get away with it?" Harvey asked.

"I've been preparing and peppering from the start

so that suspicion wouldn't be a problem. Remember, we were supposed to check in on Anna regularly for Trent. I was getting a little extra on the side. I brought over groceries that my mom bought, and I've told my mom how I've spent lots of time with Anna watching movies and talking. I told my mom it was so sad what Anna had been through, that she was such a nice lady, and it made me feel good to help her out. My mom is so proud of me. That kept her away, and it gave me an excuse to be here. I was even planning to tell my mom that she no longer had to come cleaning here because I was also doing it.

"At some point, Anna would write a check—and a big one, too. I'd show it to my mother and proudly proclaim that Anna insisted on paying my university tuition and living expenses upfront if I promised to buckle down and be serious about my education. I'd tell my mom that Anna knew how badly I wanted to go back to school, but a different school—somewhere out West. I would say that Anna knew how hard it would be for my mom to pay for schooling when it was tough enough to pay tuition at a state school here.

"I had also started to tell my mom that Anna was beginning to call me her daughter. I said that I sometimes didn't know if Anna thinks of me as a daughter or thinks that I really am her daughter. I've planted seeds into my mom's head to make her believe that Anna is often confused. I've said that a few times she's even called me Lainey. It's a small town and word gets around. I'm sure Anna's hairdresser, the post office clerk, and people at the pharmacy have already heard things."

"What were you really going to do with the

money?" asked Harvey.

"Get the hell away from here. I'm not being stuck here in these backwater snow-covered boonies for any longer than I need to be. I already have an airplane ticket. It was a thoughtful gift from dear Anna."

"But you don't yet have the check yet, right?" asked Harvey.

"That's right. You being here has shortened my timeline and changed a few plans. But it's okay; I've got it figured out. Everything will still work out okay because I'm calling the shots now. Nobody else, it's just me now."

Chapter Twenty

The Lawyer

Cassie disappeared from my limited line of vision. A few minutes later, I heard the front door open and close, and I felt a cold draft blow through. Being tied up and with my cheek pressed against the table was a severe constraint. Anna was out of it. Cassie seemed to have a plan for us that wasn't going to end well. How could I save us?

"Anna," I hissed. "Can you hear me?"

She groaned.

"Anna, we are in deep danger. Cassie has tied us up. She's been pretending to be Lainey. I think she is going to kill us. Do you hear me, Anna?"

Another groan.

"Anna, please fight with every ounce of strength you have left to break through the fog. If you get the chance, you'll need to fight for your life. I swear to you that I will do everything I can, but it will take the two of us to overtake her."

Even if I do get a chance to break us free, how am I ever going to get Anna away from Cassie? I've got to try and stall Cassie for as long as possible, so the gabapentin has a chance to fully wear off me and to leave Anna's system.

With Anna's foggy brain, she might not fully

realize what is going on here or yet believe that Cassie has been pretending to be Lainey. If I get the chance to break us free and I need to hurt Cassie, will Anna step in to prevent me from harming who she still may believe is her daughter?

"Anna?"

"Yes."

"Anna, if we get a chance, I may need your help to get us away from her?"

"Not Lainey."

Was that a question or statement that Anna just issued? Her voice was so flat that I couldn't tell. Before I had a chance to ask Anna whether her words meant that she knows Cassie was pretending to be Lainey or just the opposite, I heard the front door open again, closing off any other chance to speak to Anna.

"Whew, still snowing and damn cold out there," said Cassie as she plopped a heavy coil of chain on top of the table. She also deposited two keys, and a pistol, on the far end of the dining table while she removed her gloves.

"Where did that gun and chain come from?"

"I have a snowmobile parked on the other side of the garage," said Cassie. "It belongs to a neighbor. He uses the chain to secure the snowmobile to a tree when he's off in the woods and to drag deer back home when he gets one." She lifted the chain and dropped it again on the table, creating a loud crash. "Pretty heavy duty, isn't it?"

A streak of terror ran down my spine.

Anna didn't flinch.

Chapter Twenty-One

Anna

I heard her, and I heard Harvey. The fog had lifted. I hoped to buy us time by not showing it.

I didn't want to believe that my Lainey was gone. But continuing to think it would be dishonest and dishonorable to the memory of my daughter. David created the memory walls for me to remember the good times. He said I should remember Lainey's life, not her death. "Honor her life," he said.

Lainey was a wonderful gift but also a tortured soul. Remembering her, and trying to honor her life, couldn't be merely remembering only the happy times. The memories of the hurt that became her couldn't be erased because that was also part of who she became. She never recovered from her father turning his back on her. I thought she had finally made a kind of peace with it, but she hadn't. Her being drawn to a man like Matthew was evidence. I thought I knew my daughter well, but there were many things I never knew. I couldn't accurately gauge the depths of her pain and sorrow until it was much too late.

Some things about her I didn't know until after she was gone. The evening we learned from the police that they presumed Lainey dead. I was in my hotel bed, wailing away. Trent sat weeping in the chair facing me.

David sat quietly nearby us both. I was crying about how it was my fault because I didn't do enough to save her when Trent suddenly burst into an angry tirade.

"Stop it, Mom!" he ordered. "I can't bear for you to blame yourself. It's not your fault. It never was your fault. It is Dad's fault that she ended up with somebody like Matthew. Dad was a narcissist, and I'm glad that son of a bitch is dead. What Dad did to us, what he did to Lainey, especially, is unforgivable!"

I had never seen Trent so angry before.

"What do you mean when you say, 'what he did to Lainey especially'?"

"Mom, there are lots of things you never knew. Lainey begged me not to tell."

"Tell me now!" I demanded.

"You never knew about the letters. Did you?"

I shook my head.

"When you go home," Trent continued, "Go as far back as you can into Lainey's closet. Hidden behind her shoes, her tennis racket, and other junk there will be a pile of letters. I'm sure they're still there. She couldn't bear to throw them away, any more than she could bear to keep them.

"We missed Dad terribly after you two divorced. We didn't know if it was that you didn't want us to see him or if he didn't want to see us. We secretly wrote letters to him saying how much we missed him, and we pleaded with him to get in touch. We wrote fantastical letters, lying about how we were the best-behaved and smartest kids in school. We were young, and we exaggerated. We wanted him to want us. We wrote how if we could spend time with him, we would make him so happy. We used the neighbor's mailbox so you wouldn't know what we were up to because we didn't know if you would be angry.

"It really didn't matter though. Our letters never achieved anything. Each letter we wrote was returned unopened. I gave up. I couldn't stand it anymore. But Lainey continued. She kept writing letters, and they kept coming back unopened. I became plenty mad at her, too. I was trying not to think about him, but I could hear Lainey crying at night. Remember how our headboards were in the same place with only the wall in between?"

I shook my head again. I remembered. I remembered her crying herself to sleep so many nights.

"But Mom, that wasn't the worst of it. When she became a little older, she would sometimes skip school, or say she was staying at a friend's house, when she really went into the city and waited outside his apartment building, hoping to catch him. She never did, then, because she didn't know that he no longer had that apartment and had taken to sleeping in his office. Once she figured that out, she began waiting for him outside his office at the World Trade Center. She was growing desperate when she didn't see him there either. One day, after she thought everyone at the company had probably left, she went up to his office to see him. I think she had probably fantasized about him sweeping her up into his arms and the wonderful reunion they would have. But that's not what happened. The glass door to the outer office was locked. She rang the bell, and a few seconds later, he approached the door. She was so happy to see him. But when he recognized that it was his daughter, he turned around and went back to wherever he had been before. But Lainey didn't give up, and she kept ringing that office doorbell. Dad must have called security on her. A few minutes later, she was escorted out of the building by the guards. Can you imagine?"

My heart broke again for Lainey as my hatred for James reach a new high. "Oh, my God! I had no idea."

"I know that you didn't know about the letters and about Lainey going to see him. She begged me not to tell. She must have figured that I was the only other person who could really know how it felt that their father turned away from their own kid. I was the person she cried to all the time, and she wanted to talk about it with me all the time. I hated her. It was too much, and I was just a kid myself. I couldn't deal with my own feelings when I was so busy protecting hers."

Trent slammed his fist on the table. "Why do you think I moved as far west as I could for college and never once came home after graduation? Lainey couldn't let it go. I wanted a new life that was free from that past misery, and that meant a life free from her. I didn't want to carry that wound around with me day in and day out anymore. Dad made Lainey feel worthless. That became her identity. I wasn't going to let it become mine."

"I'm so sorry, Trent," I cried. "I had no idea."

"Of course, you had no idea. You were so busy worrying about Lainey that you never thought of anyone else. She sucked you into her misery; it's the only thing she was ever about."

"Trent, I'm sorry if I wasn't there for you more. But right now, and at this moment, how can you say these awful things about your sister?"

He jumped up from his chair. I thought he was

going to throw it across the room. Instead, he screamed, "No more sorry! Sorry doesn't cut it anymore. I'm about to become a father. My wife is at home on bedrest carrying twins. I'm going home. I'm going to look after my wife and look forward to our future. You can stay trapped in Lainey's land of misery. I don't care anymore."

Trent stormed out of the hotel room. David touched my shoulder and said that he would have a talk with him and left.

Perception, it's different for everyone depending on his or her viewpoint or station. How many lives do we alter when our perceptions of the same situation don't match? Misperceptions are the norm, even in families, or maybe it's especially so.

It took everything in me not to react when I heard the unexpected crashing of heavy chain near my head.

Chapter Twenty-Two

The Lawyer

"Anna, can you hear me?" I whispered. "That girl's gone down the hall. I need to know that you are okay."

"I'm okay. I just don't want her to know it. Maybe somebody will find us if I can buy us time."

"There's something I have to say that I've wanted to say to you for a long time, Anna. I'm sorry. I want you to know that I'm so very sorry for how I acted toward you in the kitchen that first evening we met. I'm so ashamed of myself. I've wanted to say it ever since. I was such an asshole."

"No sorry," she answered. "No more sorry."

"I don't know how we can get away. If there is a chance for you to get safe, Anna—take it. Just take it."

"Not without you."

Footsteps. The girl was coming toward us.

Cassie untied one end of the rope. The taut line wrapped around our necks slackened marginally. "Both of you, stand up."

I managed to wiggle free of the ropes. Standing was slow going; our limbs had been uncomfortably positioned for too long. My neck had a crook in it. I noticed that standing was even tougher for Anna. Or so she made it seem.

Cassie stood on the other side of the table. She was

bundled up as if she were ready to go outside. She had a pistol trained on us. "Strip, Harvey."

"What?"

"You heard me. Strip down to your undies."

I slowly did as Cassie commanded. Anna hadn't flinched. I was impressed by her acting and strong self-control in this escalating danger.

"Good," said Cassie as she used her free hand to grab the heavy chain from the table. "Now, let's take a little walk outside. We could all use a little fresh air, don't you think?"

The snow was still falling at a fast clip, and the wind still howled. My body immediately registered the shock of frigid cold hitting me like a hundred sharp needles. Each stabbing blow took more of my breath away until I could barely breathe at all. My body fought back, refusing to breathe in the biting cold that was already attacking it from outside. Sharp pain induced by the cold shot up through my bare feet and legs.

"Over there." Cassie ordered and pointed to a big old tree fifty feet down the slope from the house.

Anna and I slowly made our way to the tree, Cassie behind us, pistol trained on us both.

"Stop!" she ordered.

We stopped. Anna blankly stared ahead while I rapidly scanned the area around us impossibly hoping to spot something that could save us.

Cassie threw the chain toward me; it sank deep into the snow nearly disappearing entirely. "Pick up the chain, Harvey" Cassie ordered. "Now!"

I reached for it and, even more reluctantly, wrapped it around my waist as she then instructed me to do. My body was already shivering uncontrollably, which made any movement more difficult. The chain, having been buried in snow, just that brief instant, was already so cold that my hands ached from grabbing it.

"Sit against the tree," ordered Cassie.

When it took me a minute to register what she was saying, she screamed, "Now! Or I shoot Anna."

As I sank into the snow, my back made contact with the hard, unforgiving bark of the tree. My butt and legs shook in response to being plunged into the freezing snow.

"Good boy. Now, pick up the chain and crisscross it around your waist and neck."

My hands became fused to the icy cold chain as soon as I tried to do so.

"Anna, grab an end of the chain and bring it back to the other side of the tree. Then do the same with the other length of chain so that we can secure Harvey to the tree."

Anna didn't move, just stared numbly into the distance. She wore no coat and had only a flimsy pair of house slippers on her feet. How she managed not to shiver was beyond me.

"Anna!" Cassie bellowed and repeated her order.

Slowly, Anna's gaze shifted to Cassie, then to me.

"Anna, now!" Cassie screamed again.

Anna made her way toward me. She leaned in, grabbed the end of the chain that I was holding by my neck, and softly whispered, "Please, hold on. Please, don't die." She brought that length of chain around to the opposite side of the tree.

Either not wanting to finish a task that would likely seal my fate, or wanting to appear as still having brain fog, she didn't complete the other half of her task until

Cassie yelled at her again.

After both ends of the chain were wrapped around the tree, Cassie moved in to tightly secure the chain and me to the tree with the lock used to secure the snowmobile.

The cold was unbearable. I wondered how long I could last.

Taking unbridled joy in my demise, Cassie said, "I wonder how much you know about hypothermia. Not unlike the grief and Alzheimer's stages we've already discussed, there are also some distinct stages to hypothermia. Your body's core temperature has already begun to drop, and your body is responding predictably to the first stage, which is defined by intense shivering. The part of the brain that controls body temperature is the hypothalamus. When the hypothalamus recognizes changes in body temperature, it initiates bodily responses to bring the body's temperature back to normal. Shivering is your body trying to generate heat. Unfortunately, outside here and bare to the elements, the shivering, which is generated by your muscles, will only result in making your body lose its heat more quickly. If I were you, I'd try to stop shivering. Sadly, I must inform you that it will be an impossible feat."

Anna grimaced at Cassie's horrifying description. It was a miniscule gesture that went unnoticed by Cassie, but it was another signal that she knew what was happening.

"The body is an amazing instrument. As your core body temperature continues to drop, your body will reduce blood flow to your skin's surface to reduce the amount of heat escaping from your body. Your blood flow will be redirected to critical internal organs, in a foolish attempt to buy time and to protect those organs. Blood flow will increase to the brain, kidneys, lungs, and heart. Your brain and heart will be most sensitive to your body's heat loss. Electrical activity will slow in those organs first as your body's core temperature continues to drop. Death will not be far off then. But take heart, Harvey, this is not a bad way to die. It will be painless. It's just like falling asleep. I sincerely hope you appreciate my kindness."

"You're a pea..t...ch, Cas..t...sie!" I said, as I willed my eyes to bore into her and to find a heart inside there somewhere.

"You are slurring your words, Harvey," Cassie continued, "another telltale sign that you are not doing so well. Your thinking will soon become confused and muddled. Once you stop shivering, and I can see that you already have less strength to keep it up, that will be another signal that your condition is worsening. Factors like body fat, age, and alcohol consumption can affect how long frostbite and hypothermia takes to set in. In my opinion, I don't think you have more than thirty to forty-five minutes left to live. I'll, of course, remove the chains after you are dead.

Cassie bent toward me and pointed her forefinger in a lecturing motion. "This can be what happens when you go chasing after your best friend's wife, Harvey— or so it will likely be the conclusion the police draw. You were trying to move in on the rich widow! Shame on you!"

I shifted my gaze to Anna. Thinking and speech were so difficult, but I had to try and reach her. "Go d-d-d-ducks."

And   hoped   she   could.

173

Chapter Twenty-Three

The Bills

"What the hell!" exclaimed Old Bill from behind the wheel of his plow. Just ahead, a car straddled the road sideways, blocking the narrow lane.

"Looks like that car's been here for a while," said Young Bill. "It's covered under a good amount of snow."

"I'm surprised the car made it this far with so much snow on an unplowed road," said Old Bill.

Young Bill added, "That driver was damn lucky not to go off the road. On the lakeside of the road, there's a near eighty-foot drop in places. Do you think the driver might still be in the car?"

Old Bill shifted the truck into neutral. Young Bill jumped out from the cab to check out the situation. The car was unlocked, and nobody was inside. No key either. It wasn't a car he recognized from these parts. Young Bill walked to the back of the car and brushed snow off the license plate. The plate was from out of state.

Young Bill trudged over to the plow's driver side window to report his findings. "Dad, if we can try to reorient the car back to the direction it should be facing and then push it off to the side of the road, there might be just enough space for us to inch around it," he proposed. "But it would be damn close. We'd need to be damn lucky too not to go off over the edge ourselves."

"I don't like it," Old Bill replied. "Let's first see exactly how much space there might be to work with here."

He backed the truck up a few feet and then drove forward over the same length to now be angling the truck's headlights toward the left side of the road, the same side that dropped off down toward the lake. The black night sky combined with the dazzle of each bright white snowflake swirling around in headlight beams made it difficult to accurately gauge the road's edge.

Young Bill grabbed a shovel from the back of the truck and made his way toward the front of the car, which faced the lake edge of the road. The fierce frigid wind had created drifts, which made it even more difficult to judge where the road ended and the drop-off began. Using the shovel to gauge the snow's depth, he tested a spot and then gingerly moved forward another foot, or so, to test again. At about the four-foot mark, the shovel kept moving on down through the snow, which gave the Bills all the information they needed. Young Bill then proceeded to shovel from the front of the car to road's edge. After shoveling the width of the car, Young Bill again went over to his father's side window.

"Geeze, Dad, I don't know. Is that enough space to work with? Plus, I'm going to have to shovel all around the car, and then some, before we can try to move it to the side of the road. Even then I'm still not sure there will be enough room for the plow to go around the car."

"Get in, son," Old Bill said. "Warm up a bit while

we think this through."

Young Bill threw the shovel into the back of the truck and shook away some of the snow that covered him before climbing back into the cab. He removed his hat and gloves, allowing the cab's toasty warmth to soak in.

"We've got to either give it a try or try to get a tow truck out here to deal with this car," said Old Bill as he poured a steaming cup of coffee from his thermos and passed it over to his son. "For a tow truck to get in here," he continued, "we'll need to back up at least half mile to the old Wheeden farm for enough room to give this truck enough space to turn around, or enough space to at least get it out of the way for the tow truck to pass. Give Harley a call. He won't be too happy being woken up but we've gotta do something."

Young Bill pulled out his cell. The signal was weak but hopefully good enough. He punched in Harley's number and winced at hearing Harley's none too polite displeasure at being woken and being asked to move from his warm bed.

"Okay, he's coming," Young Bill reported as he ended the call. "He's none too happy about it though. Wanted to know what kind of idiot would be driving a car on a lonely narrow country road at night in the middle of a snowstorm."

"I'd like to know the answer to that, too," Old Bill replied as he put the truck in reverse and began driving slowly backward toward the old Wheeden place.

Chapter Twenty-Four

Anna

When Harvey and I were still bound together at the table, and as each wave of his breath washed over me, I kept my eyes shut and concentrated on keeping my breathing slow and rhythmic. It wasn't easy because of the sizzling hot anger coursing through my veins. But at least that anger was also melting away the last of the brain fog that had been controlling me. Cassie induced the brain fog to make me believe her deceptions and to leave me unable to comprehend the magnitude of her capability for cruelty.

Clearly, she had a plan, and poor Harvey was not part of it. He was an unintended victim. What do they call that—oh yeah—'collateral damage.' My plan, until I could come up with something better, was to continue acting as if I was still groggy and confused by the drug she'd slipped to us and had apparently been slipping to me on a daily basis.

Everything now fell into place. My grieving, the only real element in all of this, induced a brain fog that distanced me from the present. Grief kept me connected to the past. I preferred the past because the people I loved existed there, and I didn't want to lose my connection to them. The pain of moving away from them and into a sorrowful emptiness was too much. The present was the door into the future, and I didn't want to walk through it. I couldn't bear leaving the past and the people I loved there. My connection to them faded more and more with each passing day. Trent had unleashed the monster. Cassie used what she learned about Lainey and the circumstances of her death against me. Intuitively, Cassie understood that it could be easy to take advantage.

The initial stages of grief and dementia have common elements, especially a fogginess that can lead to second-guessing oneself. Differentiating between grief and dementia isn't clear-cut, especially when your thinking is already muddled, or hampered by drugs, and/or manipulated by a con artist.

Cassie superbly manipulated and staged situations so that my focus was never on questioning if she was really Lainey. She shaped each scene to make me focus on the disturbing question of whether I was losing it. Trent must have told her about me having had Complicated Grief Disorder. Cassie gambled that a part of me still wondered, and hoped, that my daughter was still alive.

"Lainey" came back to me—supposedly—two nights before that first time I heard her speaking on the phone to Trent and saying that she thought I was losing it. I remember having cried through the small amount of dinner I could force down. After dumping that half-eaten dinner into the garbage, I put the kettle on, thinking a warm cup of tea would soothe. That's when I heard somebody at the front door. I couldn't imagine who it could be at that hour.

I opened the door and nearly fainted. I thought it was an apparition standing before me on the opposite side of the storm door. Under a hat and scarf, somebody was standing before me that looked so very much like my daughter. Her face was a little leaner, her gaze more direct than I remembered, but so many other features seemed unmistakably the same and unchanged by the years in between.

"Is it really you?" I managed. My eyes were hot and brimming with tears, but I was afraid to blink and take the chance that the apparition would vanish.

She smiled. "Yes, Mom, it's really me. I'm back."

I pushed open the storm door, jumped forward, and wrapped her in a bear hug. "Lainey, my Lainey. I never gave up hope." There was so much to say and so much to ask. I practically lifted her into the house. My joy, it was that powerful a force.

"Mom, take it easy. The kettle's whistling."

"Oh, right. Take off your coat and boots while I make us some tea. I have so many questions. I don't know where to start."

We sat at the dining room table. I couldn't let go of her hand. I needed to touch her to make sure she was real. I couldn't stop smiling, and she couldn't stop laughing. "Mom, could I bother you for a towel? All that snow! My hair's so wet."

I hurried down the hallway, grabbed a towel, and sprinted back not wanting to be away from her a second longer than necessary.

As we drank our tea, she explained that she had been hiding from Matthew for a long time. She didn't know until recently that he was dead. They had been out in his boat when she told him that she was leaving him. He said to her that he wouldn't let that happen. They argued, and he came at her with a fishing knife.

The next thing she knew was waking up aboard a larger boat, something like a cabin cruiser, owned by a family from New Jersey who were headed to the Caribbean.

"I was afraid of Matthew," she said. "I didn't want to him to think I was alive. I knew he would find me and kill me. Even if I came back home to you, I wouldn't be safe. Plus, I didn't know what he might do to you or Trent if he knew I was alive. I thought the only way to protect all of us was to pretend to be dead.

"I convinced the people on the boat to drop me off at their first port of call in the Caribbean so that I could call my family and get back to them. After they left me ashore, what I really did was to get a job at the marina scraping paint off boats. I had another job for a while in a restaurant's kitchen. There were lots of odd jobs along the way. I was frightened and didn't want anybody to recognize me. I kept to myself. It wasn't until just recently that I found out that Matthew was dead. I tried to track you down, but you no longer had your company or the house. I did finally manage to track down Trent. I begged him to let me surprise you. Surprise!

"I've missed you so much. And I've missed so much of my life. I'm so sorry for what I put you through. I'm so sorry that I never met David. From what Trent's told me, he was an extraordinary guy."

We talked throughout the night, at least that's what she later told me. Now, I think it's safe to assume it was probably the first time she drugged my tea. She probably laced it when I disappeared for a moment to get her the towel.

Was Cassie that brilliant, or that intuitive, to surmise everything about me based on that initial conversation with Trent? Did Trent play a more significant role, or did Cassie also have him believing that she was Lainey? After all, Cassie, pretending to be Lainey, has been communicating with Trent by phone. Didn't I hear her refer to me as "mom" when she spoke to him?

I didn't want to believe they were working together, but it wasn't only Cassie that knew of David's wealth. Trent had known it from the start. Was that why he had been so supportive of my relationship with David from the beginning? Even after I pushed David away from me in Miami, it was Trent that engineered our coming back together soon after. With Harvey and me both out of the way, Trent would have sole control over David's wealth. I had so many questions, but I couldn't ask Cassie any of them, without endangering Harvey and me more. To survive, I needed to focus on the present.

Buying time had been the only tool, in an otherwise empty toolbox, to protect us from this monster. I knew better than to believe that some knight in shining armor was on his way to save us. My buying time, by continuing to appear out of it, was the only means I had to hopefully prevent something terrible from happening next. Being tied to the table was a powerful indicator that this was only the first step to something worse.

When Cassie untied us, then ordered us to stand, having difficulty doing so wasn't entirely an act. My body was stiff from being forced into one position for too long. Once standing, I pretended to be conscious of little, but like a soldier readying for combat, I inconspicuously concentrated on surveying my surroundings. I would be ready to act if the opportunity presented.

I noticed the heavy chain on the table. There was a lock on one end. Nearby were Cassie's gloves and a miniature flashlight keychain that held two keys. I presumed one of the keys was for the chain's lock, and the other was to operate the snowmobile. Cassie pointed a pistol in our direction. I had no doubt that she would use it.

Poor Harvey suffered the indignity of being ordered to strip along with the terror of why and what might be in store. From the first step beyond the storm door's protection, shocking bitter cold penetrated the nightgown I wore, and my slippers were no match for the icy snow that permeated my every step. I didn't want to imagine how much worse it was for Harvey.

Wrapping that icy cold chain around Harvey was one of the hardest things I've ever done. His breath halted, and he winced each time a link of the chain was laid across his bare skin. The horror of Cassie calmly describing the symptoms and stages of hypothermia along with the truth of it happening in real time to the man in front of me was an unimaginable horror.

The last words Harvey uttered before Cassie marched me back into the warmth of the house didn't make sense. But he deliberately looked at me as he spoke. Was Harvey already delirious or did those words have meaning?

My zombie-like act had been meant to buy time, but time was now working against Harvey. The longer Harvey was out there in his underwear, sitting in the cold snow and tied to a tree, the less chance he would have to survive.

Chapter Twenty-Five

The Bills

"I wonder how long it will take Harley to get here," Young Bill said to his father while gobbling down the last of the sandwiches his mother made as part of a routine care package to keep her Bills' strength up on cold, dark, desolate nights of plowing rural back roads. Sometimes they got stuck, or, for one or reason or another, like tonight, it just took a lot longer to get the job done.

Old Bill washed down the last of his sandwich with a swig of coffee, before saying, "I've been sitting here wondering the same thing. I've also been thinking a lot about that abandoned car straddling the road. Anna's the only person living out here this time of year. What was that out of state car doing on this road in the middle of a snowstorm? Makes me think that either somebody was trying to reach her, quick-like, not wanting to wait for daylight or the storm to end. Remember how her car was blocked from going anywhere because some idiot blocked the garage door with a pile of wood? Suppose that she, alone as she is here, needed help and called somebody to come quick?"

"Why wouldn't she have phoned somebody local or 911?" Young Bill asked.

"I don't know," answered Old Bill. "But something

about this just isn't settling right in my craw."

"Or just suppose," added Young Bill, "that whoever owns the car is unknown to Anna and has made a surprise visit. She's fragile right now, with her husband dying and all. What if it's a bunch of hooligans or some other unwanted guest?"

"That settles it," Old Bill stated. "We're going to hoof it in to check on Anna. And it's gonna be a long hike. I don't want to bring the truck back up to where that stranded car is because then Harley won't be able to get at the car. We'll need to walk from here. First, call Harley and get an ETA. If he's close by, we'll wait a few minutes for him to pick us up. If he's going to be longer, then tell him the plan, so he understands why we aren't around when he does get here."

The call to Harley went straight to voicemail. Young Bill left the message. After giving one another a knowing glance, both Bills pulled on their hats and gloves, reached for the flashlights they kept handy and sucked in the last of the cab's warmth before starting off on their mission. Walking the first part wouldn't be too bad because the Bills had plowed up to the abandoned car, but they were walking head-on into a bitter wind. Soon that icy cold would reach deep into the hollow of their bones.

Chapter Twenty-Six

Anna

At Cassie's directive, she and I headed back toward the house. Me first, Cassie behind, she didn't even bother to close the front door. Only the storm door separated us from the elements—and separated Harvey from warmth. With pistol still trained on me, Cassie dropped the keys on the dining room table and removed her gloves, one-by-one, shifting the gun from hand-to-hand as she did so. One glove fell to the table, landing alongside the keychain. The other landed on top of the keys. I stared ahead numbly, out of sight but not out of mind.

"I thought that shock of cold air might knock the last of the gabapentin out of you. Its effects should be worn off by now," Cassie said as she shrugged out of her coat. She laid her coat across the table and pulled something from the depths of her coat's front pocket. "In any event, the effect of the gabapentin is probably much less now. I'm getting impatient. Come on, let's go into the office."

She waved the pistol and cocked her head toward the office. I started walking. "Sit at the desk," she said as we entered the room.

I obeyed while taking in every part of the room. As I glanced at the memory walls, and especially at the tilted photo in its broken frame, the frame that I had smashed, it struck me that it had been a very long time since I last felt so intensely present and clear-headed. I now saw everything in this room much more clearly than ever before.

Cassie pulled a card from the small brown paper bag that had been in her coat pocket, and she dropped the card onto the desk. On the cover, the words "Thank you" were ornately scripted in gold. Colorful floral displays swirled about the two simple words that, at this moment, began to hold so much meaning for me. I was banking on an opportunity.

"Anna, open the card. I'll dictate; you write. I'm not going to worry if your hand is a little shaky or sloppy. It can be easily explained away. Ready?"

I was ready. I wrote each word as carefully as she spoke it.

My Dearest Cassie,

Your thoughtful and caring companionship during these darkest hours has been my guiding light. I've lost a child, my husband, and now I sometimes fear that I am losing my mind. Don't worry. As promised, I will soon see a doctor. Whether it's grief or more doesn't really matter. What does matter is that you know how much your patience and helpfulness have meant to me. Allow me to return the kindness you've shown me by presenting you with a gift. I know how much you want to return to school. I will cover all your expenses. It makes me happy to help you become the brilliant psychotherapist I know you will become and to know that many other people will also be helped by you.

Love, Anna

"That should do it," Cassie said.

I closed the card.

Cassie reached for it.

"Is it okay?" I asked.

I noticed her stance was now facing slightly to the side of me. The pistol resting limply and loosely aimed at the floor. Her guard was down as she opened the card and began reading, I covertly reached down and into the trash basket, frantically feeling for the big shaft of glass I remembered depositing there. I grabbed it, and in an instant, I leapt up and out of the chair, slashing an unsuspecting Cassie across her neck.

The pistol fell from her hand. She grabbed for her neck, her short blouse rising to expose her stomach. I drove that glass as deeply into her stomach as possible. She screamed and fell forward toward me, trying to grab onto me. I pushed her way, which sent her flailing. Her head hit the corner of the desk as she fell. The pistol skidded to somewhere clear across the room. It would be a waste of precious time to look for it.

I took an instant to catch my breath and to make sure Cassie wasn't moving before quickly running out of the office through to the dining room, grabbing her coat, the keys, and getting to Harvey as quickly as I could.

Chapter Twenty-Seven

The Bills

Getting as far as the abandoned car didn't take as much time as both Bills initially thought. Their prior plowing of snow up to the car made a big difference for walking. But making their way afterward along the road and beyond the stranded car took much longer than either had hoped or anticipated. It quickly became physically draining to lift one leg out of the deep snow and to then set the other into snow just as deep. At least they had the flashlights to keep them moving safely and steadily forward.

Breathless from the cold, Old Bill said, "Gotta stop for just a minute."

They stopped. Young Bill was concerned for his father. Maybe, it wasn't such a good idea for his father to be traipsing through all this snow at his age. Young Bill tried to gauge how much farther forward they needed to go to reach Anna's versus the distance back that car. It was impossible to tell. Her house could be just around the upcoming bend or still several bends farther. The dark and heavily forested narrow road wasn't giving away any of its secrets, and the flashlights' limited beams weren't able to offer any insight.

"Dad, I'm not sure how much longer we still have

to go. I think it would be better for you to make your way back to that car. It's unlocked. You can wait there until Harley arrives, which shouldn't be long now."

Old Bill, his breathing now a little steadier, looked up and down the road while considering and weighing options.

"It's slow-moving in all this snow, and there's no landmarks to go by. So, I'm just guessing and can't be sure, but I think we gotta be closer to Anna's now than it is back to that car."

"And, if we're not, that wrong guess just might kill you. I'm going to take you back to that car, and then I'll continue on myself."

Chapter Twenty-Eight

Anna

Saving Harvey was all that mattered. Despite the biting cold, inky darkness, and swirling snow, I didn't take the time to put on outer layers or snow boots. Even though the slippers offered no resistance to the weather, and they were already soaked through from the last time I was outside, it didn't matter.

I ran outside, hooked a right at the corner of the house, and ran down the sloping yard to the tree where Harvey was tied. Haste being the priority and forgetting safety; my footing slipped, pitching me face first into the cold snow. Scrambling to my feet and now caked from head to toe in snow, I quickly recovered my footing and continued praying all the while that I wouldn't be too late. I spotted the chain around the tree, ran to the other side of it to get to Harvey and fell to my knees when I saw him. He was deathly still.

"Harvey, please Harvey, look at me. It's Anna."

No response.

"Harvey, please be still alive. Please tell me that you are still alive."

No response.

Hot tears stung my eyes.

Remembering the keys, I moved to the other side of the tree to unlock the chain. My hands were shaking so badly that it took several attempts. With the key finally inserted and the lock opened, I pulled the bolt apart and began unwrapping the chain from Harvey. I kept reassuring him that he would be okay. I laid out Cassie's down parka beside him and gently rolled him on to the coat. His body felt as cold as the surroundings. I checked for a pulse but couldn't find it. Although the jacket was much too small for Harvey, I wrapped it around him as best I could, and began administering CPR that I remembered from being a lifeguard as a teenager. I listened carefully for any sign of life in between the breaths I pumped into him, but the only sound to break through was another.

"Anna!" Cassie screamed.

I jumped back onto my haunches. My own breath now caught in my throat. I peeked around the corner of the tree just in time to see her round the corner of the house.

She took aim and a shot rang out.

Chapter Twenty-Nine

The Bills

Old Bill made a pact with his son that if Anna's house wasn't just around the next bend he would go back to wait for Harley inside the abandoned car. Just as he hoped, as soon as they turned the bend, they spotted lights from Anna's house. And just as Old Bill was about to gloat, they heard a gunshot.

"Ain't nobody jacking deer in this weather," Old Bill declared.

Flashlights at once snapped off, they quickly made their way to Anna's house staying just behind the tree line for cover. Another gunshot sounded. Young Bill poked his father's chest for attention and pointed to the figure walking down the slope toward the lake with a gun in hand. They followed her gaze and spotted Anna crouching in the snow just behind a big tree. A shadowy figure lay near her in the snow.

"I know where you are, Anna!" Cassie screamed. "You're trying to save Harvey, but it doesn't matter. It's too late to save him or yourself!"

"Stop!" came a voice from somewhere to the left of Cassie.

She instinctively swung the pistol in the direction of the tree line and fired. She looked toward the trees, waiting for any other sound. Then, she shook her head.

Maybe, she hadn't heard anything. She decided that it might just be nerves that caused her to think she heard something. As she looked back toward the tree where Harvey was tied, Anna was gone.

Anna was running downhill toward the lake.

Chapter Thirty

Anna

Cassie must have heard something, too. She shot wildly into the direction of the sound. I didn't waste another second; I knew I wouldn't get another chance. I jumped up and started running for my life. A shot rang out behind me. Cassie was in pursuit.

It wasn't until I reached the edge of the lake and wondered in what direction to run next, that I remembered Harvey's jumbled last words and what he had been trying to tell me.

I slipped and stumbled forward. Another shot careened too close for comfort. Ahead, I saw frantic flutters of movement in the dark, and I prayed it was a sign that I was headed in the right direction. In a flash, I was up again and running, but Cassie was quickly closing in. I began running zigzags to avoid her bullets. Then, I arced my direction and prayed that my usually poor sense of direction had been usurped by my adrenaline. I willed my eyes to adjust to the dark. The moonless night could be a curse, but I banked on it tonight being a blessing.

I had to slow down now. Doing so was dangerous but necessary. Diverting my attention away from Cassie and her gun to focus on my every step now felt ludicrous. As soon as I felt a slight give and heard a small groan underneath me, I carefully laid my body down despite my every neuron screaming in rebellion at the insanity of my actions.

I turned my head and saw Cassie, less than thirty feet away, stop and stare at me. I was totally exposed and defenseless. I was betting my life that she would wonder why I'd do something so reckless, and that Cassie would want to take delight in shooting me at close range.

"What are you doing, Anna?" she shouted.

I remained silent.

"Did you hurt yourself, or are you out of breath and giving up?"

I offered no response. Cassie was coming closer. From my line of sight, my eyes were almost level with the ice covering the lake's surface. The ice was thin here. From my point of view, I could see the snow-covered ice begin to bob up and down, ever so slightly and subtly.

"I wasn't planning on shooting you," said Cassie. "It wasn't part of the plan at all. I was going to grant you the same peaceful death as Harvey. Wildlife would probably find your carcasses before the police. But even if you were found sooner, it would just appear that you had wandered, or ran away, and Harvey had been trying to find you.

"I'd imagined how I would be far away and get a call from my mother, she'd say, 'Oh baby, I have the worst news. I'm so sorry, but Anna is dead. They found her frozen body, or what was left of it. She was wearing only a robe over her nightgown, and just slippers were on her feet. They also found a man's frozen body. They say it was that lawyer fella we saw at her house.

Remember? Can't help but wonder what was going on there and between those two. He was found in his underwear?' The authorities would never suspect that I had a hand in your deaths."

I couldn't keep myself from asking, "What about Trent?"

"What about Trent?" echoed Cassie, all smiles. She edged closer. She was less than thirty feet from me now. "You mean my dear brother? I think we are going to both be enjoying all that money of David's. It's turned out even better for Trent that Harvey got done in, too. Trent gets control of the money sooner, and without worrying about Harvey getting in the way."

Cassie was closing in on me now. This wasn't going to end well for one of us. Soon, she would be standing over me and pointing that pistol at my head.

"But, Cassie, you haven't yet gotten any money from me and how will you if you kill me?"

"You are so naïve. There have been a couple of wired transfers to me already during these last few days. Tomorrow there will be another."

Ten feet.

"Before you kill me, tell me who else was part of this scheme."

Six feet.

A deep belly laugh shook Cassie but was cut short, when her movement caused the thin layer of ice covering the spring below her to give way. She was plunged into the icy cold water; I scrambled backward as fast as possible for the safety of thicker ice.

"Help me!" she screamed as her head bobbed up.

I didn't move.

"Help me, please!" she screamed again.

"Tell me first," I demanded. "Was anyone else part of this plan?"

The water was not only agonizingly cold; the spring's underwater current was also pulling at her. She grabbed onto my foot and tried to climb up my leg, but the current's strength was strong. In an instant, it would take me too. I kicked myself free and sent her flailing. The water current sucked her beneath the ice and away.

She had left me with more questions than answers.

Young Bill met me halfway up the hill. He had been trying to find me. It turned out that he had been hit by Cassie's stray bullet. Though stunned for a time, he wasn't badly wounded. The bullet had only grazed his shoulder. He apologized about it being a setback to getting to me faster. I thought it all had turned out for the better that I ended things with Cassie privately.

Young Bill phoned to Harley to say we needed emergency help. Harley gave up trying to hook his tow truck to Harvey's car. Ramming it off the side of the road seemed more expedient.

"What about Harvey?" I asked.

"If you mean that man out by the tree in nothing but his skivvies, I'm sorry Anna. He didn't make it."

I wondered how long Cassie had lived. I hoped her death was painful, slow, and scary.

State police and the emergency medical team sirens signaled their approach. The last thing I remembered was being wrapped in blankets and being lifted onto a stretcher.

Chapter Thirty-One

Anna

I awoke and looked down at my raw, chapped hands, wondering whose they were. I looked up to see a nurse peering down at me while fidgeting with a glucose bag that was hooked up to me intravenously. I was exhausted. All I wanted to do was to sleep and to forget.

"I have to let the police know that you are awake," the nurse said. "They want to talk to you. I'll tell them to make it brief."

She left the room and seconds later two men entered. The two officers introduced themselves. The man closest to me was Detective Sherwood. Officer Franklin remained in the background. My insides jumped into alert mode, cautioning my outer self to stay in battered mode.

"Ma'am, we can wait until morning to take a full statement," the detective said, "but there is some information we can't wait on."

Sherwood proceeded to ask about Harvey. What was his full name, where did he live, and how did I know him? Was I aware of any next of kin? I mechanically answered each question as best I could, but when he asked if I knew why Harvey had been found wearing little clothing and apparently had been tied to a tree, my self-control dissolved into sobs. The image of Harvey tied to that tree would forever stay with me as would the image of the person who orchestrated the brutality.

"I know this is painful, ma'am," the detective said. "Can you tell me about the woman with the gun who chased you? Do you know her name?

"Cassie Taylor," I replied.

"How do you know her?"

"She's my cleaning woman's daughter." I gave them Beth's name and address.

"What happened?" the officer asked. "Where did she go?"

"Dead. She's dead," I replied. "Sucked under the lake ice."

The officer cleared his throat. "Are you certain?"

I was certain. I had purposely watched and waited to make sure that evil monster would not reappear.

"Ma'am, do you have any close family who we can contact, let them know what happened and that you are okay?"

I wasn't sure anymore. Did I? I gave them Trent's contact information. I was beyond exhaustion but, at the same time, I was so tightly coiled, I began to wonder whether sleep would ever again be possible.

The Bills came in. The sling on Young Bill's arm reminded me just how real and how dangerous the last hours had been. More people could have easily died. I thanked them for being there. Arriving just when they did saved my life. The Bills were not sentimental or effusive folk. They appeared to be slightly embarrassed when I extended my heartfelt thanks. They didn't stay long. They too were exhausted.

My mind kept going over the same questions. Did Trent enlist Cassie to be part of a scheme to take control of David's money? And, if so, what was the plan? Was it to make me appear mentally disabled so that Trent could take over as administrator of David's trust? Would Trent have me locked away somewhere for the remainder of my life? Or was ending my life the plan all along? Cassie seemed to suggest that the original plan was for me to die accidentally or by apparent suicide. Trent would then immediately be the sole beneficiary of everything David, and I, owned.

Cassie also implied that Harvey's death was not part of the original plan but that it certainly provided a convenient shortcut to their goal. A sudden chill gripped me when I realized that murdering Harvey must mean that murder had been in store for me as well. I pulled the bedcovers up to my neck and more tightly around me. How could a mother ever believe that her son may have tried to have her murdered?

How could I think such a thing of Trent? Yet, I couldn't think of any other scenarios. My mind kept churning through the evidence. Trent and Cassie were communicating regularly by phone. I told Trent that Lainey was with me. He didn't reply that it was impossible because Lainey was dead. He said he wanted to speak with her. So, of course, they must have been planning all this together. Trent may have even prompted Harvey to go to me so that we could both conveniently meet our end at the same time.

Cassie said she was being paid by somebody to deceive me into thinking she was Lainey and for me to appear to be losing my mind. Cassie was twisted enough to act alone but being paid meant that she was not acting alone. Who would have a reason, other than Trent, to orchestrate such a scheme?

A nurse came into the room, checked my vitals, and told me that I needed to try and get some sleep. I gratefully accepted the medication she offered to help make it possible.

Chapter Thirty-Two

Anna

"Where is my daughter?"

At first, I thought I was dreaming, but the whisper was coming from outside me, and quite close. I cringed.

"Where is my daughter?" The voice said again as she rattled the hospital bed to rouse me.

I opened my eyes to see Beth, Cassie's mother, standing over me. "Where is my daughter?"

"I don't know."

Beth again pushed against my bed. Her face directly over mine, her voice a whisper, but her body poised, ready for a fight. "The police said you were both out on the lake ice and she fell through."

"Yes," I whispered.

"What were the two of you doing out there?"

"She chased me out onto the ice," I replied, wondering how much I could safely say to an enraged mother about her twisted and maniacal daughter.

"You crazy loon. She was probably trying to protect you from yourself, and my sweet girl likely died trying."

I wondered if I should scream for help, but thought better of it. Beth was much too close. Her hands could be around my throat, or a pillow could be over my face in an instant. I said nothing. That adrenaline running through her was nothing to mess with. Clearly, this woman didn't know her daughter at all.

"Everybody did everything for you," she said. "We kept an eye on you. I even cooked special dishes for Cassie to bring over to you. I didn't want to believe it when she said you were losing it. I wanted to chalk up the crazy behaviors she described to grief over your husband's death. Nobody is that bad unless they're getting the Alzheimer's."

I slowly inched the blanket to the top of my neck, then protectively crossed both arms over my chest.

"She said that you sometimes thought she was your dead daughter, and she was very frightened by it. My poor girl! She said that sometimes she just played along because when she tried to tell you once that she wasn't your daughter, you fell apart. You started throwing and breaking things. Despite all that, my Cassie has a big heart. She told me that she felt she was doing something good by spending time with you. It made her feel good to be helpful. She was even considering going back to school to become a nurse."

Beth bent even closer over my face, her breath hot and foul. "My girl told me in one of your lucid times, you thanked her for taking care of you, and you offered to pay her, and to pay her way through school. Imagine that! That's how good and important my Cassie was. Had I known how dangerous you could be…"

Beth backed up slightly and forcefully rattled my bed's metal sidebar.

"Did Trent know anything about what was happening to me?"

"Yes, of course," Beth said in a scoffing tone. "Cassie and I discussed it. We decided we had to tell your son. He had a right to know, and he was going to have to do something about you. He told Cassie that he was very grateful for our help. He started paying her to stay with you and to keep him updated about your condition until he could get here. He told Cassie he was planning to come. I wish he had gotten here faster. My daughter might be alive now if he had."

It was impossible to reconcile the difference between the murderess Cassie whom I knew and Beth's view of her daughter as someone close to sainthood. I knew exactly what Beth was feeling and the pain of losing a daughter. My heart broke for her.

"I'm so sorry, Beth."

Her demeanor switched from heartbroken mother to angry in less than a second. She propelled herself forward and was once again directly over me. Spittle flew from her mouth and into my face. "Sorry doesn't cut it. I've heard there's a dead man, too. Maybe I just don't buy what you're selling."

Her lack of emotional self-control and quick fury was deeply unsettling. "I'm not selling anything, Beth. It might be better for everyone if you spoke more with the police."

"When I was sorry for you that you were getting the Alzheimer's, do you know what I heard he said? He said that nobody should feel bad because what goes around comes around. He said you weren't what you appear to be. I know how you ruined your first husband. You probably had a hand in the death of this husband and your daughter. I can't help but think you likely had a hand in the death of two more people now too. Some people are just bad!"

Did Trent say those things about me?

"I think it would be better if you leave now. Please let the police do their work and come up with the answers."

As her anger rose several notches, so did the decibels of her voice, shooting from a whisper to a shout. "What gives you the right to dismiss me like I just finished cleaning your house and be gone with me now? My daughter's body is somewhere out in that lake. They're searching for her, but they say it might not be possible to find her until the lake thaws out. How am I supposed to wait? What if they never find her? All I keep thinking about is how she must have suffered."

The door opened and a nurse burst in. She ordered Beth to leave and said she would have security posted outside my door until the police could post an officer.

Looking utterly deflated, Beth gave me one last angry look and left. As she was leaving, the nurse said that my son had just phoned the nurses' station to say that he had taken a redeye, his plane had landed, and he was on his way to see me.

I thanked the nurse, rolled over on my side, and thought about Beth. I understood her anger very well. I'd felt the same when I lost Lainey. The eerie similarity of how both daughters died young by drowning was not lost on me. But that was where any comparison ended. Her murderess daughter had a twisted mind and was capable of great brutality.

I thought I had known my daughter well. Doubtless, Beth must feel the same about Cassie. But how well does any of us really know, really see, our children for who they really are. I had no idea about the bundles of unopened and unanswered letters to her father until after Lainey's disappearance. How she must have suffered in silence without anyone knowing or being able to comfort her. Did Trent really say to Beth that I ruined James and that I probably had a hand in David and Lainey's deaths? I thought I knew my son well. Could it be that I've only seen what I've wanted to see?

There was a soft knock at my door. Detective Sherwood entered. "I heard Cassie's mother was here earlier." He drew nearer to my bed. "That must have been tough."

"It was. I lost my own daughter the same way—to drowning. I know well that feeling of intense sadness mixed with anger."

"What can you tell me about what happened?"

"Not much, I'm afraid."

There was much I could say, but I didn't know yet if I should. While turning things over in my mind these past hours, I couldn't bring myself to say anything that might implicate my son in any of this. I needed more time to sort through everything that had happened and everything I had learned in the past twenty-four hours.

"She was drugging me. My recollections are hazy and full of holes. I can't much make sense of anything."

"It's our job to make sense of what happened. And I know that it might be difficult for you to remember everything. I also know that you might not even want to remember, but ma'am, I need you to tell me what you do remember as best you can."

How could I say anything without implicating Trent?

"But what if I can't even be sure about what actually happened? I don't want to give you wrong information."

206

"We have statements from the men who helped rescue you. We know that you were trying to help revive the man who had been chained to the tree. We know that Cassie had a gun. She shot at you, then ran after you. We know that's how you both ended up out on the ice. What we don't know is why any of this happened."

And that was precisely the topic I needed to avoid.

"I'm sorry, Detective. There's not much I can add."

"Ma'am, what can you tell me about the man that we found chained to the tree. Let's start there."

"Harvey was my late husband's best friend and lawyer. He came out to the house a few days earlier to go over David's estate with me."

"Why was he there last night?"

"I don't know. Maybe he said he was checking in on me because of the storm. I think I was under the influence of the drugs Cassie was putting into my tea when he first arrived."

I could hear her singing, the kids' song about a little teapot. My skin began to crawl.

"Why was Cassie at your home?"

"She often came to deliver soup and other food her mom made for me. I think Beth may have sent Cassie to also check on me because of the storm," I lied.

Another soft rap at the door, a different nurse came in to inform me that my son had arrived.

"Detective, my son has flown all the way across the country. Can I spend a few minutes with him to let him know that I'm okay?"

"Certainly," he replied. "But we do need to talk more with you. I hate to be blunt, but this is an active investigation. I think your son will understand if we

207

need to interrupt your visit. I'll wait in the hall for a few minutes. The more we speak now, the more time you will have with your son. I have a responsibility to ask questions and get answers."

Sherwood left and Trent entered soon after. "Mom, are you okay?"

The sight of my son brought on mixed feelings of intense love filled with panic. He rushed over and kissed the top of my forehead. "I've been half out of my mind worried about you," he continued. "I don't know what's been going on. The officer outside your door said they found Harvey dead, barely clothed, outside in the snow. Beth's daughter Cassie is dead. She was trying to kill you?"

Trent appeared to be beside himself. Either he was an outstanding actor, or he was genuinely upset and confused. He pulled a chair up alongside the bed. I grabbed his hand. "I don't know what to say." And that was pure truth. "I'm so sorry to have worried you so."

"That's just crazy, Mom. It's not every day people die around you. It was Cassie, wasn't it?"

"Yes, she wanted Harvey and me dead."

"Why?"

"I'm not sure," I said, not wanting to say more.

For a few minutes, we just held hands. I couldn't help thinking about the little boy who insisted on holding my hand the entire time his first visit to a zoo. Trent said he didn't want me to feel afraid in case one of the big, dangerous animals escaped their pens and came after us. "Don't worry, Mom," he said, "I'll always hold your hand and protect you." It was one of those precious moments between a mother and child, and a sweet memory that had not come back to me for a very long time. I now needed to hold on to that memory as tightly as I now held his hand.

"Poor Harvey," Trent said just as the detective again entered the room.

"Did you know Harvey?" he asked Trent.

"Yes. We first met at Mom and David's wedding," Trent responded, giving my hand a small squeeze.

"Do you know why he would have driven all the way out to your mother's home in the middle of a snowstorm?"

"Yes, I think I do."

I turned to Trent, wondering what he might say next.

"I asked him to check on Mom. I was worried about her."

"Because of the weather?" Sherwood asked.

Trent looked at me before responding. With his eyes still focused on mine, he said, "No, because when I phoned my mother to check in on her, she said that my deceased sister was spending a lot of time with her."

I shuddered and forced my head deeper into the pillow. The detective's astonished look let us know how that bit of information was the last thing he expected to hear. "Continue, please."

"My sister Lainey died a long time ago. Her body was never found. The police suspected it was a murder-suicide executed by her boyfriend. For a long time, my mother refused to believe that Lainey was really gone. She nearly drove herself and all of us crazy by continuing to look for her."

The detective wrote each detail into his notebook, asking Trent for the place, time, and other specifics surrounding Lainey's disappearance. Then, and as I feared he would, he turned to me. "Ma'am, was Lainey spending time with you?"

"Yes, no—I mean, I thought so."

"How was that?"

I explained how "Lainey" showed up one night at my home, and how a part of me never fully accepted that my daughter was dead. "This person convinced me that she was Lainey, but it wasn't until last night that I learned it was really Cassie Taylor in a wig and blue contact lenses, pretending to be my daughter."

"How would Cassie know about Lainey and think that she could get away with pretending to be her?" asked the detective.

Trent chimed in, "I think I know the answer."

This was something I wanted to also know.

"After David, my mother's husband, died, she refused to leave that beautiful new dream home they had just finished building and decorating. I was worried about her being alone, so far away from anyone, and grieving alone in that big house. I tried to convince her to move out to California with us, but she said she wasn't yet ready.

"I hired Beth and Cassie to keep an eye on my mother and to help her with the house. The day of David's funeral, while speaking to Beth and Cassie about the work in Mom's home office—I happened to comment about how much Cassie reminded me of Lainey. There are photographs in the office."

"Yes, I've seen the walls of photographs in there," Sherwood said. "I've also noticed that one was smashed and there was a bloody glass shard on the floor."

Both men looked at me to supply the answer to the

unasked question.

"The photo frame had broken earlier. It had fallen off the wall," I lied, not wanting to explain my earlier violent behavior that I still couldn't fully explain to myself. "Cassie had a pistol pointed at me. She made it clear that she was going to kill me. When I could see a chance, I grabbed the shard out of the trash and stabbed her. It's how I got away, and it's what led to her chasing me out on to the lake."

Both men looked at one another and then back at me. "We found a card on the office floor," the detective said. "It appears that you wrote a note to Cassie, thanking her for all her help and offering to pay her way through university. Did you write it?"

"Yes."

The detective continued, "What I don't understand is you said Cassie was pretending to be your daughter, yet this note indicates you were aware of her real identity when you wrote it. Can you explain that?"

Trent looked at me, question in his eyes.

"I think I passed out soon after Harvey arrived. I think he was probably also drugged and passed out for a time. It was while we were sitting at the dining room table. We were tied to each other and the table when we woke. I pretended to still be out of it, but I heard Cassie say that she had been pretending to be Lainey.

"Later, and after she forced me to chain Harvey to the tree outside so that he would die of hypothermia, she marched me back into the house, and she dictated the contents of the card. She wasn't going to let me live much longer after that. She was fabricating a scheme to kill me off for money."

Both Detective Sherwood and Trent looked to be

hanging on my every word. Then the detective asked Trent, "How often did you speak with Cassie?"

His answer sent a chill through me that rivaled the cold I endured outside only hours ago. "I never spoke to Cassie after the day of David's funeral. I've only spoken with her mother."

Those were not the words I expected to hear.

I remember he spoke with Cassie several times. There was the first time when she told him that I was losing it and then the most recent time when she answered my cell phone to talk with him. Cassie said she was being paid to get rid of me. I also remembered her saying by killing off Harvey the line to David's money would be shorter. Who else but Trent could benefit from my death?

And why would Cassie think of that or care?

"Detective," Trent added, "If you do an online search, you'll find extensive media coverage of my sister's disappearance. I suspect that Cassie may have done a fair amount of research on my sister while hatching a plan to convince my mother she was Lainey. Her motive must have been to exploit her for financial gain. The girl was clearly twisted, but I think she probably acted alone."

I knew Trent's body language, and I couldn't find a hint of falsehood in his statement. But something still bothered me. Why try to serve the detective a theory neatly tied with a bow, when by his own admission he was completely unaware about what was going on? By the look on Detective Sherwood's face, it was plain to see that he probably wondered the same.

"That's all for now. I think it would be best if you stayed here in the hospital one more night. We should be finished processing your home by tomorrow morning," he said and turned to leave. Just before reaching the door, he turned back. "Oh, by the way, we found Cassie's cell phone. It was in the pocket of the coat that was underneath Harvey. Her phone history should tell us whether she acted alone."

I saw the tiniest flinch in the set of Trent's jaw.

****

We spent some time talking about Trent's wife Karen and the girls, and their life in California. It was blessedly normal conversation that was a much-needed respite from the otherwise tense and agonizing time passing within these banal four hospital room walls. It was further relief when Trent asked if he could leave for a while to check into a hotel room and shower.

I was mentally and emotionally exhausted, but I also had some critical thinking to do. After turning things over in my mind, I made some decisions. I wouldn't go back home. Before, I couldn't see myself leaving home after David's death. Now, I couldn't see myself returning there. The love I knew there had been replaced by horror. It was now a crime scene instead of our dream home. I would ask Trent to collect some things for me from the house, and I would stay temporarily in the apartment David still kept in Manhattan. From there, I would figure out my next move.

I must have slept for a while because when I opened my eyes, Trent was dozing in a chair by the window. The jet lag must have caught up with him. I've always been intrigued by how if I stared at my son long enough, I alternately saw him again as a child, then the grown man he now is within the same few seconds. I wondered if all mothers could do the same. It was such a gift to sometimes again see that small child still residing inside the man. But I no longer trusted myself. Maybe it wasn't a gift at all. It could also be a curse given how unreliable my judgment had been by being duped by Cassie to believe she was Lainey.

Memories of Trent as a young boy flooded back. The great big, all-consuming hugs and kisses that only a wide-eyed and wildly energetic toddler can give warmed me once again. The disappointment I could see lurking in his eyes when he begged me to tell him whether Santa was real because the kids at school had said he wasn't. Trent didn't want to be a baby and still believe in Santa if Santa wasn't real. But at the same time, he fervently hoped that Santa wasn't a fabricated lie. All his hopes and fears depended on my answer. Shattering his hopes destroyed me.

It was the same when James died. My children's lives were shattered when I couldn't let them live with false hope. It was the hardest thing I'd ever done. Had we still been a family when James perished, my children would have at least grown up cherishing the memory of a loving father, but that was not our reality, and my children were unable to find any comfort or closure.

James had been evil to turn away from his children after our divorce. He unfairly blamed them for the failure of our marriage and business. He refused to see that they had nothing to do with either. His self-inflated ego was too pumped up to consider that his own behavior was our undoing. For a long time, I thought we could have made a go of it, and could have had it all, a loving family and a thriving business. For a long time, I thought he couldn't understand it was possible to have both and maybe it was somehow my fault for not being able to satisfactorily convince him of that.

But over the years I came to realize the problem was him. He was a true narcissist. Other people only existed to make him shine. He never gave half as much to others as what he demanded, and expected, to receive. If you let him down or crossed-him, he wouldn't rest until he had his revenge—no matter the cost and what it did to others. There was an evilness about him that couldn't be spotted until after he had already caught you in his web, and until after he had spun his many lies and trapped you within a web of deceits. James used people. He carefully spun plans to catch them, and he easily turned you away if you no longer served his purpose.

What made people become like James and Cassie? I didn't know much about her life, and I never knew much about James's family or early life either for that matter. All I knew was that his father had died when James was young, he was an only child, and he wasn't close to his mother. They were from a small town on the outskirts of Wichita. The times I'd asked about her, he'd only said she was more interested in spending time at the bar than with him. She was more interested in the attention given to her by the town drunks than she was helping her son to become something.

His grandmother raised him, and when she died, just after he graduated high school, he left and never returned. I wanted to invite his mother to our wedding. I held out hope to meet her and for them to reconcile, but James insisted that she was dead to him and wanted nothing to do with her. At the time, I thought she must have been an incredibly terrible and hurtful mother for James to feel the way he did. But, over the years, and after I experienced how easily James could turn his back on family, I've wondered if there might be more to the story.

Both James and Cassie had a careless disregard of others. But there was one difference. Cassie had been a killer.

My son, what about you? You are not like Cassie. And I feel terribly guilty for even wondering if you might be like James, a person who always got somebody else to do his dirty work.

Chapter Thirty-Three

Anna

When it was possible to go back to my home, we received the all-clear from Detective Sherwood. He requested that Trent and I notify him if or when we choose to leave and stay anywhere else. He said that only a few loose ends remained to be tied and it was mainly procedural that he would know how to reach us.

Trent had booked flights the day before for both of us. He didn't want me to go back to my home. Going back there was the last thing I also wanted, but I now had some things to attend to first. Trent didn't think it was wise for me to go back to that house all alone and wanted to come with me. "Too many gruesome memories," he said.

I couldn't let on that I felt that way too. I told him I needed to put everything into perspective and to say my final goodbye to the life I had known with David. That much was the truth. I wasn't planning on staying there long, but I wanted to be alone for a little while. I told my son I would spend most of my time in the city at David's apartment, collecting my things there and putting both properties on the market.

We argued back and forth a while, but ultimately, he capitulated after I promised to join him in California within two weeks. Trent flew back west to his family, and I reluctantly accepted a ride offered by Detective Sherwood back to my home. I could tell that he too thought me a little strange for wanting to go back to that remote and ghostly home alone.

The journey back home had me on edge, particularly when I saw Harvey's car upside down over the embankment. The police didn't yet have time to remove it. Detective Sherwood noticed the tears welling up in my eyes.

By now, we were on a first name basis. He said, "Anna, this might not be a good idea—you coming back here alone. Is there somebody you can call to stay with you?"

"My son wanted to stay, but I told him I needed to be alone for just a little while. By the way, I don't know where my cell phone is, and that's one of the things, I need."

He reached into his pocket and pulled out my cell phone. "We found it. I meant to give it to you earlier."

It was fully charged, which I wasn't expecting it to be after all this time. "We checked your phone, of course," he said. "Procedure. Everything was just as you described. Cassie, while pretending to be Lainey, never spoke to Trent on your phone—like she led you to believe. Cassie let it go to voicemail and then probably listened to the message or read the transcription."

I scrolled to the voicemail and read the transcript myself, thankfully relieved to learn that Trent had been truthful about not speaking to Cassie. As Detective Sherwood noted my relief, I detected that my reactions were under surveillance. Did he surmise that I had questions about my son's involvement?

And, more importantly, did he have the same questions himself?

As we pulled up to the house, I noticed that the woodpile was gone from in front of my garage. Detective Sherwood said the Bills had insisted on moving it for me. The detective led me down a freshly shoveled path to the front door. We each carried bags containing basic staples—milk, eggs, bread—and a few other things that I purchased from a convenience store just after leaving the hospital. He opened the door and stood aside for me to enter.

I instantly was hit by the feeling of total disconnection to the space that had been my home. Every carefully planned and thoughtful detail that David and I infused into these walls was now gone. Every loving moment we had shared here together was now overshadowed by memories of more recent horrors. Maybe Trent had been correct that it wouldn't be healthy for me to return here.

As if knowing what was going on in my mind, Detective Sherwood cleared his voice and said, "I can take you back to town. You can pack some clothes while I'm here. I'd also be happy to help make arrangements for you to join your son in California."

"Thank you, detective, but I'll be okay. I don't plan on being here more than a day or two. Then, I'll be heading to our apartment in Manhattan. You, of course, know my phone number if you need to reach me."

"Okay, call me if anything comes up," he said as he dropped my house keys on the foyer table and turned back toward the door. He placed his hand on the knob, but then turned back toward me for a second, just staring.

"Detective?"

"One last thing, I forgot to ask your son if he has a Gmail email account. Do you know if he does?"

"Not that I'm aware of. Why?"

"My guys found the email address 'Blackwood1again@gmail.com' listed as a contact on Cassie's phone. We are still going through everything on it."

I hoped he didn't notice the involuntary grab I made of the foyer table to steady myself. I quickly tried to mask my reaction as I pretended to have been reaching for my keys.

"Probably doesn't mean anything," he replied as he turned back to the door and left.

I stood in the middle of the living room looking out over the lake. It was still frozen over, except for the small area where the spring created a small pool and where Cassie met her death. It seemed like a hundred years ago, and it seemed like yesterday. I shivered at the memory and how close I came to dying.

Poor Harvey. He had only tried to help me, and he died trying. He didn't deserve what happened to him. Some of his last thoughts were about how to protect me and trying to tell me to lead Cassie out on to the thin ice where the waterfowl congregated.

It was still so difficult to believe that a person could be so evil. I would never be able to wrap my head around how a person could be cold-hearted and delight in the demise of another person. James had been the only person I had known like that and I had thought him to be a rarity. I fervently hoped most people were still good.

Cassie had been expecting a handsome reward for

her efforts. She had motive. I hoped Detective Sherwood found the explanation of getting money out of me as a satisfactory explanation for a motive. But I knew differently. She had as much as said that somebody was dangling a bigger payoff in front of her. I hoped Detective Sherwood didn't have any suspicions. Though I had a strong feeling, he might. Therefore, I needed to do something—and fast.

I packed two suitcases. Into a duffle bag, I packed my laptop, along with Harvey's files, and made sure there was room enough for the few more essentials I hoped I wouldn't need. Mechanically, I emptied the refrigerator and trash. As I shut off the water, I also shut off the pipeline to my feelings and tears.

I slowly walked through the home, and life, that David and I built together one last time. I made myself remember only the good times, the times that he and I shared. I gazed around the master bedroom and then stepped into the back of his closet, taking a moment to inhale the last of him. I opened the safe that was back there and took from it some things I hoped I wouldn't need.

I walked into the office and looked one last time at each of the photographs David hung on my memories wall. I said goodbye to Lainey, I said goodbye to David, and then said my goodbyes to Trent. It ripped my heart out to do so, but my heart was already in tatters, and I knew that soon it would be shredded more. Nothing more mattered.

Before leaving our beloved home for the last time, I pulled out the laptop and sent an email.

—*I'm on my way*—

I wasn't sure if my car would start after not being

used for so long so was surprised when the engine roared to life without any hesitation. I loaded a destination into the car's GPS system and started, with one singular purpose driving me forward.

I drove westward, while my mind journeyed backward in lockstep with each milepost I passed. Distant memories flashed forward, grabbed me, and became acutely real once more. It was as if some part of me deep within was resurrecting scenes from my past to warn me against what might lie ahead. Taking one hand off the wheel, I reached up and felt my face.

I recalled with astounding clarity the painfully tender black eye James gave me the night he delivered that punch and the feeling of my eardrum exploding as he slapped my head from side-to-side, supposedly knocking some sense to me.

That was what became of us, and what finally ended us. Back then, I ignored one too many exit signs. Then, I was intent on making things work. Now, I would be intent on making things right. We both had failed our children.

I tried to be both mother and father when James broke promises to attend Lainey's recitals, Trent's basketball games, or sometimes even birthdays if they happened to fall during the workweek. Weekends were usually also often off limits. A round of golf with a potential client was much more enticing than spending Sunday with the family. Or James might instruct the nanny to take the kids elsewhere for the day. I would be the last to learn if he wanted to host a pool party or barbecue for a favored client. Dinner parties, pool parties—any party for the purpose of entertaining business clients seemed to be the only reason James wanted to be at home.

When he was home, he preferred the kids to be absent or to be as quiet church mice if they had to co-exist in the same space. We all walked on eggshells. From the time they could first walk, they developed the knack of shrinking away and walking softly when their father was nearby. If they forgot, as children do, severe repercussions followed.

Even so, Lainey couldn't get enough of being near her father. Her little lips trembled each time he said he couldn't join in some family thing. "That's all right, Dad. There will be a next time," she'd say with a bravado as lacking as his feeble excuses.

I now knew too well how Lainey internalized her father's lack of love. She filled that space by finding a man who watched over her like a hawk and who dominated her every move. She confused control with love. His interest in her was all consuming, and her hunger for a man's love and approval was insatiable. A perfectly deadly match.

When little, Trent also tried to make up for his father's apparent lack of interest by trying to convince himself, and everyone else, that his father was an important man with lots of responsibilities, which was why he was so often not around. "So many people depend on Dad to help them," he'd say. "Dad works hard for us. He loves us, and he works hard to give us a good life."

I still didn't know how, or if, Trent internalized his father's words and behaviors. Not knowing sometimes bothered me greatly now. As a boy, Trent could hurl back the hurt in another direction—usually mine. Or, he would essentially repeat the same nasty words James used. I remembered Trent storming into my bedroom one morning, saying, if I went to work more often, then Dad could spend less time at work and more time here with him. I wasn't pulling my weight, and it was all my fault that Dad would again miss…

I couldn't head-off what happened to Lainey. I needed to be damn sure about keeping Trent from harm, or from doing harm. I promised myself I would try to shield the children from James and his wrath or apathy. I was foolish to believe I was doing the right thing by those kids.

For a one-millionth time, I recalled again the morning when James came into the master bath just as I was coming out of the shower. "Anna," he whispered into my ear, "you are still a beautiful woman. You will make sure that you are by my side at dinner with Kendall and his people tonight. Wear the black dress I like and don't disappoint."

I began to protest that it wasn't possible because it was parents' night at the school. I had to be there. I had wanted us both to be there. I told him about this night weeks ago and had pleaded with him not to schedule anything that might conflict.

He turned me around, looked squarely into my eyes, and calmly issued, "I'm done allowing you to let me down and I'm done allowing your behaviors to continue. Your actions are taking down the business. From now on, you will do as I say and when I say. Don't taunt me. Do you realize how easily, and with just a few simple words, I could alienate both of those kids from you? They would do anything to please their father. It would be so easy. Don't tempt me. I might just do it for fun. They see how damaged you are."

Too stunned, and surprised to respond, I simply stared at him open-mouthed.

"Seriously," James said. "Pay more attention to the business. Kendall likes your proposal. He wants to meet the brains behind it. Just remember, I'm the brains behind you, and you will make sure to give proper credit when credit is due."

They see how damaged you are.

Those words now echoed back to me with new meaning. Even though that sentence was seared into memory, and often recalled, it wasn't until now that I realized the significance of those words. I was damaged. I had let James damage me. As a result, we damaged the kids.

And I was complicit in the harm done to them.

The memory of the next day then spun into view. I was in the front yard with the kids. They were trying to teach our dog the stay command. It was extraordinarily funny to watch. The kids' inconsistency at commanding when to stay, or come, confused Pepper. She did, as she did best, and just played along. I laughed as I watched the three of them enjoying their newfound game. It was times like these that made everything worthwhile. But those times never lasted very long.

Our heads all turned when we saw James pull into the driveway in an expensive and shiny new car. As usual, I knew nothing about it beforehand. By then, he no longer included me in anything that mattered.

Trent was awed by the spectacular new vehicle. "Wow!" he exclaimed. "Is that new car ours?"

He opened the door behind on the driver's side and dove into the back seat just as James shut off the engine. James immediately jumped out of the car, reached into the back, grabbed Trent by the scruff of his neck, and flung him into the grass. "Keep your grimy little body out of my new car! And I better not ever see any of your filthy handprints on the outside of it, either. Stay away from it!"

Trent splayed out on the lawn, fought back tears, and rolled himself into a tight little ball. "I'm sorry, Daddy. I promise not to ever go near, or touch, your new car. I'm sorry."

James smiled at me with a look that said, 'see what power I hold over them.'

I ignored his smirk and quickly gathered both children to remove them from their father's ire. I remember sidestepping the scene by asking the children if they each wanted to make their own pizzas that evening and suggesting we go into the house to see what toppings there were on hand.

Just before reaching the door, I turned in time to see his scowl as he narrowly missed sidestepping a pile of dog poop. Poor Pepper was trained but being near James, when he was angry, could literally scare the crap of out her. He had that same effect on all of us.

The next day Pepper was gone. I pleaded with James, but he refused to tell me anything. It was as if she suddenly vanished into thin air. It wasn't possible that she could have run away or gotten lost from the safety of being inside the home.

Nevertheless, that's the story, and excuse, I was forced to tell the kids. They were heartbroken, and they cried for weeks afterward. I helped them make and put-up lost dog signs all around the neighborhood, at the library, and in the grocery store—all the time knowing James had done something to make sure we would never see her again. The lingering and crushing hurt the children experienced from losing Pepper was unbelievably painful to watch, and my guilt at being complicit in the lie was equally hard to bear. While the kids were in school, I called shelters and veterinarians, I drove aimlessly around, hoping to spot her. But she never turned up.

Distractions were my go-to behavior. I stupidly thought that I could be the distraction, and bandage, my children needed each time their father inflicted a wound. I didn't handle anything the way it should have been handled. I've often told myself I did the best I could, or knew how to, at the time. I was full of excuses, then. We all lived in a bubble of excuses—one after the other blown into the air, wishing that sooner or later the lousy excuse would pop and vanish to be remembered no more.

Poor excuses made for their father's behavior produced poor and warped behaviors in each of us. Poor excuses, lies, and hurt—are these the real legacies we leave our children? Is this what prompts some people to reach for a better life and others to only repeat what was done to them?

Maybe, Trent felt staying far away from me would help him heal. Perhaps it's why I saw Trent so infrequently after he moved west for college. Distancing himself from me might help him to find a new and better life. The thought speared me, but there was a chance it might be true.

Was it possible that I barely knew my son anymore? I really wasn't sure what kind of man he had grown up to be. I didn't see Lainey, the woman, until it was too late. Might Trent have problems or be a person

I no longer recognized because of his scarred childhood? I feared for Trent and now, hating to admit it, I also feared finding out more about him. I harbored so many unsettling thoughts brought on by questions that I didn't yet have answers about.

That little boy forgave his father for every hurt James inflicted. Trent suffered every indignity resolutely. Being his father's whipping post at least meant that James was, at that moment, paying attention to him. I feared Trent's every humiliation became something he believed was earned. With all my heart, I hoped that Trent had not become the man he adored as a young boy. James didn't deserve their love or adoration. But he took it, tromped all over it, and walked away without any remorse. What if Trent had grown into a man just like his father? That man was also now a father himself.

Remembering gave me a resoluteness and a new resolve about my decision to do what I was about to do now. The strength of character and conviction I lacked back then was gone, dead and buried. Over these past days, I'd grown a protective shell of steel and the courage to act.

Time spent driving gave me the perspective of the distant past to caution me about the days ahead. Forging a plan beforehand was vital. Walking into any situation without forethought would be foolhardy and dangerous. Time changes people, and I no longer knew what changes time had brought to him.

Part of me was frantically scared to find out. But another part of me longed to make sure my theory was correct. Lives depended on it. I was driving myself crazy trying to predict what I would face. I now needed, more than ever before, to have faith in my abilities to finally do the right thing.

I passed another milestone.

Chapter Thirty-Four

Anna

I sprang awake in a sweat, my muscles tight and sore. I had forgotten how different the outside world can feel when my hearing aid was out and in its charger. Neither sleep nor consciousness could ever be fully realized. It was easier to do without my hearing aid while in the comfort and safety of my own home. But tonight, in this hotel room, I felt too exposed even though I was totally alone and not a living soul could know where I am. Still, I felt exposed and frightened. Could it be ghosts from the past or souls still living that scared me so? I didn't yet have the answer, and I wasn't yet sure if there was an answer to be found.

Once the kids were out of the house, the impersonal and unfamiliar hotel rooms that I stayed in during business travels brought me more peace and sleep than I found at home. It was one of the reasons that I traveled so much. The dark and the utter silence I experienced without my hearing aid in those impersonal hotel rooms dulled my senses enough to still my mind and to bring me peace. Then, it was what I had to do to survive. Now, the sensory deprivation felt threatening.

It struck me now how things had flip-flopped from the norm for me then in contrast to the norm most people knew. Was the norm that most people lived by now finding its way back to me? Because now, I questioned whether my impromptu road trip might be too impulsive, crazy, and perhaps even dangerous. Any sane and normal person would not consider what I was planning. Did I have the courage to do what I was planning when I couldn't even find the courage to sleep here in this hotel room?

My hearing disability must have been a real help to Cassie. It made me shiver to think how many times she easily made her way into my bedroom without me knowing. I cursed myself for thinking about this now. Cassie was dead, and she couldn't hurt me. Only my own thoughts and fears could hurt me tonight. This was neither the time nor place to be afraid of anything.

But maybe these thoughts, as terrible as they were, might be a warning from me to plan better and to perhaps plan for the worst.

I turned on the bedside lamp and looked around. The room was typical of most hotel rooms with muted colors covering the walls and carpeting. A banal picture hung here and there to poorly imitate a well-decorated space that somebody would feel comfortable about calling home during a short stay. My suitcases were nearby and the duffle bag even closer. Nothing was frightening. I was safe. Most importantly, nobody knew where I was at this moment.

I couldn't let my confidence slip away. To close my eyes and to turn on my side where the least of my two damaged ears might still hear some small sounds should be of some small comfort, but I also knew anyone trying to disguise sounds would easily be able to do so around me. Anybody might become a little jittery to let themselves fall asleep in the absence of any light or sound. I assured myself that being uncomfortable under these circumstances was completely normal, which encouraged me to approach the whole of my situation more logically. I tossed ideas around, and decided on a plan, taking into account every possibility I conceived might happen.

I began to feel empowered, realizing that facing my fears had led to productive thinking and critical problem solving. Tonight, was not a loss. My plans were improved. I was now sufficiently tired. Tomorrow, I would make the necessary preparations. I still had driving, and thinking, time ahead of me to hone and refine.

Planning ahead was preferable to only seeing behind me, which was most of what I had done today. No more of that tomorrow. We can't change what we see in the rearview mirror, but we can make sure that when we move forward, the destination is the place we intend—then let go, and let God, to take over what will happen from that point on. So, I let myself doze with the lamp still on while repeating over and over—*I can do this. I must do it.*

****

Anger now became the fuel propelling me forward the nearer I came to my destination. How cruel somebody could be to conceive of a plot to mislead another person into believing their deceased child was still alive was inhumane and unforgivable. What kind of monster could be so vile to devise such a plan? If a person could do something so horrible as this, there could be no conscience or soul existing within. What other plots might be hatched and what other people could also suffer? I intended to end this.

Fuming led me on. I might have made the drive in much shorter time, but I also knew that I had to make sure I was rested enough to stay on top of things and level-headed enough not to make any costly or dangerous mistakes. Trent didn't yet expect me. I had time on my side. It was my turn to be calculating.

I forced myself to break up the drive by checking into motels along the way. Each day, I checked in with Trent by texting to let him know I was doing okay. I didn't want him to hear my voice because its shakiness might betray me. I spent several hours each night on my laptop, researching, becoming familiar with the unfamiliar landscape ahead. Again and again, I pored through the files Harvey prepared for me to learn if there was something there that I had overlooked or could use to my advantage. I rehearsed what needed to be said and the questions I would ask. I didn't want anything to throw me. I needed to be well-prepared. I would only get one shot at this.

The day had come. I had arrived. That had to be the house, I thought as I slowed down to pass by. I let myself drive by only a couple of times. It was a rural road with few other cars on it, and I didn't want to draw unwanted attention. The house wasn't at all what I expected. It was in desperate need of a paint job and a new roof with a sagging front porch sloped dangerously. There was a beat-up car in the dusty driveway. I noted its color, make, and model.

Along with everything else of late, it all needed to be slowly absorbed. I would not allow any emotion to bubble up. *Keep a grip on yourself, Anna.*

I found a motel on the edge of town and on the same main road. A diner and gas station were situated beside it. All three properties had seen better days. After settling in, I decided to familiarize myself with the town's layout a little better. Thankfully, it was a small town—a one of each town—one grocery store, one department store, one hardware store, one dive bar, one hairdresser—a few more ones of a kind and not much more. Everything was aligned along the main drag. It would be difficult to find a less interesting place, and it was difficult to imagine anyone choosing to live here. With enough luck, I wouldn't need to wait too long to accomplish what I came to do and then leave this desolate place.

There was one big problem with this one-horse town. A stranger was likely to be noticed, remembered, and likely even talked about. If I didn't spot him soon, somebody might spot me. I invented a cover story to avoid any problems. I was an older woman taking her time driving through because I needed to build up some courage before meeting up with a long-lost family member that was about a half day's journey farther. I thought the cover was creative until I realized that it wasn't too far from the truth. To make sure any gossip would be of the kind I could direct and might even help me, I made an appointment with the town's hairdresser.

Booking time with Betty was the perfect plan. She might have had only one chair for doing hair, but there were four other chairs for waiting nearby. It was unlikely that her business was so robust that she would need so many chairs to accommodate waiting clientele. It was soon apparent that although she may be cutting and styling hair, she probably earned a loyal following by providing the venue for a coffee klatch. She'd made a quick phone call after I walked in. Within ten minutes of my arrival, all four seats were occupied with local women who apparently knew one another quite well and were not at all surprised that I was there. None appeared to be waiting for an appointment. A couple of the women freely walked over to the coffeemaker and poured themselves each a cup.

Once everyone was comfortably seated, Betty began, "So, honey, what brings you to our little town?"

"I'm just passing through. I think covering up the gray, along with a trim, might help me to feel better about myself and stronger to move forward. I'm embarrassed to say that it has been quite a while since I last visited a salon. As you can see, it's much overdue, and I could really use some help."

All four women moved a little closer to the edge of their seats. I had successfully gotten their attention and piqued their interest.

"You're in good hands," said Betty. "I'll have you bursting with color and courage before I'm done." Through the mirror in front of me, I saw her cock an eye toward the four women sitting nearby.

"Betty's the best," one of them said.

"I wouldn't trust my hair to anyone else," another woman chimed in.

I couldn't help but wonder whether this tiny town even offered an alternative choice of hairdresser. So far, so good, I had quickly engaged with the entire group of women. All would now, hopefully, feel included and comfortable to join into any conversation.

"I guess I've landed in just right place at the right time," I said. "It's nice to meet all of you. I'm Anna Blackwood," I added, purposely using the surname I had when married to James.

Each of them gave their names and a "pleased to meet you" response. The woman to do so last added, "Where are you headed?"

"To see my son. It's been a long time since I've seen him. He and my husband didn't get along. They had a falling out, and we became estranged. But my husband recently died. So, I'm hoping to reconnect with my son. I hope we can start over. I've missed him so."

Mothers-all, every eye brimmed. A collective murmur of surprise and sadness rippled through the group.

"Anyway, I decided to take it slow and drive across country so that I could spend time with my thoughts, build up my courage, and rehearse the things I want and need to say." Which wasn't at all a lie.

Decidedly, the group's energy took a polite turn away from casting out prying questions. Betty broke the awkwardness, "You say your name is Blackwood. That's also a name from around these parts, too."

Bingo.

The big-haired blonde, wearing about a dozen jangling bangles, shook her melodious wrist in my direction. "Yeah, Jimmy Blackwood, that's right!"

I nearly laughed aloud. The pretentious James I knew wouldn't be caught dead letting himself be referred to as 'Jimmy'. "I don't know," I said. "My son did come out this way to stay with his father's sister when all the trouble started, but I don't think she lived near here."

"It can't be the same Blackwood family," one of the other women said to the others. "Can you imagine old Esther Blackwood raising anybody's son? She couldn't even raise herself off a barstool long enough to raise her own son. Not surprising that she's dead already nearly twenty years."

The well-coiffed heads all bobbed affirmatively in unison.

Betty stopped foiling my hair and looked at the group. "Jimmy ran off as soon as he could. Remember? He went East. Somehow, he got himself an education, a good job, and a loving family. Those good looks could get him anything and he knew it. He had to be the most handsome thing this town ever produced, and it gave him all the confidence in the world. He had a good life while it lasted. It stills sends shivers through me to think he lost his whole family—his wife and kids—in a house fire. He tried to save them and failed. He nearly died trying, and he's left with the burn scars to prove it. Maybe he died inside himself that day, too.

"It was at about that same time that his mother died. Jimmy came back here to nothing and with nothing. He moved into his grandmother's house, and he's pretty much kept to himself. Being disfigured like he is from that fire; he just isn't comfortable around other people. People say he's an angry man, but I guess he's earned the right to be. Still so sad."

The timing was about right for James to have shown up back here. I guess he didn't get away unscathed on that horrible day, 9/11. It made sense that his narcissism would be dealt a severe blow if he were now disfigured and then chose to operate from the shadows. I had no pity. How dare he feign love for the family he threw away. He was soulless.

The blonde woman chimed in again, "When he first came back, some of us who knew him as kids tried to be helpful and extend a welcome, but he wanted no part of any of us. He called us ignorant rednecks. Remember Trish? She was always so hung up on him when we were kids, I think she convinced herself that she could save him, make him happy again. That's when Jimmy convinced her to sell off the farmstead that had been in her family for generations, and she got a good price for it. Then, she moved in with Jimmy. Before that year was out, she was gone. Word was that he was usually drunk and a lot of times rough on her. I've heard that she escaped from him with not much more than the clothes on her back. He lives like a recluse and probably on her family's money. Folks say she was too afraid to fight him for it."

Learning that James was a recluse was a key finding. If I were to pay a visit to dear "Jimmy", there's not much chance of anybody finding out. I could quickly end his miserable existence, and likely nobody would discover his remains for quite some time afterward. Although, that also meant the reverse could also be true. If things didn't go as planned, nobody would have any idea that his house would be the place to look for finding me. The rest of the world believed him dead. I was beginning to not feel quite as brave as a few minutes ago.

The scary reality of James being alive was starting to settle in.

Another of the women, one who had not yet spoken, suddenly piped up, "Jack, my husband owns the bar across the street," she said as if to provide me with context, "and Jimmy's in there a lot, practically every night. Just like his mother use to be—isn't that strange? But unlike his mother who slobbered all over anybody sitting near her, Jimmy always sits alone at the far corner of the bar. Jack says that sometimes he can get some conversation going with Jimmy, but only if he's in the mood. He never talks about his past, but you're right that he's all anger inside. When he has too much to drink, he starts spitting strange poetry and going on about getting revenge while slamming his fist on the bar. That's when Jack usually tells Jimmy to go home and sleep it off."

Betty then asked if it was rib night at Jack's tonight. When his wife indicated it was, Betty leaned into me and said they were the best ribs in the state and if I liked ribs, I shouldn't pass them up.

"Sounds delicious!" I said, wondering if I'd ever again have much of an appetite.

Betty smiled as she admired how her creation was coming along.

"Tell Jack he'll be getting a new face with a pretty hairdo in there tonight."

The conversation turned to the weather, how busy Betty was going to be because of some upcoming wedding, and a kitchen one of the women wanted to renovate. While they discussed this and that, I had time to think about James. In some way, it was shocking to confirm my speculation that he might indeed be alive. In another way, fear and dread crept up my spine.

Betty smiled into the mirror again at the final results of her work, then spun me around to face the women. With my hair trimmed, colored, and styled, and though a bit too poufy for my liking, I did feel like a different person. I would need to be a different person to do what had to be done.

"You look wonderful," they exclaimed. "Your new 'do' should give you that extra shot of courage you need," said Betty.

"I certainly hope so," I replied.

****

I stopped at the liquor store and bought a bottle of whiskey before heading back to the motel. Once back in my room, I went online to do more research. After that, I spread myself out on a mattress that had seen much better days and many more bodies than I cared to think about. I mentally walked through my next moves. I questioned myself about what I hoped to achieve and whether I had enough gumption to go through with it. This could go wrong in a hundred different ways.

I found myself thinking in terms of marketing campaigns. There were distinct phases: research & preparation, the campaign launch, reward or adjustments. I was the phase one expert, but James had it all over me when it came to the launch. Rewards or adjustments had always been the phase up for grabs and mostly dependent on how well we had each done our work in phases one and two. I was determined to call the shots on every phase of this particular campaign. The launch could be tonight, and I suspected that it wouldn't take too long to learn if it succeeded.

I knew James well, so well, I could predict his behaviors. But I also wasn't fooling myself that he may have changed over all this time. Who he was now, if entirely different than I expected, could derail my plan. I also hadn't given enough thought to my own physical danger. The women at Betty's had described him as an angry loner, which meant nobody knew him or his limits anymore.

James was an angry man when I divorced him, and I had divorced him because of his mental and physical abuse. It was evident that his temper had not improved over time, but was it now worse? I knew I was treading in dangerous waters. Could I trust myself to defend myself against James, if needed?

I reminded myself that my anger was the weapon necessary to fend off Cassie. I would need to rely on my outrage over how he plotted against me using Cassie, plus my anger over James' complicity in Lainey's death. His abandonment of her was what sent her down a path that ultimately ended her life. It was because of him that my daughter was gone. I would risk my life, and do whatever it took, to keep him from doing harm to me, Trent, or my grandchildren.

I got up and readied everything, poured myself a shot of whiskey for fortification, and then filled the water glass again, topping it off with more liquid. I was banking on that drink being necessary later. But, first things first, right now I was banking on the notion that James still loved ribs. I made one last check of the room and one final check of myself. Launch time.

There was no denying my nervousness. I realized how jittery I was as soon as I tried to start the car. I needed to center myself before moving forward. I took one deep breath and then another. I wondered if I was losing it. Why wasn't I going to the authorities and letting them handle this? I couldn't find a satisfactory answer to that question, and I wondered if I was a complete fool. Maybe, I should just keep driving west, go to Trent like I promised, and let the authorities deal with James. It would be safer.

But would it? Me linking Cassie to James had been accidental. As soon as I checked my phone and learned that Trent and Cassie had not spoken my trust in Trent was restored. It was shortly after that when Detective Sherwood asked me about the 'Blackwood1again' Gmail.

Suddenly, the pieces fit together. James always had to be number one, and he always 'won'. 'Blackwood1' was the username he'd always used at the agency. I had been 'Blackwood2', the second-rate one as in just another Blackwood or 'Blackwood-too'. He never missed a chance to try to put me in my place and to show that he was bigger, better, and best. It was one of those telltale examples of narcissistic James. It had been one of the many signs I had seen only after looking into the rearview mirror of our marriage.

Although I recognized that email address as a bright red flag, it would be meaningless to anybody else. His choice of username was a clear message directed at me. I was sure of it. If I had told Detective Sherwood what I thought when he told me the email address, I'm sure he would have dismissed me as a mother willing to say and do anything to protect her son—even blame Harvey's murder on a dead man. I knew that even if I could convince the police to investigate, it would take time, which would give James enough time to cover his tracks and probably set up Trent even deeper.

James had me questioning if my own son might have had more dealings and deals than he let on regarding Cassie. I was ashamed that I wondered if Trent had anything to do with wanting Harvey and me out of the way. The James I knew would delight in my feeling of guilt and shame. The inconceivable was true. James was alive and framing his own son as the mastermind in a plot to get to David's money faster and conspiring to murder me was part of the plan.

I still didn't understand what the ultimate endgame was for James, but I was sure he was behind everything. Or I would be sure once I could see him. And with that thought, my guilt multiplied. I was forced to admit to myself that I couldn't fully believe that James was alive and that all of this was the result of James plotting until I saw him for myself and confronted him about it. I felt guilty that a part of me still suspected Trent.

It was vital for me to keep in mind that James also knew me well. Had he led me here? If so, what kind of trap might have been set-up and is waiting for me?

Though I was filled with anxiety and hesitation, I pulled away from the motel and drove toward town. The ladies had been correct about Jack's ribs being a draw. There were a lot of cars already parked around the building. One of them was the same car that I saw parked in the driveway of the old house where I believed James lived. My stomach clenched. Was I about to come face-to-face with a ghost? His life and death caused so much hurt. What kind of damage might a ghost be capable of inflicting?

As soon as I entered the bar, a waitress breezed by, all smiles, and told me to sit anywhere I liked. Luckily, I managed to arrive just as a young couple with a toddler was leaving. Their booth was to my left and in the far corner. I liked the idea of a wall behind me and to one side. I was close to the entrance if I needed to make a quick exit. And, I had a perfect view of the left side of the horseshoe-shaped bar.

There, on the last barstool, sat James Blackwood. As much as I thought I had prepared myself for this moment, the shock of seeing him again after so many years rattled me. It was surreal to be facing somebody long presumed dead. I thought about Lainey and how I wished it was her that was still alive after being presumed dead for so long. I welcomed the anger bubbling up within me as my hatred for James again flared at the thought of how he not only abandoned his children, but he also had the unabashed gall to have somebody imitate his dead daughter. James was ruthless. And I would be a fool not to remain conscious of that fact.

The same waitress breezed by again. "Tonight's rib night," she announced as she dropped off a menu and bowl of peanuts still in the shell. "If you like ribs, gettum while we've gottum—they're real popular."

"Yes, I've heard," I replied. "Everyone at Betty's told me so earlier today."

"I pegged you for a stranger to our little town," said the waitress. "Guess I got it wrong."

"No, just passing through," I said, then ordered the ribs and a glass of wine.

I was sorry when the waitress walked off with the menu. It was big and tall and would have provided me with excellent cover. I pulled my e-reader from my purse. It wasn't as big as the menu, but it would have to make do providing cover for my face. I pretended to read and wondered what I was going to do once my ribs came. James had not looked my way since I'd arrived. Hopefully, the glass he nursed would continue to absorb his attention.

More than twenty years had passed since I'd last seen him; he looked older. Although he carried a little more weight, he appeared to have filled out rather than become heavy. I surprised myself by acknowledging that he was still handsome. From this vantage, his profile was unscarred, and his advanced age merely made him seem more distinguished.

The waitress delivered my glass of wine, smiled, and said my ribs would be out shortly.

I gazed out again over the top of my reader to resume my spying. James was alive and choosing to live in a place he always couldn't wait to leave. Why had he chosen to make the world believe that he had died along with thousands of others on that horrific September day in New York City? How could a person live with themselves knowing the devastation they caused to others, not to mention dishonoring the memories of those who did perish that day?

My dinner arrived. I didn't have much of an appetite, but it would look terribly strange if I didn't appear to eat. Thankfully, everyone in these parts ate ribs with their fingers. I somehow managed a one-handed rib-hold while still pretending to read. The ribs were indeed delicious, which made forcing myself to nibble slightly less of a chore. Just as I was getting close to finishing my dinner, Betty, followed by a man that I assumed was her husband, entered. She scanned the room, and when her eyes settled on me in the first booth to her left, a smile lit her face.

She pranced toward me; the surprise of it caused me to lower the reader. "Anna, wasn't I right about those ribs?"

Her booming voice caused several people to turn and look at me, including James. His head turned ever so slightly in my direction as if the noise was just a mere annoyance not worthy of his full attention. Even so, I immediately slid farther into the booth to be less in his line of sight. It was a close call, too close, and now, all I wanted to do was leave.

"Yes, Betty, they are delicious. Thank you so much for the recommendation."

She beamed and was just about to introduce me to her husband, when I interrupted, "Oh dear, I didn't realize the time. I need to get back for an important call. I'm so sorry, but I don't know the server's name. Could you ask her to bring me the bill?"

Betty looked disappointed but quickly recovered. She wished me well, and they were off. A minute later, the waitress was at the table, I immediately paid in cash and left her a generous tip. After a last glance back to the bar to make sure James wasn't looking my way, I quickly slid out from the booth and out of the building. I fumbled around in my purse for my keys, cursing, and growing faint from forgetting to breathe.

Finally, now behind the wheel after what seemed like an eternity, I roared the engine with a little too much pedal to the metal, my tires squealing as I pulled away. I let out a mighty sigh as I realized I had made it away from there without James noticing me. I checked the rearview mirror just to be sure. There were no cars behind me. I saw that I was driving much too fast and forced myself to slow.

I had learned what I needed. James was alive. I should just grab my things from the motel and drive on to Trent's. I wouldn't stop until I reached him. But no, I couldn't. I'd only accomplished part of why I came here. Now that I knew for sure that James was still alive, I needed to confront him. He needed to see he wasn't going to get away with anything. He wasn't going to ruin any more lives. I would do what I needed to do to make sure of it.

Those were wonderfully courageous words to tell myself, and to try to convince myself of, even though I desperately wanted to listen more to that part of myself telling me to get the Hell out of here now and let the authorities deal with it all. But I knew I couldn't. I knew I wouldn't. Too much was at stake.

I checked the closet, the bath, and the windows immediately upon entering my motel room. The place was indeed empty, and the windows were locked. I made sure that everything I might need was in easy reach or at the ready—just in case. I looked over at the bottle of whiskey on the small table in front of the window and the full glass waiting. My heart was pumping hard. I commanded my body to relax. I had to take control of myself if I were to take control of the situation. I pulled back the covers and started to get into bed while still wearing my clothes. Be prepared, I thought. Stick with the plan. But then I decided that I needed to pretend as if nothing in the scene were wrong or out of the ordinary.

I took my hearing aid out and inserted it into the charger on the bedside table. Teeth brushed, pajamas on, I crawled under the covers and shut off the light. Then, I turned the light on again. One small concession to pretending courage should be permitted. My hearing disability kept me from being woken by noises that would easily wake other people. Keeping the light on would make me feel safer. With covers pulled up to my chin, I closed my eyes and willed my body to relax, but there was still just too much adrenalin pumping through me to do so.

Deliberately, I turned my attention away from

where I was and mentally transported myself to seeing Trent and the girls. I was looking forward to seeing my granddaughters. I wanted to be a regular part of their lives. It was something I've always wanted. But I'd also wanted them to experience a happy grandmother who enjoyed doting on them. I was too afraid that every little girl behavior they displayed would only make me remember Lainey and that I would be too sad to be the loving grandmother they deserved. David knew this about me. The memory walls, his reassuring voice, and his warmth had lifted me out of my grief over Lainey. I had become ready to get to know my grandchildren. Just before he died, David and I spoke of it being a priority in the new year ahead. Nothing was going to stop me from keeping that promise to myself now.

Once this business was over, I would only look forward. I drifted off, letting my imagination play with the fun times I'd have with my granddaughters.

They were my future.

Chapter Thirty-Five

Anna

I turned over, awakening slightly to adjust my pillow. As my head settled into the folded pillow, a jolt of panic ran through me. I forced myself to remain still, even though every nerve screamed at me to jump up and run. It was precisely how I felt as a child after a bad dream or seeing a shadow move on the other side of my bedroom window, only later to realize that it was just the silhouette of a tree branch swaying in the night breeze. That's it—that's what is wrong. I'm in darkness.

The light on the bedside table next to me was no longer lit. I couldn't hear anything. I was on my bad side. My better ear was smushed into the pillow, forcing my deadened ear that I received courtesy of James and his boxing of my ears when he assaulted me all those years ago into a role it couldn't handle. I also couldn't see anything, so I suddenly had no idea of time or space. I was trapped inside myself.

There must be an obvious explanation. Perhaps the bulb needed replacing. *Think, Anna. If there were somebody here, they would be doing something— wouldn't they?* No, not everyone. This is how James would play it. Quietly planning, taking his time, enjoying the moment, making sure my fright would keep me disoriented and unbalanced. He was always big about the element of surprise.

Anna, listen to yourself. You are going to feel so stupid, though quite relieved, when you reach up to turn on that light and find out the bulb has gone bad. You need to find out why the room is dark. There is no possibility of going back to sleep until you do. Before moving think through precisely what you will do. Reach up and turn on the light, grab your hearing aid from the charger during your arm's downward motion, and then check that everything is as it should be.

You can do this. One-two-three. Come on, Anna, one-two-three.

I nearly knocked the lamp off the table after I reached too quickly to turn on the lamp. I grabbed my hearing aid as my arm came down and quickly inserted it into my ear in one fast move. That's when I realized that the light had not come on. It was a bad bulb all along. That's why the lamp was no longer lit.

Laughing aloud, I chided myself. "Anna, you are such a scaredy-cat—you are such a silly old woman!"

"Or, maybe not so silly." The soft, measured response came from somewhere in the dark.

My breath caught. My hand slowly groped around under the covers for my cell phone. I had kept it close for the—just in case—that was now somewhere in the room with me. David's pistol, taken from the gun safe at the back of his closet, was loaded, and there too. I drew both closer.

I waited.

Nothing.

Taking small breaths and making no other moves, I waited.

Nothing.

As my eyes adjusted to the dark, I dared not move my head, but I was sure there was nothing above me or in my peripheral vision. There was nothing behind other than the headboard. If anybody were in the room, they would have to be in the hall leading to the bathroom—in front of me, between the bed and the door to the outside.

I wished I was losing it. I wished I could chalk the voice up to one of the auditory hallucinations I'd experienced when I thought I might be losing it. Could it be that I was just scared, and my mind was playing tricks on me now?

There was only one way to know. I kept my hand wrapped around my phone and sat up.

I couldn't see anything, but I immediately felt his presence.

"Anna, my dear, how long it has been? I'm so sorry to have woken you."

I screamed at hearing James' sickly-sweet voice coming from somewhere in the dark.

He started laughing.

"James, please!"

The floor lamp in the corner by the small table in front of the window clicked on. He'd positioned the floor lamp's on/off button to be near his foot.

"Please what?" he asked at the same time as the lamp lit.

I screamed again.

The left side of his face was horribly disfigured. Had I not already heard his voice; I wouldn't have been sure this was really the man I once knew.

I gathered myself. I had carefully rehearsed what to

do. This wasn't exactly how I expected it to happen, but nevertheless, it was the time. I pressed the record button on my phone app. At least, I hoped that's what I had done. I had carefully and blindly rehearsed where on my phone to find it if I encountered a situation where I was unable to see my phone.

"You always did know how to make a showy entrance. How did you break into my motel room?"

"It's a small town. Everybody knows everybody. I woke Robbie, the night clerk, and told him that his cousin, who happens to be a recovering alcoholic, had fallen off the wagon at Jack's. I thought it best to let him sleep it off here before facing his wife in the morning. Robbie gave me his master key and told me to pick any room but number 27. I could leave the key in the room with his cousin. Robbie wanted to get back to sleep."

"I'm guessing there was no cousin?"

"You're still smart, Anna—don't believe it if anybody tells you that you are losing it."

"Then you loosened the bulb in the table lamp next to me. It wasn't as if you were taking any big chances doing so, because you remembered that I probably wouldn't hear you without my hearing aid."

"Oh, Anna, give me more credit. It was dramatic and perfect. I assure you that I haven't lost my flair for staging."

"Those scars. Did you get those on 9/11 or was it when you were valiantly making desperate attempts to save your wife and children from a house fire?"

James gave a little smile. It was cockeyed and creepy. The half of his face that was disfigured by burns no longer moved in unison with the opposite side.

"I was badly burned. But I did escape. Just as I was nearing a crowd of people to ask for help, I realized that I had been presented with a perfect opportunity to escape my life. After all, because of you, the agency was finished. Creditors were on my back. I was about to lose what little was left. I had been stashing away some funds back here in a shell account created to save what I could. That's when I realized that I had just been handed the perfect excuse and means to shut the door on it all by disappearing."

"That sounds just like you," I taunted. "You've always been an expert at shutting doors, shutting out others, and disappearing acts."

"I was surprised to see you tonight at Jack's," he said. "What made you think I might be connected to your recent troubles, and how did you find me?"

"You're a good actor. I didn't think you recognized me, but you aren't quite as clever and creative as you give yourself credit for being. Several clues: your new email address was the first and the second clue being an unswayable belief that my son is innocent. The third clue, the recognition about how closely Cassie resembled Lainey physically and how much she resembled you in every other way. How I found you was remembering the name of the Midwest town, you long ago said you were from. I tried to phone your mother when we thought you dead. I found out that she had died the month before. It stuck with me. I took a chance that you might be alive and here."

James was eyeing the whiskey bottle and full glass next to it.

"Go ahead," I said. "Help yourself."

"I think I will. Thank you for your hospitality," he

said while raising the glass as a toast and then downing the whole drink at once.

He quickly poured himself another. He began passing the glass from hand-to-hand, occasionally taking a swig. I remembered this as being one of his nervous gestures.

"Why?" I asked.

"Why what?" he sneered as he poured himself more whiskey. Again, he swallowed it in a single gulp.

"Why did you do any of this? Did you follow my life? Why did you enlist Cassie to pretend she was your dead daughter? Do you have no shame? Was Cassie also your real daughter?"

His laugh was long, low, and full of disdain. "Oh, please. I was long past having the slightest interest in any of you after you tried your best to ruin me. Then I happened to see the news one night. That's when I learned about Lainey and when I saw your tear-stricken face pleading for any information that might lead to finding her. I was sorry, of course, to hear about her, but I wouldn't say I was surprised. She was always weak and needy—and it was you who made her that way. By lavishing too much affection and attention on her, you turned her into an emotional cripple. I also saw Trent standing behind you on some of the newscasts. He turned out to be quite a good-looking guy. He resembles me, doesn't he?"

"Nothing about my son resembles you!"

James laughed.

"Cassie—now that was somebody who resembled you inside and out."

James snickered. "I spent some time with her mother. Beth was barmaid at a little place near the New

York apartment. I must have let on a tad too much about where I was from and where I was headed. Beth dressed my wounds that day best she could. Years later, this girl who had a close resemblance to a younger Lainey, if only her hair and eye color could be made to match, showed up here, saying she wanted money for college. She was smart and twisted, that one. I paid her tuition. Something told me to keep tabs on her. She could either become a threat or prove to be useful.

"I was surprised to learn just how much pleasure it gave me to see you turned into such a wreck when Lainey died. That's when I started to follow you on the news and online. I'll say this—you did an excellent job of using your public relations skills to draw a lot of media attention. It brought me joy every time you cried, pleaded, and begged. It was sometimes even a turn-on, and it got to be like a drug. I couldn't get enough of it. The worse you felt, the happier I became. You were finally getting the kick you deserved.

Listening to him made me increasingly confident that I could pull the trigger. My left hand, the one still underneath the bed covers, angled the pistol so that it was pointing directly at James.

"Then, and I don't know how you did it, but you snagged that wealthy guy. You finding happiness was not something you deserved, but I was encouraged again when your new husband died suddenly. By that time, I really wanted to see you suffer more. Cassie was a real find. You have no idea what a twisted girl she was. I did a little digging into her background. Did you know that she was thrown out of school because of suspicions about her involvement surrounding the apparent suicide of her roommate? She was ripe for the job of torturing you and driving you insane. I gave her money to move near you. It was easy to have Beth tag along because she was easily influenced by Cassie's wants. Maybe her mother was a little afraid of her too. I sometimes wondered if the pleasure Cassie got out of the job I gave her was more interesting to her than the money. She even asked me if I minded if you didn't live through it."

James sat back in the chair and began turning his head from side-to-side as if he wasn't feeling okay.

"So, you were paying her?"

James raised his head and just glared at me.

"You were paying her?" I asked again.

His voice turned colder. "No."

Of course, he was.

"Trent was paying her," James said, the creepy lopsided smile again spreading across his face.

"I know that Trent was paying for Cassie and her mother to clean the home and to watch out for me. But I know that it was you who also paid money and the promise of more to get me out of the way," I said, and quickly pressed the stop record button on my phone.

"Anna," James slurred, "Our sunny boy was fronting the cost of getting you out of the way so that he could get to David's money faster."

"I don't believe you."

"That look on your face tells me you just might. I'm really enjoying this."

I had not spent adequate time going over the files Harvey had prepared for me when I should have done so. With everything that was being done to disorient me, it was quite likely that I wouldn't be able to comprehend what was in the files anyway. So, I made a point of studying them during every stop I made on the journey out here. I found account information. Harvey had been transferring money to Trent. Over two-hundred-thousand dollars had flowed from David's account to Trent since David's death. There was indeed something going on that I didn't understand.

"Maybe I'm not as smart as you. Why don't you lay it out for me?"

I didn't really expect him to do so, but maybe the drinking made him less careful and loosened his tongue. On the other hand, James always did like to boast and pretend to be all-knowing.

"Cassie and I were kindred spirits when it came to the enjoyment it gave us to see you suffer. The kick of seeing somebody suffer was usually her payoff. So, she didn't question it when I said it was mine, too.

"Cassie didn't matter much to me in the long run. If all went as planned, she would be Trent's problem. I wondered how thrilled he'd be when he learned about the resurrection of his long-lost father, his new sister, and the information I could take to the authorities. That information was going to provide Trent with good reason to support his dad in his old age. Of course, affording to support me might also mean needing to find another way to dispose of you. Can you see the bonus in that for me? I'd get the kick out of seeing you dealt with, and I'd have a free lifelong stream of income afterward, a win-win," he slurred.

James paused, cocked his head to the side and added, "Of course, I'm always open to tweaking plans. I could decide to keep away from Trent."

"So, let me understand this correctly. You'll blackmail Trent over his paying Cassie to get rid of me if I don't pay you blackmail to stay away from Trent?"

"I win either way. Hey, maybe we sweeten the deal with a little lovin'. I bet you've missed me." He stood and began to sway counterclockwise as if his feet were caked in cement.

"Poor, poor little Jimmy. My, you're a little unsteady there, little Jimmy boy," I taunted. "I doubt you could get it up."

James lunged at me but missed. He lay sprawled halfway down the bed by my shins.

I quickly got up from under the covers. Phone still in one hand and the pistol now in the other.

James rolled over onto his back after several unsuccessful attempts. "What did you do to me?"

"A little something I learned from Cassie. Although I admit that I don't really know how much of the drug is a safe dosage." I smiled. "Could be, I gave you a little too much?"

"Dead men can't die."

I pointed David's pistol at him. "Shall we test that theory?"

"Please, no! Don't!" James tried to cover his face, but his arms wouldn't cooperate. Still crying, he could only manage to turn his head away from me.

So easy to pull the trigger, so tempting.

Then he stilled. Lights out.

I quickly changed into my clothes, shoved my pajamas into the suitcase I had repacked earlier, and shoved the pistol into the duffel bag. Using my phone, I took several photos of James sprawled out on the bed and then left.

Chapter Thirty-Six

Anna

I began driving and thinking about next steps. A few hours after dawn, I left the Interstate in search of gas, coffee, and some breakfast. I settled into the booth of a cute little restaurant and began poring through Harvey's files one more time. There it was. I stared at the page until I could decide about what to do next. A lot of money had flowed to Trent. Why? Two eggs and three cups of coffee later, I was finally gassed up enough to find out.

I pulled out my phone and called Detective Sherwood. I explained where I was and what I had been doing, though skipping over a few of the details. I wondered if he thought me crazy when I told him about James still being alive and conspiring with his daughter Cassie.

I wasn't surprised to hear the touch of doubt in his voice. That's why I had recorded the confession. I told the detective about the proof I had, what I done to get it, and that he should expect emails from me containing a photo of James and his recorded confession as soon as we hung up. I then told him about the email address being the clue that drove me here, and I pleaded with him to have James arrested as soon as possible. He was dangerous. My son, his family, and I were all in danger.

After reassuring the detective that I was safely on my way to Trent, he agreed to look into everything and to act if it all matched what I had just reported.

Next, I phoned Trent to tell him that I would be arriving the day after tomorrow. He asked what flight I would be on so that he could pick me up at the airport and seemed more than a little surprised when I told him not to bother because I was driving out to him. I used the excuse of needing my car once I got there. I could have gotten there earlier, but I needed a little more time to myself first. I needed to think about how I would tell Trent what I had learned. I knew that in the end, the chips would fall where they may, and any attempt by me to control the situation would be futile. I still had to try. Trent was my son.

After driving most of the day, I pulled off the highway and into what looked like a pretty little community. The scenery and landscaping were much different than in Kansas, which elevated my mood and let some hope creep into the crevices surrounding my darker thoughts. I was too exhausted to drive more. I'd had little sleep the night before. This motel felt clean and much more welcoming than had the last. That made me wonder again, for the one-hundredth time that day, about James and what today had been like for him.

Shortly after an early dinner, I received a call from Detective Sherwood. James was in local police custody and being questioned. I thanked him and asked to be kept updated. I hung up and wondered whether James being locked up would help me to sleep peacefully or would the thought of what he might say to the police make rest impossible. I was also nervous about the next day. I would be seeing Trent, and I still had no idea how I would broach the subject of James or Cassie. I tossed and turned throughout the night.

I was on the road again early and only hours away from confronting Trent. I phoned him to say when I expected to arrive. Since it was the middle of the day, there was a good possibility that nobody would be home. Trent informed me that it would be the case and gave me directions to his office. We would meet there. Meeting at his office was also preferable to me. I wanted the chance to speak with him alone before seeing the rest of the family. I scolded myself when I realized that I was driving much more slowly that last hundred miles and when I recognized that I was trying to distract myself with innocuous thoughts about mundane topics like—how what they say about California always being "sunny" must be true. Anything that kept me from obsessing over how the next few hours might play seemed thoughtworthy.

It had been more than a year since I'd last been here. David often had business out this way. One time, we had decided to tack on a small vacation by visiting Trent and his family at the tail end of David's business meetings. The visit had been wonderful. I remembered David commenting during the ride back to the airport how he really enjoyed spending time with Trent and the family. He said that Trent and the grandkids couldn't feel more like actual family than if they were biologically connected.

I remembered how David turned to me, smiled, and said that we should make more effort to visit them more often. David's loving ways were special. I never forgot those words he said that day. I wondered what this visit would bring. David had loved Trent like his own son. I hoped that Trent was worthy. I had to believe he was.

After taking a couple of wrong turns, I spotted the address and pulled into Trent's office parking lot. I was right on time. I had barely entered the building when Trent rushed toward me and swept me up in his arms.

"You made it! I'm glad you're here, Mom. I still can't believe you drove all the way across the country by yourself and not even telling me about it until you were two-thirds the way here. Something could have happened to you, and nobody would have known."

I cringed, feeling stupid for being so reckless. "I'm sorry, it was not a good decision, but at the time."

"It's okay. You are here now, all in one piece, and that's what matters."

Trent escorted me into his office, and I gratefully slumped into one of the cozy leather chairs in front of his desk. But only a second later panic was trying its best to settle into me. "Coffee, tea, water, juice—what can I get you?"

I answered that tea would be perfect and then asked where I could find a bathroom to freshen up. Trent pointed to a door on the other side of the room. I needed just a little more time to gather myself and my thoughts, though I knew that had run out of time. There was nothing left but to wing it. I returned to my chair just as Trent came in with my tea.

"I thought we'd do a late lunch/early dinner," he said. "You must be hungry, and the girls are dying to see you. Then, later, you can relax and turn in anytime you want. After all that driving, you must be exhausted."

I told Trent it sounded like a good plan. We made small talk about the girls as I sipped my tea. Trent was so tanned, healthy, and vibrant looking. The climate and lifestyle here certainly agreed with him. Trent had a gift for telling stories. He had me laughing at tales about the twins' antics. It was impossible not to be completely enthralled. He radiated love for his life and everyone in it. I wanted to bask in his glow for just a while longer. The truth was, I was afraid to extinguish that glow or be permanently removed from it.

No more pussyfooting. Time to jump in.

"Trent, I had another reason for driving here beyond what I've already told you. I don't know how to begin. It might be a shock."

"Now, you are scaring me. Just come out with it."

"I drove through Kansas on my way here. I had a hunch your father was still alive and somehow involved in all that mess with Cassie. I was correct about both. Your father is alive, and Cassie was your half-sister."

Trent placed both hands on the edge of the desk and pushed himself back some. His eyes were still looking in my direction, but I didn't think he was any longer actually seeing me. He was somewhere else or perhaps just trying to process my words. I wished I had special powers to see inside his head. How much of a shock was this to him? Was it a total shock or not a shock at all? Maybe, he thinks I am losing it. I was desperate to know, but he wasn't saying anything. I tried to study his body language.

After what seemed like an eternity, he brought both hands up to his face, nervously rubbed his forehead, and then ruffled his hair. "I don't understand."

I laid out the details for Trent about my initial suspicions, my finding his father alive and then confronting him. I said I had recorded him and that his father was now in police custody and under investigation for conspiring with Cassie in the attempted murder of me and the killing of Harvey.

"What! What are you saying? I'm sorry, Mom, but all of this is just so difficult to believe and understand."

Trent stared intently into my eyes while I repeated everything once again. I showed him the photo I took with my phone. I expected his initial reaction would be astonishment that his father was still alive and wondering why he let the world, and his family, think him dead. I was surprised, because it seemed an odd response, when instead Trent asked, "Why would he target you?"

"Revenge. He always blamed me for whatever went wrong—the divorce, his business souring, him no longer being the shining star of the advertising world. He saw me on the news talking about Lainey's disappearance, and it pleased him to learn I was suffering. He kept track of me, and he simply couldn't handle it when I found David and happiness again."

Trent remained silent for several minutes. Processing the news, I assumed. I hoped. "And Cassie? What did he say was in it for her?"

"He said she was twisted and took pleasure in torturing people."

"That was her only motive?"

"Not exactly, she was also being paid."

My words hung in the air. Trent was now clearly shaken.

A few more minutes passed. I looked around the room to give him time to think. From the corner of my eye, I caught him beginning to stare at me intently as if he were trying to make up his mind about something.

Just then, his cell phone rang, startling both of us. Trent swiveled in his chair so that his back was to me. I couldn't make out the conversation. He was whispering, and it was unsettling. Why had he turned away and begun whispering?

He spun around back toward me after a few minutes. "Sorry about the interruption, Mom. What you've been telling me here is really crazy stuff. It's a lot to take in and to make sense of. I'm going to need some time to process. It sounds like something out of a movie."

His response might be considered reasonable to some people, but I didn't think it was at all normal. It was as if Trent were hearing a story about some other people, but this was about his father who was presumably dead to him as little as an hour ago. He now finds out that his father is alive, and his only response is, "it sounds like something out of a movie"?

Could Trent have been involved in a scheme with James and Cassie to get rid of me? I couldn't believe that my son would do that, and I felt guilty and ashamed for even having the thought. But the idea kept hanging there and, as much as I wanted to, I couldn't dismiss it.

"Let's go!" Trent said suddenly.

"Where?"

"I promised you a meal. You must be starving."

I followed him out of his office and then out of the building. He asked for my keys as soon as we were outside. He said he wanted to get my luggage.

"It's not necessary. I'll follow you."

"No, we can take care of the car later."

It seemed a strange and unnecessary idea. Why

shouldn't I follow him home? I'd just have to come back for it later. But I did as I was told and climbed into the passenger seat of his car. We drove in silence, and it was unnerving. I made a couple of safe comments about the weather. I asked if he was familiar with a restaurant we passed and a few other nonsense topics just to make small talk and to obliterate the uneasy silence. Trent supplied curt comments and quick answers. Conversation wasn't flowing. Then I noticed us heading in a direction different than we should have taken to get to where Trent lived.

"This isn't the way to your house, is it?"

"There's something I want to show you."

"What?"

"Just trust me, okay?"

If only he knew how much I wanted, and was trying, to trust him. I wanted nothing more. I closed my eyes and tried to relax. I thought I heard Trent release a little sigh as if me zoning out might help him to relax some too. There was no more pressure on either of us to talk or be congenial.

I knew that I had to be more direct in my questioning of Trent. I needed to find out if he had been paying Cassie. I needed to find out about all that money that had flowed to him via Harvey from David's account. But now was clearly not the right time.

We made a sharp turn, slowed, and stopped. We were in the driveway of a home that I'd never seen before. It was big, beautifully charming, and oceanfront. Trent shut off the engine and unsnapped his seatbelt. He took my hand in his and said, "I never imagined today starting off the way it did."

"I'm sorry."

"There's no turning the clock back now."

"What are you talking about, and where are we?"

"Follow me," he said as he got out of the car.

He grabbed my bags from the back seat, which only confused me more. I nearly had to run to keep up with him as we made our way to the house. Once inside, Trent set my bags down. That's when I noticed the floor-to-ceiling windows stretching across the entire expanse of the wall in front of me and framing the most magnificent ocean view, I'd ever seen. I gasped.

"Beautiful, isn't it!" Trent exclaimed. He seemed wonderfully happy with my reaction.

"Everything about it is beautiful. The view is incredible, and the décor is amazing—the furniture, the lighting, everything is exactly my taste. It's spectacular, yet cozy and homey. There's so much warmth and character in this space, and it's a perfect balance to the expansive and amazing view beyond. I wouldn't change a thing if it were mine."

A grin as wide as a Cheshire cat's spread from ear-to-ear on Trent's face. Before I could say another word, he grabbed my hand and began leading me throughout the main floor of the house. The kitchen, the dining area, a guest bath—everything was so well laid out and well-appointed. Everything was constructed of beautiful materials. It was then that I realized what was going on. Trent was showing me his new home. I knew that my son made a good living, but I also knew he couldn't afford a house like this and with a view like that. A sinking feeling hit the pit of my stomach as I realized where the money must have come from and certainly much more would be needed to cover costs like these.

What was his plan? Was it to woo me with the

beauty of this place and his palpable excitement over it, so that by the time I learned the truth, I would be okay with it? That wouldn't happen. It couldn't happen. What Trent failed to realize was that James would be soon singing to the police that Trent was paying Cassie to get rid of me. Trent had the biggest motive, and this house was a testament to it. James would put as much of the blame as possible on his son.

I suddenly felt very unsteady. I grabbed a stool from under the expansive marble kitchen island and sat down. Trent turned toward me, his face falling further with each step.

The fact that my son had conspired to kill me was fighting to sink in. My own son wanted me dead so that he could get to David's money. James had told the truth, and I didn't want to believe it. I still didn't want to believe it. I couldn't ever imagine my son being a cold-hearted criminal. It didn't match the person I knew and loved. And, to think that in his eyes, my life meant nothing to him.

How could that be possible? But it must be true. It also explained Trent's strange reaction to the news that his father was still alive. He didn't seem shocked when I told him. The only visible reaction he had when I delivered the news was a sudden coldness and detachment that emanated from his eyes. That coldness and indifference must have been aimed at me. What do I do?

"Mom, are you feeling okay? What's the matter?"

I couldn't look at him. "May I have a glass of water, please?"

"Sure thing."

What do I do? Do I play along with this charade?

Or do I confront my son? Am in danger if I do?

Trent returned with the glass of water.

"Just feeling a little woozy for a moment. It's been quite a strange and awful time for me these last few weeks. I guess it's all just now catching up with me.

"Of course," he said. "How insensitive of me to not think this just might be too much and maybe not the best time…"

"There are things that I'm not able to understand right now. Something is bothering me. You didn't seem at all surprised when I told you that your father was not dead. How could that not be a shock to you?"

"I suppose looking at it from your point of view my reaction might have seemed a little strange," he said as he lightly dragged his hand along the edge of the marble countertop. Then, he turned and walked toward one of the kitchen windows that looked out over the beach below. He just stood there, watching for several minutes. Several long awkward minutes passed, and I was no longer sure that he was going to say more.

I was interested in hearing his explanation. Could it be that he was still searching for one? Finally, he turned back toward me. "Look, I don't know how to explain this to you so that it might make sense."

"Can you please give it a try?"

"My father died a long time ago. He was dead to me long before 9/11. The fact that he's magically alive now changes nothing for me. He's still dead to me, and if he came anywhere near my family, I'd make him dead for real with my own two hands.

"Mom, I was shocked to hear that he's still alive. But I guess that I also just have so much anger in me still about him and what he did to us. That anger surged back through me in that same instant. Not wanting to be that angry boy again and fearing that I could easily become him again, is what shocked me the most.

"While we were sitting there in the office and when I heard from you how that man cared more about torturing you than feeling sad about losing Lainey, I had to work very hard at keeping my anger in check. I have a wonderful life and a beautiful family. I'm happy. I'm loved, and I don't want him to change me back to how I felt, and who I was, before. And I won't let my family have less than they deserve. They deserve the best, and I include you, Mom. You deserve the best."

Words and feelings poured out of Trent like a waterfall. I had never heard or seen him be so forthright and expressing so many emotions. My heart went out to him, and I nearly jumped up from the stool to wrap him in my arms, but I sensed he wasn't finished.

"Can you imagine how hard it was for me to learn that you nearly died at Cassie's hands. I arranged for her to be there to help you. It was because of me that any of this happened."

"Trent, no, you can't think like that."

"But I have, and I've tried to push it away. Or maybe not fully take it in from the start is a better way of saying it. I couldn't face, and still can't face, thinking about how close I came to losing you. I've been, we've all been, looking forward to you coming here. Then today, I find out that I nearly lost you again. You confronted a madman, alone, without letting anyone else know what you were up to. That was totally dangerous and completely foolish. Haven't you been through enough? I don't want to lose you again."

"Again?"

"When we lost Lainey, I lost you, too."

"Oh, no. I never meant…"

"I know, Mom. I get it now. I can't imagine losing one of my daughters. It would break me in two. I don't know if you would have ever made it through it if it weren't for David. You were suffering so bad that I don't think you noticed how tough losing Lainey was on me too. I had lost my father, my sister, and my mother. I'd finally found a wonderful woman to share my life, and I wanted you to be happy for me and to want to be part of our lives too, especially when the twins were coming along."

"I'm so sorry, Trent. It was unforgivable of me to make my deceased child the focus of my life and to ignore my child that still lived."

Trent again took my hands in his. We both looked down at those clasped hands remembering the same memory from so very long ago.

"No more sorry, Mom," Trent said, beginning to cry as he continued. "Everything was finally coming together. We were a family again. It was all because of David. He pulled you through your grief over Lainey. And he was focused on us being a happy family. He's the man that I want to think of as being my real father."

"You do? I knew that he loved being with you and the girls too. He told me he wanted for all of us to spend more time together and not just because it was what I wanted. He said that he wanted it too. But how did you know that? I don't think I ever told you and I don't think he had a chance to either."

Trent came over and hugged me. "Let's continue the tour," he said, taking both my hands and pulling me off the stool to lead me forward. That ugly feeling and questioning why we were in this house and about the money came back at me. The thought was such an awful intrusion amid these beautiful moments we had just been sharing.

"There's another thing that I don't understand. How are you able to afford a house like this?"

"I'll tell you in a minute, but first I need to ask you something."

I was starting to feel a little woozy again. We stopped just in front of a door leading to another room.

"You've seen most of the main floor. What do you think of the house so far?"

"It's beautiful. I can't imagine a more beautiful space and a more beautiful location. It's exactly what I would want for myself. But, and please forgive me, I know that you earn a good living, I still don't understand how this could be your home?"

"It isn't."

"What? Whose is it, then?"

Trent opened the door to the next room.

"Step inside."

It was a beautifully decorated library. Sunlight pouring in from the oceanside streamed across the room. My old beloved beat-up camera was atop a table next to a comfy reading chair. Photos, lots, and lots of them, lined the walls. They were duplicates of the same images that lined my memory walls back east, including my two favorites—nurse Lainey and our beach picnic. There were also photos that Trent must have taken the day David and I married. Also, and notably, there were also lots of empty frames hanging on the wall too. I was astonished. I turned to Trent. He was smiling happily through a veil of tears.

"David should be here," he said on a choke. "He was so looking forward to this moment."

"I still don't understand."

"This house, it's for you. It's the surprise he was planning for you and the surprise you said he was going to tell you about just before the heart attack."

"The surprise!"

"I helped him through every stage of it—finding this spot, contractors, permits...We had a lot of fun planning this for you. You were both finishing up on the lake house. David knew it would be too much for you to take on building and furnishing a second house so soon. He said that he knew your tastes as well as his own because of the lake house.

"Working on this project with David gave me a chance to get to know him better. I'm so grateful that I had that chance. It was such a shock when David died. This place was nearly done by then. Harvey and I talked it over. Harvey kept David's cash flowing to finish up everything. He knew it was what David would have wanted for you. Harvey was in on the secret too. He was a good guy."

Harvey had been a good guy. He didn't try to pull any wool over my eyes. The transfer of funds to Trent was clearly documented in the material he gave me. Harvey had been transparent. James and Cassie were the types who chose to operate in murkiness and deceit. Never, should I have believed anything either of those two said to make me mistrust Trent. My attention returned to my son.

"We both wanted to see David's dream finished. We knew that it would be good for you, too. David had carefully planned every little detail, and all I had to do was to follow his plans. There's a door behind you that you should open. David dreamt of this day. He often spoke about his plan to show you around the house. He would leave this main floor room for last. So, I've tried to do this just as David would have wanted."

I turned and looked at the door. I was bewildered. I couldn't imagine what more could be in store for me.

"Go on, Mom."

I opened the door, and my breath caught as my gaze traveled over a superbly outfitted darkroom. I couldn't believe my eyes. All the necessary chemicals were lined up and labeled. Trays were neatly stacked on the table and waiting to be used. My fingers traced the outline of the enlarger, and they began itching to bring an image to life. I was crying now too. This was David's parting gift to me, and it was as if I could feel his presence. I could clearly imagine the look and love he would have had on his face as clearly as if he were standing before me once again.

I could almost hear him asking me, "Anna, what do you think? Do you like it? Is it everything you need?"

I missed David so much, and I loved him even more now knowing how close he and my son had the chance to become. Of course, James had tried to blame Trent as being part of a scheme to kill me. He was taunting me again and enjoying watching me suffer. I wasn't too surprised that David had done all of this for me, and for us. That's just the kind of guy he was. David was one of those rare human beings that gave light, warmth, and love to everyone he met. He, like Lainey, left us much too early.

I carefully closed the door on the darkroom, still not being able to totally believe that it existed and what a wonderful surprise it was. I looked at the empty photo frames on the walls. Each one energized me. I moved to the window and looked out at the spectacular view of the sparkling ocean and sandy beach below. There, I caught sight of Trent's wife and the girls on a blanket. It looked as if they were preparing for a picnic.

"Is that…"

"It is. They're waiting for us."

I grabbed the camera and checked it. Of course, it was already fully loaded with film. David always thought of everything.

"Let's go. I want to hug my grandbabies. We've got lots of new memories to make."

Chapter Thirty-Seven

Three Years Later, Anna

My life had come together. The properties back east had been sold. Trent now managed my affairs. I enjoyed living in California. I sometimes thought of myself and everyone around me as part of a patchwork quilt—worn, but steadfastly warm and cozy.

I found a peace and contentment I couldn't imagine, and had just been on the road to finding, before I lost David. I saw my son's family often. I felt like a child myself again when the twins and I played on the beach, when we screamed in unison at scary movies or had fun making a mess baking in the kitchen.

Trent and I have found one another again. The boy I loved is long gone, but the man he became is a treasured gift newly opened. He raised himself because I wasn't there, or wasn't enough, when he most needed me. David's gift to me of this new home is special, but the ultimate gift is rediscovering my son. Knowing David, this was likely at the root of his intentions. David had tugged at the bow that kept Trent tightly wrapped. Loosening his tight shell and enabling me to unwrap his many protective layers happened during discussions out on this deck while enjoying a sunset and wine in hand or while walking along the beach with the girls running happy circles around us.

Some talks were raw and painful, some delicately warming. All, chipped away at the edges of images that I had formed in memory. Images that turned out to be untrue or changed when Trent's different perspective was overlaid upon that moment in time. The way I had framed some memories distorted the true nature of the moment. The last thing a mother wants to do is to cause harm to her child. Yet, we do, and we cannot avoid it. For they are caught in the web of our existence, just as much as we are, but the angle they see things from is not the same. We think we shield our children from experiencing our pain, only to later discover that our doing so inflicted a different, and sometimes deeper, wound.

Unwrapping Trent necessitated unwrapping myself—exposing, recognizing, and laying naked my own many layers. I was both victim and culprit. Trent bravely exposed each of his scars. My bravery was to look upon his every wound, feel it, and respectfully accept how I played a part in inflicting that pain on my own beloved flesh.

During one of our beach strolls, he asked me something that I'd never thought about until then, but I've thought much about since. He asked me why I was so drawn to living nearby water. I replied that I loved looking upon its raw beauty that is never still and always changing.

"But, Mom," he said, "water isn't just beautiful, it's also brutal. Lainey disappeared under water. It took her away from you...from us. You don't think about that when you look out at the sea?"

"No." I replied, "Water also took away her look-alike, Cassie. Saving me."

Life is incongruous. Everyone wants to have lived a full life. Isn't that what people whisper to one another to ease their sorrow about the lifeless person on display and framed inside a casket? "He lived a full life." The other person nods in agreement, turning his gaze to the gleaming casket and whispers the expected reply "That he did."

What's not said and what's left hanging in between is the part that we don't want to recognize or confirm. Living a full life means experiencing many happy times and suffering through the lows. Those happy times that make you so incredibly glad to be alive stick with you. So too, does the suffering. Open wounds may scar over but never disappear. Your scars either become a part of you or you become them. If you are lucky, your suffering will show you how to treasure the warmer moments more.

When I remember living on the lake, I remember swimming with David. I remember David's favorite word. Often, I think about that word and the granular truth of it. "Interstitial," the unseen that lies in between is everything. It's both the terrible and wonderful unseen that holds us and keeps us.

Every time I witness a beautiful sunset out over the ocean, I remember the quote by Paulo Coelho, "Beautiful sunsets need cloudy skies." I had been working hard in therapy. I had new friends that I enjoyed spending time with, and I never tired of sitting on the deck and watching the waves as they greeted the beach in all their many moods. I saw things differently now.

My change in perspective was helped along by another, and the final, gift from David. My love of photography was revived in that perfectly outfitted darkroom he had constructed for me and had intended to surprise me with. I felt his encouraging spirit supporting me when I developed and printed my first roll of film after decades of barely remembering that this had once been an essential part of my life.

Blindly, and with only my fingers to tacitly guide me inside the changing bag, I instinctively popped open the film's cannister and nimbly loaded the roll of film onto a reel without any fumbling or needing to make successive attempts. That cherished old meditative and soulful state was brought on again by the smell of the chemicals and reliving the slow, deliberate, step-by-step process of bringing carefully chosen beautiful memories to life filled me once more. The first print I attempted in my new darkroom was from my first day here. It was taken down below on the beach, and of my granddaughters, all smiles as the wind blew lightly through their hair. I felt reborn as I watched their young faces come into focus under my enlarger.

Another evening enjoying a glass of wine and watching the setting sun begin to dip below the horizon, I again, as always, raised my glass in a loving toast to David and Lainey for having graced my life for as long as they did. I was a stronger and better person because of them. And, as I also did most evenings, I blew two kisses out to sea—one for each of them—and I'd recall a particular memory, usually different each time, that again made me remember their lives and to still feel the warmth of their love.

****

I was walking out of the pharmacy one day when I caught a glimpse of somebody who looked so very much like Lainey and Cassie. She was turning a corner on a downtown street. She turned, looked directly at me, and smiled just before she rounded the corner and disappeared. I quickly crossed over to that side of the street, nearly getting run over by a car in the process. I turned the corner, but nobody was there. There weren't any people on the sidewalk. No people were sitting in cars. There were no doorways that somebody might have slipped into to hide from me. I knew that it was not unimaginable that things like this might continue to occasionally happen. Of course, it hadn't been Lainey and, of course, it certainly hadn't been Cassie.

But I couldn't let it go, maybe because it had not happened for quite some time was the reason that it bothered me so. There was nothing sinister about the episode, but still, it was jarring all the same, and that's when a long-forgotten question suddenly bubbled up into my consciousness.

Later that day, I phoned Detective Sherwood. He was surprised to hear from me. I asked him if the plane ticket to California that Cassie had purchased using my credit card had ever been used. Not only was the detective surprised by my call, but he also said he was surprised to learn about the plane ticket. It wasn't something I had told him about back then. It wasn't even something I remembered until now.

Detective Sherwood said he would try to look into it, but he also said that after the passing of so much time, it might not be possible to learn anything. To complicate matters, I too was no longer entirely sure of the dates, the airlines, or the specific destination airport. The detective promised to cast a wide net, but he said the chances of finding out anything were slim. He reminded me that it wasn't unusual that Cassie's body was never found, given the circumstances of her death, and that I shouldn't fixate on the question of whether Cassie could still be alive. He didn't believe she could be. He assured me that neither Lainey nor Cassie could still be alive.

Six days later, Detective Sherwood phoned. He reported that the airlines did come back to him with some information. He was amazed that they could. He asked me to sit before he delivered the news that the ticket seems to have been used. I grabbed the scruff of my neck and stiffened as an icy chill swept through me. The thought that Cassie could somehow still be alive was unnerving. That flight was to California, here, and that realization stopped me cold. In a calm and measured voice, Detective Sherwood cautioned me that the accuracy of the airline's findings was dubious, at best, and to not place much importance on their information.

"Dubious," it's a word I've repeated to myself millions of times since. I struggle with the terrible fear and anxiety that word conjures inside me and yet I also still cling to the sliver of hope that hides deep within its meaning.

****

The twins decided that an amusement park adventure was what they wanted to do on their birthdays. I tagged along, not for the rides, but to be part of their fun and to enjoy their whoops of carefree laughter and joy. Images that would become keepsake treasures.

That thought led to an idea. Sarah and Sammy thought my darkroom was some kind of secret magical place, and they were unendingly curious about it. I kept the room locked as a precaution because of the chemicals kept there and the danger they could present to curious, clumsy youngsters. They thought it must be magic to create photographs in a darkened room, and they couldn't understand why a whole room was needed to make pictures when everybody else just did so using their phones. To them, their Granny had extraordinary powers. They would be thrilled watching images magically come to life.

When we arrived at the amusement park, I handed Sarah and Sammy simple cameras and instructed them to each shoot their own roll of film. I promised to develop the film rolls later that night, and the next day they could be in the darkroom with me to see their photographs materialize and be part of Granny's magic. Both girls jumped up and down squealing with excitement.

Karen and I laughed, when Trent commented how maybe the photography adventure might be even more fun, and far less expensive, than the amusement park rides. The kids wanted to go on nearly every ride, even the ones they were thankfully too small to yet join. We, adults, were surprised at how they gave such serious, studious thought to deciding on, and framing, each photo they took in between rides. Clicks were calculated. None seemed taken in haste or wasted.

It was a long, but enjoyable, day, and that evening, as promised, and although I was exhausted, I developed their rolls of film. As I hung the films to dry, I wondered what scenes they chose to expose. But I wouldn't cheat and study the negatives so that I could be honest when I exclaimed my surprise at seeing each image the next day.

The next day, Trent and the twins arrived for brunch. Karen was given the gift of sleeping-in—in consideration of, and in appreciation for, the excellent planning and execution of the event filled activities of the day before.

Brunch was filled with fun and silly recollections of yesterday.

"I loved the roller-coaster! It was the best ride." pronounced Sammy.

"No, it wasn't," argued Sarah. "You were a fraidy cat. You screamed the whole time. Bumper cars were the funnest!"

"No, they weren't, and you screamed too."

"Okay, enough. If we're done here, how about we go into Granny's mysterious chamber to see how she produces magic?" asked Trent.

"Yeah," shouted the twins in unison. Trent wrapped his arm around me, and we headed down the hall toward my mystery lair. Truthfully, I don't know who looked forward to this more—me or the girls?

I had laid everything out beforehand to minimize necessary preparations that might bore or confuse young minds. After settling the girls onto stools carefully positioned to observe, I theatrically waved my magic wand, which were actually tongs, and began to work my magic. The girls were mesmerized by their Granny's powers, gasping each time they saw one of their own creations slowly come into focus and materialize before them. Trent, standing behind them, cast a grin over the scene that seemed wide enough to engulf and embrace us all. He too thoroughly enjoyed the wondrousness and the innocence his beautiful young daughters reflected.

One look at Trent and I knew we were both thinking the same—*this is one of those times that becomes an unforgettable memory.*

As I brought the next print into focus under the enlarger, Trent leaned in closer. "Sammy, who are you waving at?"

"I took that photo." announced Sarah. She's waving at Kissee-Face."

"Yup, Kissee-Face," echoed Sammy.

"Who is Kissee-Face?" asked Trent.

"She's the lady that always blows kisses to us," Sammy said. "So, we call her Kissee-Face."

Trent and I locked gazes. While I concentrated on bringing the image into sharper focus, Trent asked, "Girls, how do you know her? When do you see her?"

"She's always around. Sometimes she's in the supermarket," said Sarah.

"Sometimes she's there when we are getting onto the bus after school," added Sammy.

"Last week, she blew us a kiss from across the street when we were playing in Bailey's front yard," said Sarah. Sammy shook her head up and down.

"She's awfully nice," continued Sarah. "She's just there sometimes. She blows us kisses, and then she's gone."

"See," Sammy pointed, "there's Kissee-Face."

I concentrated on fine tuning the focus to that part of the photograph.

That's when I spotted her. My stomach flipped. I looked up at Trent. His mouth agape and his unsteady stance made me fear that he might fall over and knock the girls from their stools. He had spotted her, too.

I looked again at the image under the enlarger. The ghostly image of a woman appeared in the upper right corner. Only part of me could explain away why she looked like an apparition. I could say to Trent that my over-magnifying an area of the image's distant background would, of course, generate a more grainy and diffused appearance. But what couldn't be explained away was who it was.

It wasn't just a likeness; it was her, and she was clearly blowing a kiss to my granddaughter.

PITY ME NOT

Pity me not because the light of day
At close of day no longer walks the sky;
Pity me not for beauties passed away
From field to thicket as the year goes by;
Pity me not the waning of the moon,
Nor that the ebbing tide goes out to sea.
Nor that a man's desire is hushed so soon.
And you no longer look with love on me.
This have I known always: Love is no more
Than the wide blossom which the wind assails.
Than the great tide that treads the shifting shore.
Strewing fresh wreckage gathered in the gales:
Pity me that the heart is slow to learn
What the swift mind beholds at every turn.
(Sonnet 29 by Edna St. Vincent Millay)

A word about the author...

Colleen Coyne writes stories about everyday people wrestling darkness. She often imagines plots and characters while passing long hours confined to an airplane seat. She has spent considerable time in the air as an international trade specialist, expanding markets around the globe for New England and Mid-Atlantic seafood. Her marriage to Dane also keeps her hopping between homes in the USA and Europe.

Colleen's home base in the U.S. is in Mystic, Connecticut. Watching spectacular sunsets while enjoying a glass of wine with family and friends at her home on the Mystic River is one of her most favorite things. Bewept is her second novel.

Thank you for purchasing
this publication of The Wild Rose Press, Inc.

For questions or more information
contact us at
info@thewildrosepress.com.

The Wild Rose Press, Inc.
www.thewildrosepress.com